With my
Warmest Best Wishes

Ted Sherrell

SECRETS FROM THE COUNCIL CHAMBER

Also by Ted Sherrell:

Ted Sherrell's

Secrets
from the
Council
Chamber

UNITED WRITERS
Cornwall

UNITED WRITERS PUBLICATIONS LTD
Ailsa, Castle Gate, Penzance, Cornwall.

British Library Cataloguing in Publication Data:
A catalogue record for this book is
available from the British Library.

ISBN 9781852001919

Printed in Great Britain by
United Writers Publications Ltd
Cornwall.

To my darling Ann
the love of my life,
my dearest friend and my inspiration
and
to our lovely, loyal, devoted family
– all treasured.

Contents

I

The Conker

The mayor had, that evening, entered the chamber in good spirits
for he had anticipated a short session – relatively speaking, at
least. He had had a briefing from the town clerk, Cecil Conway,
that afternoon and the agenda for the regular monthly meeting of
the full council appeared to be the lightest for months so,
optimistically, Frank Jackson felt that with deliberations starting
at 7 o'clock, he should be on his way home before eight. Such a
fervent desire betrayed a somewhat strange paradox in the man; a
member of the town council for over 20 years, now serving his
third stint as mayor, there were none who derived more
satisfaction, fulfilment and pleasure from civil life than he did.
He enjoyed deep involvement in the community, the every day
scenario of people stopping him in the streets or in shops
commenting on this, complaining about that, making suggestions,
sometimes 'venting spleens'.

As mayor, he, along with his charming, gentle wife Adele,
enjoyed, generally, the official events – opening fetes and so
forth, attending shows and official dinners, giving out prizes;
even the fraught business of, say, the judging at baby shows did
not faze them, though the dangers involved when incurring the
wrath of the outraged mothers of those infants who had come
second and beyond could induce terror in many a brave heart. The
fact was they were sociable people, who enjoyed social,
communal occasions. The stark reverse side of the coin with

Jackson, though, was that, whilst he enjoyed his deep involvement in town matters, he disliked formal meetings; he always had. He had ever felt that any half decent councillor did most of their work – certainly the bulk of their positive contribution to their electors – outside the chamber. Thus the briefer the meeting, the happier he was, and if he had an excuse to miss one altogether, such as it clashing with a civic event – then the latter would always take precedence in his diary, and he would hand over the chairing of the meeting to the deputy mayor, Douglas Denny.

This evening, though, he was confident matters would be reasonably painless and tolerably brief; within a few minutes of wishing the town clerk a brisk greeting, however, mild despair was engulfing him. For Cecil Conway had put before him a letter which had only arrived at the council offices late that afternoon. 'It'll have to come under 'Any other business', Frank – at least, that's how I see it. You're the mayor, of course, so it's a matter for you really, but it's something the council should know about. Not a big issue, mind you, but it's one of those daft things which can cause aggravation and problems beyond their importance.'

'And be debated for hours,' rasped the mayor. 'The sort of nonsense everybody wants to comment on – has a view on. Tell them the town hall's got to have a new roof and we're looking for a six figure sum to put things right, and nobody will say a word. But something like this, well . . .' he tailed off wearily, shaking his head. 'You're right though, Cecil, they've got to be told about it. Any other business, as you say. You'll have to read it out – in full. Not that it's very long. And it's nonsense, of course – and they'll go spare. Most of them will anyway, though one or two will be sort of sympathetic – you know the ones.' He glanced at the town clerk who nodded his agreement – oh yes, he knew the ones all right.

The meeting as set out in the agenda did move along at a decent pace as the mayor had anticipated. Faster, in fact, for by 7.40 they had arrived at the dreaded 'Any other business'. Had not that wretched letter arrived, then proceedings would have been over in less than a further minute. Still, it had to be

10

confronted. Frank Jackson cleared his throat, and said in a tone devoid of emotion, 'We come to any other business, Ladies and Gentlemen. We have one item; A letter arrived in the office here late this afternoon which needs to be brought to the attention of the Council. I will ask the town clerk to read it out. Mr Conway, please.'

'Thank you, Mr Mayor,' said the clerk, sitting beside him. 'I'll read the letter in full – fortunately, it's not long.' He stopped, then looking towards Jackson, 'I'm sorry, Mr Mayor, but it's just occurred to me, that this item should be taken 'In Committee'. There are possibly legal and financial matters involved here – matters of, of, of, well, in a sense, a sensitive nature which could, could, well possibly, could cause problems in the future. Indeed, could be prejudicial in the future – prejudicial against this council, that is. You have read the letter, Mr Mayor – just before the meeting. Probably you will have drawn the same conclusions as myself – that, initially, the press and public be excluded whilst the matter is discussed.'

For a few seconds the mayor appeared nonplussed, but rapidly regained his composure. He nodded; 'Well, yes, I suppose you're right. I'd not thought in those terms, but as you say, I only read it a few minutes before the meeting started, so I didn't have time really to think of it in that light. But it is probably the right course of action when considering its contents – though not that dreadful or dramatic,' said he, hastily, aware that Ruth Blythe, the long serving reporter of council affairs for the local paper, was sitting at the back, pen in hand.

With her keen 'nose' for a story, Ruth would already be sensing something; thus was the mayor anxious to put her off the scent. This was a forlorn hope in reality, as that good lady, excellent, perceptive, experienced reporter that she was, generally would ferret out any council business which would be of interest to, and possibly against the interests of, local readers. She was already aware there was a story here somewhere – a letter delivered that very day which clearly was causing consternation to mayor and clerk alike. Something was afoot –

and she did not doubt her ability to find out what it was, although it might take a few days.

'Yes, though the letter is not – not earth shattering or, or alarming in any way' – it was rare he was so indecisive as this, but the town clerk's strong suggestion regarding the letter be read, and considered, 'in camera', had briefly neutralised his usual urbanity. 'No, no,' he stuttered – 'though there is nothing of major – well, no major problem, I feel as there are, as Mr Conway says, financial and legal issues involved, it would be better to take this item in committee. Do I have a proposal that we do so?'

The deputy mayor, Douglas Denny, rose to his feet. He nodded slowly, but there was a pained expression upon his face. 'Well, yes, I will propose we go into committee, but with some reluctance. I've said before that I feel there are times we go into what is, in effect, secret sessions, too easily – too quickly. Often when we've done so, the issues which are brought before us could be debated in full view of press and public – though, it has to be said, that it's not often there are members of the public here unless we as a council have done something daft – or, at least, dafter than normal' – Noted for his acerbic humour, was Councillor Denny – 'or have wasted council tax on some silly project. We are the elected representatives of the people, Mr Mayor, and wherever possible all we do, all we debate, all we decide, should be done out in the open. I'll be blunt – if it was just the town clerk recommending we exclude press and electors, I'd not go with it.' He fixed the officer of the council with a somewhat hostile glare, he having little regard for Conway, considering him to be overpaid and, if not incompetent, certainly not really 'up to the job'. He had not, during the ten years he had been a councillor, made any attempt to disguise his opinion. Not unnaturally, the clerk had never warmed to the elected man and whilst treating him with a cold courtesy, had as little to do with him as possible. 'However,' continued Denny, 'I do trust your judgement implicitly, Mr Mayor, so if you, having read the letter, feel its contents, at present, should not be made public, then I will go with it.'

'Thank you, Mr Denny. Do I have a seconder?'

12

Councillor Sidney Bartlett, 'Father of the Council' in terms of both service (33 years) and age (82) half rose from his chair; 'Yes – yes, Mr Mayor, I'll second it,' said he a little falteringly. 'Like Councillor Denny, I don't greatly like this – this – well, this constantly running towards secrecy in what we do. We should always try to do things, to conduct our business, in an open fashion; this isn't North Korea – folk have a right to know what we're doing. Years ago, when I first came on this Authority . . .'

'Thank you, Mr Bartlett, for seconding the motion,' interjected the mayor hastily. When Sid Bartlett started to cast his mind, and tongue, back to the days of yore when first he was elected, urgent action was required if the meeting was not to become bogged down with his reminiscences – usually of a time when the sun, metaphorically, never set – according to him at least. 'I'll put it to the vote – all in favour.'

A slightly deflated Sidney Bartlett sank back down onto his chair – also slightly offended. A man of his service and experience deserved the courtesy of being allowed to have his say, he reasoned, but then that was Frank Jackson. He was basically a good mayor and sound chairman the veteran councillor was willing to concede, but not the most patient of souls – and always in a hurry. He raised his right arm whilst his burly posterior was sinking into the comfortable chair.

'Carried,' stated the mayor noting the crop of raised arms waving before him. He looked towards the back of the chamber. There were no members of the public attending (not an unusual situation), just Ruth Blythe at the press desk. 'I'm sorry about this, Mrs Blythe – sorry that we have to go into committee on this. Still – it'll let you get home a bit earlier tonight,' he said, somewhat lamely.

His apologies to the journalist, though, were genuine. Ruth Blythe was held in high regard by him, indeed by most councillors. The quality of her writing and her accuracy were of the highest standard. In fact, many a councillor who couldn't remember exactly what they said in a debate, would wait for the local paper to come out on a Thursday and, if they were quoted, would read word for word exactly what had come forth from their lips during the heat of verbal debate. Even more often she would inform councillors exactly what the authority had decided at the end of, often, protracted and confusing discussion, they, themselves often being a touch uncertain. The mayor had commented to his deputy some months previously, that they could do with somebody of Ruth's intelligence and perception on the Council: 'No thank you, Frank,' Denny had retorted. 'She would make the rest of us look like a bunch of idiots, a woman with a sharp brain like she's got.'

Seeing the door of the chamber closing behind the journalist, the mayor turned to Cecil Conway. 'If you would read the letter, please, town clerk, then we will all be in the picture – and hopefully be able to chart a way forward.'

'Thank you, Mr Mayor.' Cecil Conway made little effort to mask the dread he felt as he began to read, his tone akin to that of a weary vicar leading a funeral cortege into a church. 'They'll go spare when they hear this,' he had commented to other staff in the office after he had read the letter that afternoon. He would assuredly be right. He cleared his throat, looked closely at the missive held tightly in his hands, started with the comment, 'It's not very long – and certainly very much to the point. It is from a Mrs Sharon Milner of Swallow Avenue – that's one of the roads in the new estate on the edge of the town.'

'I fancy we all know where it is, Mr Mayor,' rasped the deputy mayor, acidly. 'And it's not a new estate, either, as it's been there five or six years now. Let's have the letter, please, just read as it's written without any superfluous comment from Mr Conway. We want to get home tonight.' He fixed the officer with a glare of some malevolence, one which was returned.

Conway opened his mouth to reply, but he was forestalled by the mayor who wanted to get on with the business and was not prepared to have his, and the Council's, time wasted with verbal sparring between these long time protagonists.

'I feel the town clerk was only trying to be helpful, Councillor,' he snapped, fixing Douglas Denny with the type of look which spoke volumes (although essentially an easy going man, Frank Jackson was no fellow to argue with when he was

14

annoyed, and his fellow councillors were aware of it). 'However, I fancy we all know where Swallow Avenue is, Mr Conway, so I would suggest you proceed with reading out this wretched letter – immediately.'

'Very well, Mr Mayor,' replied the town clerk, a model of meekness. 'It states as follows: Dear Sir, I wish to complain regarding a major safety issue in the park, close to the children's play area. There is a horse chestnut tree quite close to where the swings are. This is in a dangerous condition and needs attention immediately, on safety grounds. Unfortunately, it is already too late for the welfare of my six year old son, Caleb, as he, this afternoon, suffered injury whilst walking with me near the tree. The full extent of his injury is something which, at the moment, I do not know, as I am writing this letter to you just half an hour after this so worrying accident, and I will not know the full extent of his injuries until I have taken him to the doctor. I tried to summon an ambulance but they were unable to attend – shamefully – for well over an hour for some reason, so I immediately phoned my GP who said he would see me at 4.30pm (thus am I dropping this letter into your office on the way to taking my son to his surgery). Clearly I do not know as yet what injuries have been done to him with this missile falling onto his head. It could just possibly be concussion, but the power with which the object struck him on the temple makes me fear he could suffer permanent brain damage. My husband and I will assuredly be seeking legal advice with a view to suing the council for keeping such a dangerous tree in a public park close to an area used by young children. This, though, is a matter for the future. In the meantime, I demand (and I have my husband's full support on this having just spoken to him on the phone at his place of work) that this unsafe tree, a danger to public health, be cut down immediately before any other dangerous objects can fall and cause serious injury to any other child. It has occurred to me throughout the 2 years I have lived in this town that this huge tree is inappropriate in the park. It is much too large and obtrusive, is ugly, and, now it is autumn, it becomes potentially lethal as its hard brown seeds, the size of golf balls, hurtle down from it –

especially if there is a wind. If one should strike a child, as it did my Caleb, then its danger to the public cannot be exaggerated. I trust that upon receiving this letter from myself with, as I have already stated, the full support of my husband who works for the local health authority, action will be taken within the next 24 hours to take down the tree, before harm can be caused to anyone else. However, I state here and now that even if it is razed to the ground, my husband and I will still seek compensation and damages from the council, through the courts if necessary, for the injuries to our son. Yours faithfully, Sharon Milner (Mrs).' The clerk ceased reading and looked towards Frank Jackson – 'That's the letter, Mr Mayor, and now that councillors have heard its contents they will no doubt understand why I – why we – felt it advisable to take this item in committee. There are, as I said, financial and legal matters involved and we appear to be dealing with a lady, a couple in fact, who appear to wish to make life difficult for this council.'

The mayor nodded – 'Quite right,' said he. 'Clearly we are dealing here with people who are, shall we shall, a little difficult and who could cause problems – and we don't want any more of those than we have already got. I feel . . .'

'Brown seeds – the size of golf balls?' The words came, suddenly, from Sidney Bartlett, who – along with some other members of the council – had been somewhat bemused by the contents of the letter. 'What's the woman on about?'

'Conkers, Mr Mayor, that's what she's on about,' interjected the town clerk. 'That's what this lady told our Sally in the office as she was leaving after having handed in the letter. Her son was hit on the head by a conker – though why she couldn't say so in the letter is beyond me. Brown seeds, indeed.'

'What – a conker – her boy was hit by a conker? That's what this is all about, a conker? Is – is – is this woman serious, Mr Mayor?' spluttered the veteran Bartlett. 'Being hit on the head by a conker would hardly give a dormouse a headache.'

'I fear she is totally serious, Councillor,' replied the mayor wearily. 'And if she is, then unfortunately, we must be also. The letter is legitimately submitted to us – she clearly has every right to do so – and we have to decide what action to take on the matter.'

'That's easy to decide, Mr Mayor – we take no action at all,' snorted Councillor Tom Gaskell. 'The town clerk should write to this lady suggesting she stop wasting our time. We've enough real problems in the town, enough demands on our ever smaller budget and, of course, our time, without having to listen to and consider idiotic letters like this one.'

'If Mr Gaskell's making that a proposal, then I'll second it,' cried Julia Bennett, on her feet with alacrity. 'To have our time wasted in this way is intolerable. It's hard to get into the mind of someone as absurd as this.'

'If it's the woman I think it is, Mr Mayor, then she's just a troublemaker – simple as that. And somebody who thinks she's got twice as many rights as anybody else,' interjected Jim Sparks. 'Big, fat woman – late thirties, Yorkshire accent, if I'm not mistaken.'

The town clerk nodded. 'Well, yes – that could describe the lady, I suppose. Certainly she's a touch, shall we say, on the large size, and she definitely has a north country accent. And she was, I have to say, somewhat aggressive.'

'Yes, that's her, all right,' snapped Councillor Sparks. 'Came into my newsagents a few months back and bought a daily paper. The next morning she was back again with the same paper, obviously read from cover to cover – you could tell that from the state of it – and wanted her money back because, according to her, there were inaccuracies in the television listings. As if that was my fault. I gave her short shrift, of course, but it didn't put her off coming back. I remember last December she came in and bought a pack of Christmas cards; the next day she was in again wanting her money back because the cards were religious, mentioning God and Jesus. I pointed out to her that it was his birthday, so it only seemed reasonable for Him to be mentioned on the card. She was having none of it, though – she said she did not believe in religion and, again, demanded her money back.'

'Did you give it to her?' asked Tom Gaskell.

'Not likely – I just swapped the pack with Jesus on for one

with a fat robin on the front – although it was a lot thinner than her. Then there was the time she came in one morning for a get well card, but brought it back in the afternoon saying the lady she'd bought it for had just died – so before she could ask for a refund, I swapped it for a sympathy card. The woman is trouble, truly a pain. There was another time . . .'

'Thank you, Councillor,' interjected the mayor. He was not averse to hearing Jim Sparks' reminiscences as they were usually quite entertaining, the newsagent ever able to 'tell a good tale,' but it really was time to move the meeting on – an hour or two watching television, plus a liberal measure of single malt in his hand, was calling loud and clear. 'I am not sure if we can get away with doing nothing about this, but that is what has been moved and seconded, so I'll put it to the meeting.'

'Well, before you do, Mr Mayor, I feel we should perhaps discuss this a little more.' The intervention came from Councillor Jack Dawson, a respected, quiet, reserved man who spoke only when he had something relevant and, usually, sensible to say. 'I agree that this lady's complaint would appear to be absurd and a waste of our valuable time, but we live in an age when litigation, selfishness and intolerance are all too much to the fore. So whilst my heart says, yes, let's throw this silly letter in the bin where it belongs – metaphorically, anyway – my head suggests that perhaps we should discuss the matter more fully; and take our time in doing so. Clearly that will not be tonight. However, I note we have a special meeting of the Full Council in a week's time to discuss the outline structure plans sent down from the District Council – well, the Government really – that in the next ten years we plan for an extra thousand homes in the town plus industrial units and so on. That in many ways will be a waste of time because our opposition to it all – and it will be opposition as we all know – will be largely ignored at District level, totally ignored at County, whilst, the Government will never even have heard of us. However, seeing as we have to meet, we could perhaps put the meeting to some positive purpose by deciding what we are able to do about this preposterous letter, the threats contained therein and our magnificent horse chestnut tree. In the meantime, though,

18

it would possibly be prudent to get our Works Department, in the morning, to put a temporary fence around the tree, obviously following roughly the circumference of the circle where the conkers will fall, just to ensure there are no further incidents of this nature. Not that I believe for one moment there will be, but it is perhaps wise to err on the side of caution – 'belt and braces', as the saying goes; sadly there are those around who see local councils as a soft touch in terms of compensation and suchlike.'

'Sound reasoning, Councillor Dawson,' opined the mayor. 'Nonsense though it is, you are right to be cautious – and that we discuss it at next Tuesday's meeting is, I feel, a good idea. The main item, the future planning issues won't take long – we've discussed it all so much in the past, and at great length I might add. I see no problem there, Mr Conway, do you?'

The town clerk shook his head. 'None, Mr Mayor; I'll add the item to the Agenda. Also, if it's the wish of the council to go along with Councillor Dawson's suggestion that a fence be put around the horse chestnut, then I'll instruct Mr Benson, the Work Superintendent, first thing in the morning. It'll not take them long.'

'The speed one or two of that crew work, it'll take them the rest of the week,' a cynical Sidney Bartlett muttered to Tom Gaskell sitting next to him.

'Mr Mayor, whilst I fully see where Councillor Dawson is coming from on this, I feel there could still be danger from the tree even if it is fenced off,' said Councillor Liz Crosby. 'I mean, we're talking of children here; unless it's the sort of fence you would put around Dartmoor Prison, some of the more adventurous would probably get over or under it to pick up conkers and suchlike and, in consequence, could get hit by a falling conker or suchlike. And whilst I'm as angered as anyone else at the troublemaking foolishness of the letter the town clerk has read out, there are perhaps others in the community who will try to cause problems for us, and gain money from us. With that in mind, would it not be better if in the morning, members of the outdoor maintenance staff get a few ladders and strip the tree of conkers.'

'No, no, no, Mr Mayor,' cried Councillor Sally Gilbert, to whom trees were God's supreme creation. 'That would be a terrible thing to do – almost sacrilege. It would be like destroying a field of corn, or trampling over a garden ablaze with flowers. Conkers are its crop; they must be left to fall naturally, then harvested. Also, men up ladders amongst the foliage inevitably would cause damage – break off small branches and suchlike. I'll go along with Councillor Dawson's idea – reluctantly – that it be fenced temporarily, but nothing beyond that.'

'Mr Mayor, if I might intervene here.' Cecil Conway was on his feet, an expression of concern upon his face. 'The fact is this cannot happen as there is no way we can have men on ladders picking the conkers off that tree. Health and safety would have a field day if we even tried. To do what Councillor Mrs Crosby suggests would, in reality, cost us a fortune – and by the time we were actually able to do the job, most of the conkers would have fallen anyway. Scaffolding would have to be erected all around the three – it is far too high for us to use ladders. The hiring and erection of the great amount we would need for such a large tree as that horse chestnut would cost us thousands – and probably take a couple of weeks to achieve; they're always busy, these scaffolding firms. So, with respect, Mr Mayor, in terms of both time and cost it is a non-starter.'

'Is the town clerk saying, Mr Mayor, that nobody on the council is allowed to go up a ladder?' There was a note of incredulity in Tom Gaskell's tone when he voiced the question.

'Oh yes, Mr Mayor,' replied Cecil Conway, 'They can go up ladders, but only to a height of – of, well, I'm not sure about this, but I think, about 12 feet or so. The Works Supervisor would know, cleary, but I believe the stipulation for this is that they have been on, and passed, the ladder climbing course.'

'What's that, Mr Mayor – ladder climbing course? Did I hear that right?' exploded Sidney Bartlett.

'Well, yes, Councillor, I fancy you did,' replied the mayor with as much urbanity as he could muster. 'I do believe that these days, members of our outdoor staff are expected to do such training – along with other courses.'

20

'What other courses?' Councillor Bartlett's face suggested he was on the brink of apoplexy.

'Oh well, these days there are courses run for local government employees in the handling of much of the equipment they use in their work – mowers, strimmers, chainsaws, the polishing machine we use on the town hall floor and, well, much more. It costs us a pretty penny, I'm afraid, but the law demands it these days,' came the reply from the town clerk, gazing at the far wall of the chamber so as to avoid the glares and expressions of disbelief he knew would dominate the features of most councillors.

Frank Jackson came to his aid by trying to move the debate away from a subject which he knew would outrage many members – indeed, outraged himself. He wanted, though, to get home that evening, thus it was important to keep to the immediate topic of debate, the horse chestnut tree. 'Sadly, Councillor, this is the safety obsessed climate in which we now live – well, the public sector does. If private industry and small firms adhered to all this nonsense, then there would be bankruptcies everywhere and millions more on the dole. All this, though, is beyond the control of this council and the town clerk, so I want to move this meeting on to a decision as to what we do this evening. We've had a proposal that, in the short term, we fence around the tree and discuss the matter more fully at next week's meeting; I shall put this matter to the vote.'

Before he could do so, however, he was interrupted by Sidney Bartlett, whose thought processes were still dominated by the, to him, absurdities of ladder – and other – courses, tasks which, to him, were simple and could be, to the average person, mastered after a few minutes of tuition. 'What's the town clerk saying, Mr Mayor – that all our outdoor staff have to go on ladder climbing courses? And even when they've done it, they're only allowed to go up twelve feet?' There was a rare blend of astonishment, frustration and sheer anger in his tone.

'Well, yes, Mr Mayor. That's it – in theory, at least,' replied Cecil Conway, clearly ill at ease having to give an explanation on a legal requirement with which we had no sympathy – it was plain daft in his view, but there was nothing he could do other than to fulfil his duty as the council's chief legal and administrative officer by pointing out the dictates and restrictions imposed by law. 'In reality, not all our staff have been on the course. Two of the chaps refuse to go on it because they – they – well, they suffer from vertigo, and cannot stand heights; two others have not long been with us and have yet to do the course, which leaves three who have successfully passed it. However, only one is available at the moment, due to holiday and sickness, although the gent on leave, Jimmy Combes, is back to work next Monday. The fellow sick, though, Derek Mortimer, will be off for a further three weeks, at least.'

'What's wrong with him?' enquired the mayor.

'He's broken his collar bone,' replied the town clerk.

'How did that happen?'

The officer appeared a touch embarrassed, gazing everywhere about the chamber except at the faces turned towards him awaiting his response. 'Well – well – well,' he stuttered, 'unfortunately he had an accident whilst watering one of the hanging baskets outside the town hall. He, he, somehow slipped – and fell off the ladder he was standing on. Very, very unlucky – he was only about six feet up; he fell awkwardly.'

There was a stunned silence about the chamber as members were pondering whether to laugh or cry at this Pythonesque news. Silence, however, was broken:

'Mr Mayor, this debate's going on forever – I've got a home to go to, and I want to go to it before midnight.' Arthur Phillips, good councillor though he was, assuredly had never been a patient man. 'And it's not only tonight that's wasting our time, the same thing will happen next Tuesday, you can be certain of that. A decision has to made, so let's make it here and now. Personally, whilst I'll agree some trees are impressive and well worth keeping, this horse chestnut in the park, though big, is nothing special. All it does is make a mess with all the conkers this time of year, and gets in the way of the mowers when they're cutting the grass. So why don't we cut it down, like this woman is demanding. Granted she's a pain, but she could still be right.

Hopefully there's one or two on our staff who've passed the chainsaw course – if not, there's plenty of folk around who'll do it for us. Whatever, let's have it down – I so move.'

The sudden and dramatic intervention by Phillips had taken all by surprise and for a few seconds silence reigned. It was broken by a shriek from the lips of Councillor Sally Gilbert – 'No, no, no Mr Mayor. Chop down that lovely tree – no, no that cannot be allowed to happen. I'm shocked Mr Phillips can even suggest such a thing – it would be a, a, well a grotesque act of vandalism. We must not do such a thing – I'm appalled it can even be suggested.'

Cecil Conway was on his feet with alacrity, aware he had information which would halt in its tracks this deviation in the debate. 'Mrs Gilbert can be assured, Mr Mayor, that the horse chestnut is safe from the woodman's axe,' said he, with a forlorn attempt at levity. 'As soon as I received this letter this afternoon, late though it was, I contacted Miss Davison, the 'tree lady' at the district council. Fortunately I caught her just as she was about to leave for the day. She checked with her records and confirmed, as I suspected, there is a preservation order on the tree. In consequence, we would have to go through a complicated, time consuming process just to have a branch lopped off. It would take almost an act of Parliament, or of God, to chop down the tree itself.' Again a lame attempt at humour had come from the town clerk's lips.

The mayor, though, was impressed. 'Thank you, Mr Conway, for that; and thank you for your immediate action in ascertaining the status of the tree. That has clarified matters considerably. Increasingly it looks as if Councillor Dawson's proposal of temporarily fencing then a discussion leading to a decision at next week's meeting is the way forward. Thus, I put this to the meeting – all in favour?'

Most members thrust their hands into the air, though by no means all. None, though, when invited to do so voted against.

'Carried,' announced Jackson, pleased that at last he had been able to get a grip on this tedious, unnecessary debate and, in consequence, bring it to a conclusion. It was time to do likewise to the meeting. 'I fancy, Town Clerk, that concludes our business for the evening.'

'It does, Mr Mayor.'

'Good – then I declare the meeting closed. I'll see you all next Tuesday, when we do it all again – in the meantime, I wish you goodnight.'

'Mr Mayor – a thought has just come to me.' Cecil Conway was on his feet again.

'I have declared the meeting closed, having been told by yourself there was no further business,' rasped the mayor, testily.

'Quite so, and I'm sorry to jump to my feet in this way, but I've just had a thought regarding this, this nonsense with the conker which yourself and other councillors might feel would be a sensible precaution to take.'

'The town clerk's not suggesting we issue everybody in the town with steel helmets, is he?' enquired Douglas Denny – often to the fore in bringing humour to proceedings, though not always with success.

Cecil Conway gave a weak, weary smile – he was a courteous man but not a lover of comedy – then proceeded to explain his thought processes: 'I fear that such provision of headgear would bankrupt this authority, Mr Mayor, but it would, I feel, be a wise and relatively modest expenditure of public money if we were to take advice from our solicitors. I hadn't thought of it until a few minutes ago; possibly I should have – but this entire business has come upon us all of a sudden like a whirlwind. I apologise, Mr Mayor, for bringing this up at – it almost is, literally, the eleventh hour – but in a situation where we are being threatened with being taken to court and suchlike, it would certainly pay us to know where we stand legally. Whether we could be held responsible for any injuries to this young lad – thus, whether or not we can be sued.'

After hearing what the official had to say, the wave of annoyance which had swept over the mayor at Conway's belated intervention just a minute before passed rapidly on its way to be replaced by a measure of approval, even admiration. 'Old Cecil really is on the ball tonight' he mused to himself before saying,

'Thank you, Mr Conway – what you suggest makes sense. To be forewarned is to be forearmed, as the saying goes. I rarely like to involve our legal advisers any more than we have to as they are never cheap, but in this instance we would be foolish if we did not. Members agree?'

A series of grunts came from the committee which the mayor took to be assent (certainly nobody appeared to object). Thus did he decree – 'Carried. So, Mr Conway, you'll consult our solicitors and bring their legal opinions to the meeting next week.' He looked quizzically in the direction of the official who nodded briskly:

'I will, Mr Mayor – hopefully such legal advice will help to point us in the right direction when it comes to making a decision on this matter.'

'Yes – hopefully.' Frank Jackson was, basically, a 'glass half-empty' man, and whilst the clerk's advice they consult their solicitors was essentially sound – wise in fact – he expected little in return except for a very substantial bill for 'services rendered'.

The following Tuesday evening saw Ruth Blythe leave the meeting early – something she rarely did. This time, though, she could see nothing coming from the debate on the structure of the town in terms of planning and development for the future which she had not reported in the past – many times. Thanks to Frank Jackson's tight chairing of the debate (members being permitted to speak once only on the issues, and to a maximum of 5 minutes in accordance with standing orders) the meeting would not be interminable but, due to the fact virtually every councillor wished to speak on the matter, the debate would not be brief. Not that the experienced, shrewd journalist minded – she had sat through some prolonged, tortuous council debates over the years, but usually was rewarded for her patience, able to harvest an unguarded quote from a councillor, a surprise decision on the part of a committee, an original idea from a member and so forth. On this night, though, nothing like this was happening – and there was no way it was going to. Every councillor who spoke said

b

virtually the same on the matter that they had said on numerous occasions before – and she was all too certain that nothing new or original would come forth.

If there was any news to be had from the evening, anything to grab the attention of the paper's readers when it came out on Thursday, it would, she was fairly sure, be contained in the second item on the agenda, tantalisingly entitled, 'Letter received on October 10th – to determine a course of action.' The problem there, though, from Ruth's angle, was that the 'course of action' would be decided 'in committee', with herself and members of the public excluded. She had sufficient confidence in her own investigative abilities to feel she would, eventually, find out what the letter was all about, but knew that such would be in the future.

Thus, before the conclusion of the meandering debate being held in open committee, did she pack up her pens and notebook, bow her head respectfully to the mayor – who responded in his habitual courteous fashion with, 'Good night, Mrs Blythe – thank you for coming along,' – then leave the chamber.

She was correct in her surmise that there would be no surprises regarding the outcome of the debate and vote on the public issue of the Future Development Plan; as she expected – indeed, as the mayor expected – it was passed with a reasonable majority, nobody, whether for or against, changing their views, or their comments, on the matters.

Formally the council moved 'into committee' – though there was nobody to eject from the chamber – and the vexed issue of what to do about the 'dangerous' horse chestnut tree in the park was addressed. The mayor looked towards the town clerk: 'I believe you've consulted our solicitors on the matter, Mr Conway. What is their view – their legal judgement and advice? Sadly the age in which we live means we do really have to make sure where we stand legally. A few years ago we would not have had to worry too much in that direction, but these days we as a council – as councillors as well for that matter – have to cover our backs. Some bugg. . .' he stopped momentarily, suddenly realising he was chairing the town council, then continued, 'some people will sue at the drop of a hat.'

'Or a conker,' rasped Douglas Denny.

Frank Jackson smiled – 'Indeed, Councillor – at the drop of a conker. Anyway, what does our solicitor say?' he enquired, looking in the direction of the town clerk.

Cecil Conway cleared his throat – at great length, which was a sign that he was aware the news he was about to impart to the council would not be well received. 'Mr Mayor – well, Mr Mayor, our solicitor was a touch, well, ambiguous – he felt that whilst possibly he could give a view, an opinion, the situation was a touch – well a touch uncertain so he felt it would be wrong for him to give definite, decided legal advice.'

'Now there's a surprise,' snorted Douglas Denny, to nobody in particular but certainly to the meeting at large. His opinion of the council's solicitors – all lawyers, for that matter – was possibly even lower than that which he possessed for the town clerk. 'All we ever get from this fellow is vagueness and big bills.'

'I'm not sure that's at all fair, Mr Mayor,' retorted the town clerk. 'Mr Adamson has been the council's solicitor for very many years, and his firm has given us legal advice for decades – usually good, sound advice it is too. He is, though, a man to err on the side of caution – rightly in my view. It is crucial we, as a local authority, avoid the 'fools rush in' scenario, one which might well cost the council tax payer a good deal of money and get us, the council, nowhere. He feels that whilst the issue clearly is not a major one, he suspects that the lady involved here – the lad's mother – is simply angling to get some sort of compensation from this council. He doubts she has a case, unless her son was badly injured, which seems most unlikely, but still feels we should ensure that our approach leaves no loopholes which she can exploit. With that in mind he suggests that we seek the advice of. . .' he ceased talking, briefly, and cleared his throat, aware that what he was about to say would incur the wrath of some members: 'Well,' he continued, 'well, seek the advice of counsel specialising in this kind of situation to know exactly where we stand on the matter. This, probably, is quite sound advice as we have so many different issues of law coming in here – health and safety, human rights, European Court of Justice, and, and, so on, Mr Mayor.'

27

'Sound advice? Sound advice? Counsel? Douglas Denny did not so much speak, as explode. 'Counsel – good grief, these people are even worse than solicitors – they'll charge you a grand just for telling you the time of day. No, Mr Mayor, no counsel – let's make our own judgement on this. We're not idiots on this committee, not fools. We've got, between us, a fair old reservoir of knowledge and common sense, so let's have nothing more to do with legal advisers – let's just make a decision; and that, I feel, is a very simple one – we do nothing. This entire business is nonsense – a fuss created by a hysterical, or possibly scheming woman, out to embarrass this council, or extort money from us.'

'I doubt whether it's possible for us to do nothing, Mr Mayor,' interjected Councillor Liz Crosby. 'As the town clerk said, there are all these laws, legal bodies and so forth in place these days, so many of which can cause trouble for councils no matter how responsible and careful we are. So, whilst I have no enthusiasm for spending public money on lawyers, perhaps we should take the advice of counsel.'

'I would have thought, Mr Mayor, that information is very relevant as to the condition of the young lad whose head was struck by the conker,' interjected Jack Dawson. 'I trust,' he continued, a wry, gentle smile playing around his lips, 'that he is not lying in a hospital bed in a coma.'

The Mayor snorted – 'I very much doubt he is, Councillor, but the point you make is a good one. It certainly is something we should be told about. Have you heard anything Mr Conway? As Councillor Dawson says, it certainly is relevant.'

The blank expression upon the features of the official showed, plainly, he had no information on the matter – though he was rapidly realising he should have pursued enquiries in that area. He was saved in his somewhat embarrassed confusion by Councillor Sally Gilbert.

'Mr Mayor, in that direction I can possibly supply information which might be helpful. My granddaughter is in the same class as the boy allegedly struck by the conker. She tells me he was at school the following day, fit as a fiddle. Clearly, he suffered no ill

28

effects from – from the conker attack' – a rare attempt at humour from serious minded Mrs Gilbert.

The Mayor's expression brightened considerably. 'That, Councillor, is very helpful news, indeed – or it seems so to me, at least. It's probably why we've not heard anything back from his mother since she dropped in her wretched letter.'

'And we'll not hear anything more from her either, I bet,' rasped Douglas Denny. 'That's shot her fox, all right. Woman's nothing but a trouble maker, that's clear; but she's caused us problems we could do without – and money too, what with having to involve solicitors. Then there's the fence around the tree; we've had to put it up, now it'll cost us money to take it down.'

'Well, no, actually it won't cost us anything to take down. As I reported to you just before the start of the meeting, Mr Mayor,' said the clerk, his normal urbanity reasonably restored. 'The fact is the fence was pulled down by vandals – or large parts of it anyway – within 24 hours of being erected. Mind you, it was theft as well as criminal damage, as several of the fencing stakes and some of the fence itself have disappeared. The matter is now in the hands of the police.'

'A lot of good that'll do,' snorted deputy mayor Denny; his lack of faith in the competence of officials had long been quite universal. 'They'll log it at the station, or put it on a computer – and nothing will be done. For years they've said they're going to have regular patrols of the park, but the reality is that they're about as regular and frequent as the coming of Halley's Comet; total waste of time. Whatever, as I said earlier, I feel we should do nothing more on the matter, Mr Mayor, a view strengthened by Mrs Gilbert's very timely information that the boy was at school, and perfectly well, the following day. I'll formally move we take no action – and leave that fine tree in place.'

'Seconded, Mr Mayor,' grunted Sidney Bartlett. 'Nonsense, all of it.'

'I'm not sure we can be seen to take no action at all,' commented Jack Dawson in his soft, measured way. 'That it is 'much ado about nothing', as the bard would say, cannot be denied. That it has wasted our time and some public money, likewise. We do, though, as we are only too aware, live in strange times – times when everything we do comes under public scrutiny as never before. Although this Mrs Milner would appear to be making a mountain out of a molehill (perhaps it's even smaller than that) and certainly would seem to have no case against this council in any direction, it is probable that even if she does not actually pursue any case against us, or make any claim, she could still 'bad mouth' us to people, stir things up and the like. Councillor Sparks' experience of her in his shop shows that she is the type of person who could cause a fight in an empty room; thus whilst I feel there is little if anything we need do in a positive way – certainly we should leave that magnificent tree in place – we should perhaps appear to be taking the matter seriously and will be keeping an eye on the horse chestnut, indeed on all trees on our property, and will take immediate action if even the slightest danger would appear to manifest itself. Perhaps we could issue a statement in general, and to the media and local paper in particular, that we are aware that there can be some small danger from trees and the like, especially in windy weather, with possibly branches and suchlike falling from them, and in consequence all will be under regular inspection and scrutiny from our staff and, and, and tree surgeons.'

Douglas Denny snorted. 'I love that title, 'tree surgeons'; most of the folk who call themselves that do not know much more about trees than the average badger. It's just that they own chainsaws and want to make a few bob from them. Still, I see where Mr Dawson is coming from and in general I agree with him. If he's willing to propose we go down this route, then I'd be happy to second him.'

'So Councillor Dawson is suggesting we – well, we monitor things; for that's basically what is being proposed – only it does sound a lot better than keeping an eye on matters. Yes, I'll go with that. It means we're – well, we're on the ball, but it's not really going to cost us anything.'

There was general agreement at Jim Sparks' comments, the mayor included. Nodding his head, he said, 'Yes, I feel that's an excellent way forward, Councillor Sparks. We monitor the trees and, of course, all matters in our parks to ensure there is no danger to the public, even in a minor way.'

'Constantly would be better, Mr Mayor, would you not think,' interjected Sally Gilbert. 'We monitor all of our property, indoors and out, constantly; that way, as I see it, we leave no loopholes.'

The mayor smiled, then nodded again. 'Perceptive of you, Mrs Gilbert,' said he. 'You are totally correct; constantly is the word the council tax payers will wish to hear – so that is what they will hear. Ladies and Gentlemen, we have a proposal that we monitor – vigilantly is a word which could be added to this, do you not agree gentlemen' – he looked in the direction of proposer Dawson and seconder Denny, received from them nods of agreement – then continued, 'So I put the motion to the vote – all in favour? Those against?'

'Unanimous, Mr Mayor,' reported the town clerk.

'Good, good. You'll issue a statement, Mr Conway, as suggested earlier regarding our policy – our determination to ensure that everybody is safe when accessing our parks, playgrounds and buildings? And as soon as possible?'

'It will be done first thing in the morning, Mr Mayor.'

'Thank you, Mr Conway.' The mayor looked at the assembled councillors; 'This has been an unnecessary and, frankly, annoying situation Ladies and Gentlemen, created by someone who would seem to feel their rights are greater than their responsibilities to fair play and the wider community. However, this way forward will ensure that this council is very receptive to the welfare and interests of the people of the town – and will have cost us relatively little. I wish you good evening, Councillors, and thank you for your attendance.'

There was a general returning of the mayor's 'good evening', but the last word lay with Jim Sparks – 'You cannot beat a good 'monitoring', said he, to nobody in particular, as they made for the exit. 'The cheapest and most painless council policy known to mankind.'

II

The Flagpole

Frank Jackson glanced, covertly, at his watch. Twenty to nine –
and there was football highlights on television at half past nine,
it was certainly dragging on tonight. The longest meeting for
months, in fact. It was Sally Gilbert's fault as usual. Trees – that
was all the woman thought about. She had been on the council
six or seven years and he'd rarely heard her talk about anything
else.

And she had to choose tonight, when there was already a long
agenda, to read out a list of fifty different trees and shrubs she
thought the council ought to buy to plant in the park. All in Latin,
too. Nobody had ever heard of any of them; and who cared
anyway. Like Arthur Phillips said, half of them would be ripped
up by vandals within a week, and the rest would die of root rot
with all the rain they had; but nothing would stop her reading out
her infernal list and now here they were at least half an hour later
than they need have been – and Cup Football was less than twenty
minutes away.

Cecil Conway didn't help either. He'd take a thousand words –
and half an hour – to say good morning, would Cecil. Quite a
competent town clerk in his way, but he could always bring
complications to the simplest problem. And time; like just about
everybody connected with this council, Jackson mused, he was a
master at wasting it.

'So that's the gist of the letter, Mr Mayor,' droned the town clerk, referring to a communication from the town Civic Society, suggesting the council put on some exhibition, mooted in the vaguest of terms, in the town hall regarding local heritage. There was a noteable dearth of enthusiasm amongst councillors.

'It would have been a damned sight quicker if he'd read it out,' muttered Councillor Tom Gaskell, his mind, likewise, upon the fast approaching Cup highlights.

'So what's new?' retorted Jim Sparks, sitting beside him. He moved upwards slightly from his half reclining position, raised his voice slightly, and gazed at the mayor.

'Move no action,' he said.

'Thank you, Mr Sparks,' replied Frank Jackson. 'Do I have a seconder?'

'Can I hang a hat on this one, Mr Mayor?' Councillor Mrs Julia Beckett hauled her considerable bulk to its feet. 'You see, whilst I agree we should take no action on this letter, I do feel that there are one or two points raised. . .'

'Do I understand you're seconding Councillor Sparks' proposition, Mrs Beckett?' interjected the mayor.

'Well, yes, in a way, but. . .'

'Thank you, Mrs Beckett. The motion's been proposed and seconded – all in favour?'

There was a communal grunt, a few arms moved in desultory fashion – and Town Mayor Jackson smiled happily, 'Thank you, ladies and gentlemen – the motion's carried. Now if there is no other business, I declare the meeting. . .'

'Hang on,' cried Douglas Denny, clambering noisily to his feet. 'I'd like to ask the town clerk why the Union Jack on the town hall tower was flying at half mast yesterday on the occasion of the Queen's birthday?'

'I've had no notice of this question, Mr Denny,' rasped the mayor fiercely. 'You've been on this council long enough to know that it's customary to give me notice of anything you wish to bring up under 'any other business'.'

'I appreciate that, Mr Mayor – and I apologise. But I've been unable to contact you. I did phone your home at lunchtime but your wife told me that you've been away on business for a couple of days and would not be home until early this evening – just in time to attend this meeting.'

'Yes – yes, well that's quite true. Anyway, what's all this about flags at half mast? It's the first I've heard about it.'

'It's obvious you've been away, Mr Mayor, else I reckon you'd have heard about it, all right. In fact, I've been pestered all day about it – people stopping me in the streets, telephoning me at home and so on. I reckon you must have had numerous complaints here in the office,' said Denny, looking at the town clerk.

'Well – yes. There have been a few residents making comment about it,' replied Cecil Conway. 'It's the sort of silly little thing which people tend to get worked up about.'

'Silly little thing, be damned!' roared Denny. 'I don't call a deliberate insult to Her Majesty the Queen a 'silly little thing'.'

'Likewise to the Mayor of Pontville sur la Mer,' interjected Councillor Nigel Hollins, Chairman of the Twinning Committee. 'It almost caused an embarrassing incident when the French party were here last week.'

'In what way, Mr Hollins?' asked Frank Jackson, a further furtive glance at his watch causing him to write off the first half of the match.

'Well, Monsieur Mallion, the mayor, looked up at the tower as the town band was playing the French National Anthem, saw the Tricolour at half mast and thought we were deliberately insulting him – and France. It took a bottle and a half of Scotch to convince him that obviously the wind, or something, had made it slide down the flagpole.' He glanced malevolently at Conway. 'I complained forcibly to the town clerk and he told me he would look into what had happened. I might have saved my breath by the look of it. The fact is, we pay our officers very generous salaries, and have a right to expect a little efficiency in return.'

Cecil Conway jumped to his feet, his glasses almost falling off in the process. 'Mr Mayor, I must protest at Councillor Hollins' grossly unfair attack. I would remind him – and everybody else on the council – that my salary is far lower than many other town clerks serving towns no larger than this one. Also, a couple of years ago, you will remember that I volunteered to forego my annual increment to help the town's finances after the extra expenditure we incurred when we had to replace the town hall floor because of dry rot, and have a couple of new windows.'

'And whose fault was it we didn't have enough money to do the job properly?' retorted Hollins. 'If the town clerk had put a sensible amount in the estimates to do the job then the crisis would never have happened. £5,000 he put by, Mr Mayor, and in the end it cost £52,000. If I ran my business. . .'

'Mr Hollins, please – that's enough,' snapped the mayor, his gavel having a rare outing as it thundered against the polished block of wood provided. 'We're in open council at present. This sort of thing should be discussed at committee. Not that we're going to go into committee,' he added quickly. 'The town hall floor and windows are an issue over and done with. . .'

'Thank God,' muttered Councillor Mrs Liz Crosby.

'. . .and I see no need to resurrect it. The question at the moment would appear to be, why are the flags being flown at half mast, and what are we going to do about it?'

'Perhaps I can help, Mr Mayor,' said Conway, his composure regained. 'We have had a few problems with the flagpole on top of the town hall tower. I know that the works supervisor tried to put the matter right twice last week when the Tricolour would go no further than halfway up the flagpole, but he's had a number of other problems to deal with, and hasn't been able to give the matter his full attention.'

'I don't care what his other problems are – sorting out that flagpole would appear to be a priority,' said Hollins. 'After all, we can't go upsetting folk the way we are at present. But then the works supervisor should be here in person to tell us what the problems are and why he hasn't solved them. Where is he?'

'I'm afraid he's off sick,' said Conway. 'A nasty bout of the 'flu.'

'That's a pity – but I know there's a fair bit of it about,' replied the mayor, wearily. 'Obviously we can't really discuss this without the works supervisor being present, so I would suggest it be put on the agenda of the next Properties Committee meeting, when, hopefully, Mr Benson will be over his 'flu and can tell us exactly what the problems are regarding the flagpole.'

'Well – er, unfortunately, Mr Mayor, the works supervisor will be unable to attend that meeting.'

'Why?'

'Because he'll be on holiday,' replied the town clerk.

'Marvellous, isn't it?' muttered Tom Gaskell to Jim Sparks, slumped in the seat beside him. 'Benson seems to spend a third of the year sick, a third on holiday and a third drinking tea in Cecil Conway's office. It's a miracle this town doesn't come to a complete halt.'

'Well, then, I propose it be put on the agenda of the next full council meeting in a month's time,' said the mayor, impatiently. 'All agreed?'

A series of grunts and nods affirmed that the council did, indeed, agree. 'That appears to be the end of our business tonight,' snapped Jackson, a glance at his watch showing that the second half highlights of the game were still within his grasp. 'Will somebody move the Common Seal?'

'So moved,' said Councillor Sparks.

'Thank you,' replied the mayor. 'And thank you for your attendance, ladies and gentlemen, I declare the meeting closed at 10.15pm, and wish you good night.'

Frank Jackson called the meeting to order.

'Good evening, Ladies and Gentlemen,' he intoned.

'Evening, Mr Mayor,' came the mumbling replies.

'We're pleased to welcome the Reverend Gladstone, Vicar of our parish church, to lead us in prayer.'

The parson glanced cursorily at the ranks of councillors, and at the half dozen council tax payers – most of them regular attenders – who had come to view and listen to the deliberations of their elected representatives, sadly reflected that the only time he ever saw any of them in church was at funerals, then lowered his head and mouthed his usual call for the Lord to bestow wisdom upon the very mortal members of this council.

The Reverend Gladstone duly said his piece, was thanked by the mayor, and wasted no time in making good his escape from the chamber. Frank Jackson, meanwhile, was looking at item 2 upon the routinely listed agenda.

'Apologies for absence?'

'I have only one, Mr Mayor,' replied Cecil Conway, 'from Mrs Gilbert; I'm afraid she's unwell.'

'Thank heavens for that,' muttered Tom Gaskell to his eternal neighbour Jim Sparks. 'That means there'll be no trees tonight. Be able to get home at a sensible hour.'

'She's probably suffering from Dutch Elm disease,' whispered Sparks, grinning broadly at his joke; 'or it could be ash dieback.'

'Item 3 – Minutes of the meeting of the full council held in this chamber last month. These have been circulated; is it your wish I sign them as a true record?' The mayor glanced around the chamber, took in the slight movement of hands and a few muttered 'ayes,' and quickly penned his signature to the bottom of the relevant page of a large minute ledger.

'Mr Mayor, before you sign the minutes,' said Mrs Beckett, getting to her feet, 'I would like to question the wording of minute 72.'

'You're a bit slow, Mrs Beckett,' said Jackson sternly. 'I've already signed the minutes now as being correct.'

'Well, yes, I appreciate that, and I'm sorry for not getting up before – my attention was distracted by somebody slamming a door elsewhere. It's just that I feel that whilst the minute isn't exactly wrong, its clarity would be greatly improved if in the last line of the minute the word "suggested" was used rather than "proposed".'

'It means the same thing,' said Tom Gaskell.

'No, it doesn't, Mr Mayor,' argued Mrs Beckett, stoically. 'There is a subtle difference which I believe would be more in keeping with the subject of this minute. It is, after all, rather sensitive.'

'The woman's daft,' muttered Jim Sparks. 'Imagine wasting the council's time with nonsense like that.'

'Imagine reading the minutes,' replied Tom Gaskell. 'I've been on the council for nearly twenty years and I've never read the minutes yet,' he continued proudly.

'Members agree we change the words as suggested by Mrs Beckett?' asked the mayor. He took the grunts to mean that they did agree, and altered the minutes accordingly.

'Item 4 – Matters arising.'

'There are none,' intoned the town clerk.

'Item 5 – verbal report from the works supervisor concerning the flagpole on top of the town hall tower.' The mayor glanced at the gnarled figure sitting on his left.

'Mr Benson, please.'

'Thank you, Mr Mayor,' said Billy Benson, his deep, melancholy voice immediately casting its usual pall over the proceedings. A small, rather round-shouldered man in his late fifties, council meetings for him held all the joy of a tooth extraction. His only vision of the future now was to see retirement seductively beckoning.

'Well, now, about his flagpole. You see. . .'

'Point of order, Mr Mayor.' Councillor Sidney Bartlett, at eighty two, the council's oldest member, was on his feet – a rarity in itself.

'Yes, Mr Bartlett?' asked the mayor, puzzledly.

'It's a very warm night. Could we have a couple of windows open please?'

'Yes, of course. Mr Benson before we hear your report, would you open the windows behind you?'

Benson cleared his throat, a little nervously. 'Well – er – well I'm afraid I can't open any of the windows, Mr Mayor.'

'Why not for heaven's sake?'

'Well, you may remember that back in the autumn the council decided that the windows should be nailed up to prevent them from being opened because the frames have become rotten. As I recall a small sub-committee was set up to decide future policy as to the windows – whether you wanted double glazing or ordinary windows, UPVC or aluminium frames and so on.'

'I don't remember this,' rasped the impatient Frank Jackson.

'Mr Benson's quite correct, Mr Mayor,' interjected Cecil

Conway. 'Last October, I think it was, when we decided to set up the sub-committee. I've got it all minuted.' He immediately began to toss aside the piles of folders, and sheets of paper, lying mountainously on the desk in front of him. Frank Jackson gazed at him in exasperation – would the day ever dawn when the town clerk ever found the file he was looking for?

'It doesn't matter about the minutes, Mr Conway – we'll take your word for it,' snapped Frank Jackson, making no effort to disguise the annoyance in his voice.

'I seem to remember something about this, Mr Mayor,' said Arthur Phillips. 'As I recall, the sub-committee was to meet to decide exactly the kind of windows we wanted for the chamber and then the works supervisor would be able to get estimates of cost. I can't remember who was on the committee though.'

'Mayor, Deputy Mayor, Chairman of Properties and Chairman of Finance and General Purpose, or, at least, that's the usual composition of sub-committees,' opined Cecil Conway.

'Well, when did this committee meet? I certainly don't remember ever attending or being informed of any of its meetings.'

'You would have been informed, Mr Mayor. You would have received an agenda like everybody else,' said Conway, urbanely. 'Perhaps you overlooked it?'

'It's possible, I suppose,' agreed the mayor. 'Anyway, what did the committee decide – and why hasn't it been done?'

'Well, actually, it didn't decide anything. As I recall, the first meeting was scheduled for a date in early December but unfortunately it had to be put off because it clashed with the Annual General Meeting of the local Toc H branch – although agendas would have been sent out,' added he hastily.

'What's the Toc H got to do with this council?' asked Arthur Phillips, somewhat bemused.

'Nothing directly, Mr Mayor. It's just that Toc H had booked the council chamber that evening, as I recall, so obviously we couldn't use it for the sub-committee meeting. However, we did put forward a new date for mid-January, but as members will recall, the very cold weather caused the central heating system in this building to freeze so we had to postpone that meeting as well. For some reason, the setting of a further date for a meeting of the committee has been overlooked.'

'Meaning that the town clerk overlooked it,' snapped Arthur Phillips, who always got belligerent in hot weather.

'I must protest at that, Mr Mayor. I merely obey instructions from the council. I received no further instructions as to when members wished the meeting to take place. However, I did foresee some major work being done on the windows of this chamber, so ensured that a sum of money was put by in the estimates to cover it.'

'How much?' asked Jim Sparks.

'Five thousand pounds,' replied Conway.

'Five thousand pounds,' roared Sparks. 'That wouldn't cover the cost of the sills in windows of this size. We'll be lucky if we get this job done for less than £25,000. I would have thought the town clerk would have learned something from the fiasco on the town hall floor.'

'Then there's no chance of doing it, Mr Mayor,' retorted Conway, tartly. 'This authority doesn't have that sort of money to spend at present.'

'It seems to me that we're getting nowhere fast on this issue,' said Frank Jackson. 'The fact is that we're facing the summer without being able to open the windows. I don't know who's directly to blame for this, and I don't really care. All I know is, something has to be done – and done quickly.'

'That's all very well, Mr Mayor, but we're obviously talking about a lot of money being spent on these windows,' said Tom Gaskell. 'I feel we've a duty to the council tax payers not to rush into anything, but to ensure that at the end of the day we get value for money.'

'I agree with Councillor Gaskell,' said Jim Sparks authoritatively, 'and with that in mind, I propose that this entire matter be referred to the next meeting of the Properties Committee for further discussion.'

'I second that,' said Gaskell.

'Very well,' said the mayor, with a sigh – too hot in his rather heavy suit to contemplate having an argument. 'All those in favour?' the motion was carried.

'Now perhaps we can let Mr Benson get on with telling us about the problems he's got with the flagpole.'

'Thank you, Mr Mayor,' said Benson mournfully. 'You see, the trouble with the flagpole is that it's rotten, especially the top half. That's the trouble with wood, of course – rot. Most flagpoles these days are made of metal. That's what I would recommend the council goes for next time when the pole is replaced. And it'll have to be replaced obviously; it's beyond repair.'

'That's all very well,' interjected Nigel Hollins, 'but the works supervisor's still not told us how the two flags in question came to be flying at half mast.'

'Well, that's simple enough, Mr Mayor,' replied the phlegmatic official. 'You see, the wood at the top is so rotten in won't hold the nails which hold the pulley wheel in place any longer. When we came to pull the French flag up on the morning of the day Mr Hollins is complaining about, the nails just came away and the pulley fell off. We tried to nail it back in place, but we were halfway down the pole before we found wood sound enough to take the nails. So that's why the flag looked to be half mast.'

'It didn't look to be,' retorted Hollins, 'It was.'

'Well, yes, I suppose it was, Mr Mayor,' agreed Benson. 'And the same thing happened with the Queen's Birthday, of course.'

'So what are we going to do about it?' asked Arthur Phillips.

'Well, of course, we'll have to have a new flagpole – as I said just now,' replied Benson.

'Obviously so,' said the mayor, 'and I reckon we want one as soon as possible. I feel, Councillors, that we should instruct the works supervisor to get a new one urgently.'

'How much will it cost?' asked Jim Sparks.

The mayor glanced questioningly at Billy Benson.

'Well I've not had a firm estimate, but I have had a word with a couple of builders in the town and they tell me it'll cost between. . .' he coughed nervously, and looked down at the desk in front of him; 'between three and four thousand pounds.'

'What? Did – did the works supervisor say between three and four thousand pounds, Mr Mayor?'

'That's what it sounded like to me, Mr Sparks.'

'But that's ridiculous. How can it cost money like that? After all, it's only a piece of metal about fifteen feet long,' rasped Sparks.

'It's not the cost of the actual flagpole, Mr Mayor,' replied Benson. 'That wouldn't be of any great price at all. It's the erection of it which causes the problems – and eats up the money. You see, although we can maintain the pole from the top of the tower, and put the flags on, of course, when it comes to replacing the pole, it necessitates scaffolding – and that costs a fortune.'

'But why?' asked Arthur Phillips.

Billy Benson looked at the councillor in his rather squint-eyed way. 'It just does. These scaffolding firms charge a great deal to erect it all, and then charge it out at a fair old fee for each day.'

'I wasn't referring to the scaffolding,' snorted Phillips testily. 'I know that costs a fortune. What I want to know is why we need scaffolding to start with – why the job can't be done from the top of the tower?'

'It's all to do with the siting of the pole, Mr Mayor. Because of the construction of the top of the tower, the flagpole cannot be erected on the actual roof. Instead, it's cemented down against the side of the tower – as many councillors no doubt realise – which means we have to have scaffolding, I'm afraid.'

Councillor Jack Dawson pulled himself slowly to his feet and gazed vaguely in the direction of the 'chair', through his pebble glasses, 'Mr Mayor, instead of talking about spending a small fortune on a new flagpole, why don't we continue to use the one we've got?'

'Because it's rotten for heaven's sake,' retorted Nigel Hollins. 'What do you think we've been talking about for the past ten minutes?'

'Only the top half's rotten – the rest isn't,' continued Dawson, doggedly. 'If the top half was cut off, then we could use the lower half as a flagpole. It would probably last for another ten years like that.'

'Mr Mayor, we can't have flags flying from half a flagpole. Why it would be – well, demeaning for the town. And an insult to those we were supposed to be honouring by flying their flag,' insisted Hollins.

'I must agree with you there, Mr Hollins,' said the mayor.

'I agree it would look daft flying flags from half a flagpole, but surely the easiest solution is to do away with a flagpole altogether,' said Tom Gaskell.

'We must have a flagpole,' said Mrs Beckett.

'Why?' asked Gaskell.

'Because we must. Every town has an official flagpole – some more than one. In fact every village, and probably even some hamlets, have official flagpoles. There are many important occasions which need to be marked by the flying of flags. To say that we should do away with the flagpole altogether is absurd.'

'Not so, Mr Mayor,' insisted the tenacious Tom Gaskell. 'That flagpole is the most underused piece of council property in this town. We fly the French flag when the French delegates are over here on their annual twinning booze up, the Stars and Stripes on Independence Day – though why, is beyond me – and the Union Jack on the Queen's Birthday and a couple of other occasions. An expenditure of four thousand pence would be too great for that amount of use, let alone four thousand pounds.'

'Mr Gaskell is being parochial and, with respect, somewhat petty minded about this,' opined Nigel Hollins. 'The flying of flags of various nations over our town hall is a very important aspect of the vital work of cementing relationships between ourselves and countries throughout Europe – the world in fact. And there have been many more national flags than those which Mr Gaskell has named flown from that flagpole during recent years.'

'Like the time we flew the East German flag to welcome the West German delegation who came to discuss a possible twinning link years back before the two countries were reunified,' snorted Jim Sparks. 'No wonder we never heard a word from them again.'

'That was a most unfortunate error, Mr Mayor,' said Hollins, quickly, 'due to the fact that our letter requesting a flag was sent to the wrong embassy in London.' He fixed the town clerk with a somewhat malevolent glare, before returning his glaze to the 'chair.'

'May I ask the works supervisor, through you, Mr Mayor, if our own council staff could be used to replace the flagpole. That would save some money, surely.'

'No chance I'm afraid,' said Benson, shaking his head solemnly. 'This is obviously a tradesman's job, and we've only got two tradesmen, Gordon Lashman and Henry Collins. Unfortunately, Mr Lashman, who's not far off retirement as councillors will probably be aware, suffers rather badly from asthma and would find it impossible to climb all those internal steps leading to the roof of the tower, whilst Mr Collins can't stand heights. No, there's no way we can use our own labour.'

'Then is there no possible way, Mr Mayor,' asked Mrs Beckett, 'that the flagpole can be replaced without the use of scaffolding; or, at least, extensive scaffolding? That obviously is where the expense lies.'

Billy Benson looked somewhat dubious, then shrugged his shoulders. 'I'm doubtful,' he said, 'but there is a remote possibility that it could be done in a different way – which would save us a lot of money.'

'That being?'

'Well, there's a builder in the town – I hadn't better mention his name because I haven't been able to get hold of him, as he's on holiday in Canada – who's also a trained steeplejack. Now on a couple of occasions I've known him avoid the use of scaffolding by donning a kind of safety harness and hanging over the side of one or two buildings in the town. I know that he replaced some missing slates on a high part of the church roof using this method. He's never done any work for the council, but then we've never needed this kind of specialist work done before. Whether he could use this harness method to replace the flagpole I obviously don't know. The problem, as always these days, is damned health and safety legislation – the bane of our lives.' He stopped briefly, shaking his head in mild despair, then continued, 'Still, I will certainly ask him when he returns from holiday.'

'When will that be?' asked the mayor.

'He's away for over two months, not due back until the end of June, so his sister told me when I was talking to her a few days ago. Still, as I've said, I can certainly have a word with him as soon as he returns and then report to the July meeting of the full council.'

'That sounds fair enough, Mr Benson,' agreed Jackson. 'There's no great panic about this job, although the sooner it's done the better of course. But if hanging on a couple of months is going to save us a sizeable amount of money, then it will be well worth while. Members agree that we await a report along these lines at the July meeting?' Mumbled 'ayes' and grunts of assent ruled the day.

The July meeting agreed to the planting, suggested by Mrs Gilbert, of a further fifty trees, made a decision to write a letter of protest to the county council – and the local MP – at their resolution to sell off half the playing fields of the local comprehensive school for building, and donated one hundred pounds towards a new roof for the town's Citizens Advice bureau. As to the flagpole, nothing was done because Billy Benson's mysterious steeplejack was so enjoying himself in Canada that he decided to stay for a further month, thus returning at the end of July. As the council stood in recess throughout August, it was agreed that Benson should report to the September meeting of the council.

That gathering was held on a very cool evening, much to the relief of both Cecil Conway and Billy Benson, neither of whom had made any real progress towards sorting out the windows which should open to the chamber. The holiday break seemed to have done everybody a power of good, for the meeting moved along at a brisk pace, the members exuding an air of efficiency. It was agreed that a further part-time worker be appointed to help keep the cemetery tidy, and the grass mowed – Mrs Crosby's objection that it was a silly time to appoint anybody extra to the outdoor staff as there would soon be no grass to mow thanks to winter frosts, being over-ruled, much to her chagrin.

'We do need time to train a man to handle the mowers and suchlike, Mr Mayor,' pointed out Cecil Conway, 'so if he is appointed now, then come next spring, he'll be most proficient in all his duties.'

This argument didn't convince anybody, but it was generally thought an extra pair of hands – albeit part-time – throughout the winter would be useful in order to improve the general standard of the cemetery, a most sensitive area in the consciousness of local folk; any failure to maintain high standards of care and maintenance would bring salvos of complaints.

The meeting voted to write to the county council, with a copy to the local MP, complaining about the state of the main street of the town – 'there are pot holes so deep they've got their own wildlife,' as Jim Sparks put it – and a letter was also to be sent to the district council complaining about the deplorable state of the public conveniences. 'I suspect that the public lavatories in the slums of Calcutta are kept better than ours,' as Mrs Beckett put it, rather dramatically.

Tom Gaskell, who'd travelled large portions of the world during his ten years as a merchant seaman, informed the council in general, and Mrs Beckett in particular, that having once visited Calcutta, he could categorically state that whilst there was considerable room for improvement in the general upkeep of the town lavatories, they were still somewhat better than those found in the sprawling Indian port. Mrs Beckett, at her formidable best, took issue with Gaskell upon the subject, but was eventually silenced when the mayor demanded it by slamming down his gavel.

The last item on the agenda, before 'any other business', was entered: 'Town Hall Flagpole. To determine a course of action.'

The mayor glanced at Billy Benson. 'As I recall, Mr Benson, you were going to have a word with this builder, steeplejack fellow you know when he returned from Canada, and see if he could tackle the renewal of the flagpole without scaffolding.'

'Yes, that's right, Mr Mayor,' replied the works supervisor, getting stiffly to his feet. 'Well, this chap came home at the beginning of last month, so I've been able to discuss the matter with him. And I'm glad to say the news is good – he can renew the flagpole using a safety harness which suspends him from the top of the tower. This means, of course, he'll not need any scaffolding, so the price will be radically less than the four thousand pounds mentioned recently.'

'How much less?' asked Arthur Phillips.

'This chap reckons it'll cost about twelve, perhaps thirteen hundred pounds, including the price of the flagpole.'

'Mr Mayor,' interjected Jim Sparks, 'we're treating this steeplejack as if his name's secret. Is there any reason why we cannot know exactly who we're talking about?'

The mayor shook his head. 'None as far as I'm aware, Mr Sparks. This gentleman wouldn't mind having his name made public I assume, Mr Benson?'

'No – no, shouldn't think so. Obviously there's no secret involved in all this. For members information, the chap I'm thinking of is Cohn Matthews who lives in Holly Close. He's a good tradesman from what I've heard, and I'm sure will be just the fellow we need to sort out this flagpole business.'

'If we give the go ahead, how soon can he begin the job?' asked Nigel Hollins.

'Almost immediately,' replied Benson. 'He's just got a small job to finish, which'll not take him more than a couple of days apparently, then he's got a few days spare before he starts some biggish job somewhere in the town. He reckons our job'll not take more than a couple of days at the outside.'

'That sounds excellent, Mr Mayor,' said Hollins. 'It would mean that we'd have a new flagpole in place long before the end of the month – when we're expecting a visit from the folk dance group of Pontville sur la Mer. We'd be able to fly the Tricolour in a proper fashion this time.'

'Not another blasted twinning effort,' muttered Tom Gaskell.

'If the council tax payers knew how much money was wasted on all this nonsense, they'd sack the lot of us.'

'No they wouldn't,' whispered Jim Sparks in reply. 'I'd soon see to it that everybody knew it was Hollins' folly not ours.'

'So it's members wishes that we instruct the works supervisor to ask Mr Matthews to replace the flagpole as soon as possible?'

'With a metal one, of course,' interjected Mrs Crosby.

'Naturally,' replied Frank Jackson. 'All those in favour, please show.'

'Just a minute, Mr Mayor,' wheezed Sidney Bartlett, pulling himself to his feet. 'I fancy we're out of order on this one, you know.'

'In what way, Mr Bartlett?'

'Well, it says in standing orders that if any building or maintenance work is going to cost more than two hundred pounds, then we have to go out to tender. We're talking here of over a thousand pounds – and it could be more; after all, we've not had a proper estimate from this fellow. These things always seem to creep up in price.'

Frank Jackson nodded, 'That's a very fair point, Mr Bartlett – and one which I'd not considered, I must confess.'

Cecil Conway sprang to his feet. 'I'm afraid Mr Bartlett is somewhat out of date, Mr Mayor. There probably was a two hundred pound limit some years ago – though I must say it was before my time – but the limit now is three hundred and fifty pounds.'

'Which still means we've got to put it out to tender, Mr Mayor,' rasped Tom Gaskell. 'Mr Bartlett's quite right. I don't know how the town clerk failed to advise us of this in the first place. If we go ahead with this at present, without others being given the chance to tender, then the district auditor will be down on us like a ton of bricks. In fact, we could end up in jail.'

'All, that is, except the town clerk,' muttered Jim Sparks.

'With respect, Mr Mayor,' replied Cecil Conway, 'I do think Mr Gaskell is exaggerating somewhat. Certainly the district auditor would ask questions if we contemplated spending well into four figures without going to tender, but I hardly think he'll call the fraud squad in for just a few hundred pounds over our official limit.' He smiled his patient smile at the council and resumed his seat.

'That's all very well,' retorted Bartlett, doggedly, 'but standing orders are the rules by which this council operates, and those rules should be obeyed – to the letter. If we start ignoring them here, and bending them there, where'll we all end up?'

'I agree with Councillor Bartlett, Mr Mayor,' said Tom Gaskell. 'These things have got to be done properly.'

'But if we go through all the palaver of putting it out to tender, it'll put the replacement of the flagpole back weeks – in fact, months probably, Mr Mayor,' whined Nigel Hollins.

'He's worried that he won't be able to use the Tricolour when the French twinning delegation come over at the end of the month for another booze-up,' muttered Jim Sparks to Gaskell.

'That's just too bad,' retorted Tom Gaskell, springing to his feet once again. 'As I said just now, these things have got to be done properly. And it's not as if there's any real urgency to the matter. I'm sure we can carry on as we are for the time being.'

'Mr Mayor, we cannot continue to fly flags at half mast,' observed Douglas Denny.

'Quite right,' said Jack Dawson. 'But if the council adopted the idea that I put forward in a previous meeting, we could use the existing flagpole until another is erected, and the flags would not be at half mast.'

'What idea was that, Mr Dawson?'

'To cut the top half off the pole and just use the bottom,' retorted Dawson sharply, a touch of hurt in his voice, motivated by the fact that Frank Jackson had seemingly forgotten his, to him, wise remarks of a couple of months earlier.

'Well, yes, that would appear to be a reasonable plan – in the short term,' agreed the mayor.

'Yes, quite so,' agreed Arthur Phillips. 'If Councillor Dawson is making it a proposition that we cut the top off the pole and use the bottom half until we put up a new one, then I second it.'

'Do you propose that, Mr Dawson?'

'Yes, I suppose I do, Mr Mayor. I fancy it's a good short term

49

solution. In the meantime, tenders can be invited for the erection of the new flagpole – including one from Mr Matthews. I know he said it would be only a little over a thousand pounds, but I really do think it needs to be put down on paper – for everybody's point of view.'

'I agree, Mr Dawson. You've heard the proposal, councillors; I believe you're going to second it, Mr Phillips?'

'Yes – I second the proposal,' agreed Phillips.

'All in favour, please show – carried,' droned the mayor, not taking a lot of notice as to who was, or wasn't, voting in favour of the motion. He turned to the town clerk.

'Will you be able to get tenders in sufficiently quickly to be able to bring them to the next meeting, Mr Conway?'

'What, you mean the next meeting of the council, Mr Mayor?'

'He gets dafter by the minute – what does he think we mean, the next meeting of the Fatstock Show Committee?' muttered Jim Sparks.

'Of course,' retorted Jackson, the will to live growing ever weaker within him, 'what other organisation are you in the habit of reporting to?'

'Well – quite. But what I was meaning was whether you wished me to report to the full council or the Properties Committee. It would, of course, be correct procedure to report to the Properties Committee.'

'Quite so. In that case, bring the tenders to them. I'm sure that would be in order, Mrs Crosby – wouldn't it?'

The Chairman of the Properties Committee nodded. 'Yes, Mr Mayor,' she agreed, 'and perhaps we could be given delegated powers to accept the lowest tender and put the work in hand. After all, if we have to wait for the full council to meet, then we'll waste another week.'

'That makes sense,' agreed Frank Jackson. 'Are members in agreement to delegate powers to the Properties Committee to take this action?'

'Just a moment, Mr Mayor, please,' interjected Cecil Conway. 'I've just been thinking that whilst everything proposed certainly makes sense, there is the possibility that all the tenders might not be in by the time of the Properties Committee meeting.'

'They will if you make the deadline a few days before the committee is due to meet,' pointed out Mrs Crosby.

'Well – yes, true. But that doesn't really give those tendering much time to work out their estimates, does it? I feel it's just a little unfair on them. With that in mind, perhaps it would be better if I bring the tenders to the meeting of the full council, the week afterwards, Mr Mayor?'

'We're going around in circles as usual,' muttered Jim Sparks.

'Yes, all right – the full council,' rasped the mayor testily, rapidly becoming fed up with the entire business. 'Members agree that the tenders be brought to the next meeting of this council?'

Members did, indeed, agree.

Amongst other matters, it was agreed at the October meeting of the council that Cohn Matthews' tender of £1325 for the providing and erecting of the flagpole on top of the town hall tower be accepted, the work to be put in hand immediately. His wasn't the lowest tender – it was the only one.

At the November meeting, Billy Benson revealed in his customary monthly report on the general maintenance work being carried out on council property, that Mr Matthews had, as yet, been unable to make a start on the erection of the new flagpole owing to the fact that he'd had a small accident.

'Does this fellow ever do any work?' asked Tom Gaskell. 'It seems to me he's either abroad on holiday or sick.'

The mayor admonished him for the remarks. 'Mr Gaskell, these are rather personal comments and whilst I appreciate you're saying them – well, perhaps 'tongue in cheek' would be the best way to describe it – they're still remarks which could be misconstrued, and should be kept out of open council.'

'Who said I made them 'tongue in cheek' muttered the unrepentant Gaskell to Jim Sparks.

'Apparently, Mr Mayor, Mr Matthews was just a bit unlucky,' explained the works supervisor. 'He told me that he descended a ladder from which he was working in Fore Street the very day before he was due to make a start on the flagpole, and as his right foot hit the pavement at the bottom of the ladder, he stumbled rather badly, and fell off the edge of the pavement breaking a small bone in his foot in the process.'

'He sounds like a right star,' muttered Gaskell once again. 'After all, how do you fall off a ladder when you're on the bottom rung?'

'How long will he be off work?' asked the mayor.

'Until about Christmas. He told me on the phone this morning, when I enquired as to his progress, that he'll definitely be starting work again in the New Year.'

'That's quite some time, Mr Mayor,' said Nigel Hollins, 'perhaps we should consider getting somebody else to do the job.'

Arthur Phillips jumped to his feet. 'That's ridiculous!' he cried. 'By the time we go through all the business of going out to tender, and so on, and getting replies in, Matthews will have had enough time to get over a heart transplant, let alone a cracked bone in the foot. Anyway, nobody'll tender for the job, will they? – except to do it the expensive way using scaffolding. No, it'll be a lot quicker and cheaper to wait for this fellow to recover.'

Frank Jackson nodded his agreement. 'I fancy you're right, Mr Phillips, and I'm sure most members will agree.'

Most members did, indeed, agree.

The subject of the flagpole was not a particularly burning issue at the January meeting of the council, several other problems having supplanted it in the consciousness of councillors. Principal amongst these was the vandalising of the town hall ladies' cloakroom over the Christmas period, the discovery of dry rot in the mayor's parlour, situated at the back of the council chamber and the threat by the amateur operatic society to sue the council over the partial collapse of the town hall stage, with them stood on it, during their annual Christmas carol concert. However, at the end of a long verbal report, the works supervisor did state that, unfortunately, owing to the bad weather, work had not yet started on erecting the new flagpole.

'What bad weather, Mr Mayor?' asked Nigel Hollins, genuine puzzlement upon his face. 'My wife only remarked to me this morning how mild the weather is for the time of year.'

'Well – yes, that's true to a degree,' agreed Benson solemnly. 'But it's still been rather wet and cold – not very nice weather to be working at the top of that tower.'

'Of course it's been wet and cold,' rasped Jim Sparks. 'It's always like that in January. Come to that, it's usually like that in June around here. If this fellow Matthews isn't going aloft to do this job until the weather's perfect, then I reckon Mr Gaskell here will have his way after all – the flagpole will never be replaced.'

'It's not quite like that, Mr Mayor,' replied Benson, stoically. 'All Mr Matthews is waiting for are a couple of reasonably dry, frost-free days. There's cement involved in this job, you know. It's impossible to cement around the base of the pole, down the side of the tower, unless the weather is reasonable.'

'Yes, fair point, Mr Benson,' interjected Frank Jackson quickly. The meeting had already dragged on quite long enough – and there were highlights of the evening premier league games on the box in less than half an hour. 'Let's hope the weather improves sufficiently for the job to be done before our next meeting.'

Billy Benson most earnestly shared the mayor's hope.

Late January and the early part of February brought some unseasonably sunny weather but little joy for Benson. Indeed, the February meeting of the council saw the hapless works supervisor face a torrid time. Escalating dry rot, and costs to match; the vandalising of the town hall ladies' cloakroom being followed by like treatment to the gents; the operatic society threatening to sue him personally as well as the council – were just some of the problems which were making his life a misery; and Arthur Phillips didn't help matters, for at his insistence a date had been fixed for a meeting of the sub committee which was to consider the state, and replacement, of the chamber windows – despite a masterly attempt at prevarication by Cecil Conway. Still, he was winning. He only had one final item on his list of work done – or about to be done, sometime – and the meeting would be virtually over.

'Concerning the flagpole, Mr Mayor,' he said, gazing steadfastly down at the top of his desk, 'I'm afraid we've run into a bit of a snag.'

'Not another one?' roared an angry Nigel Hollins, jumping to his feet. 'Damn it all, the Egyptians built pyramids quicker than it's taking us to replace that infernal flagpole. I thought this builder was supposed to be a steeplejack – and used to doing work like this?'

'Well, it's not really his fault, Mr Mayor,' replied Benson. 'The problem lies with the flagpole itself. Mr Matthews put the work in hand a couple of weeks back when the drier weather came, as he said he would. It only took him a day to take down the remaining part of the old flagpole and prepare for the new one, and at the end of the afternoon he told me that he would erect the new one the following day. The next morning, though, when he inspected the new pole before hoisting it aloft, he noticed a very slight crack in the alloy – and decided it wouldn't be safe to erect it. He said that if it was put up in that condition there would always be a chance that it would snap in a gale, and, of course, come hurtling down into the street. Obviously the council can't take that sort of risk, so the flagpole has been sent back to the suppliers and we're awaiting a new one.'

'And how long will that take?' demanded the irate Hollins.

'Well, unfortunately the suppliers had no further flagpoles in stock,' replied the works supervisor, 'so they've had to send to the factory for another one. They reckoned at the time that delivery would be about a month or so, this was about a fortnight ago, so it should be here in roughly another fortnight.'

'A month, Mr Mayor, just to get another flagpole. What are they using to transport this piece of metal – a mule?' Nigel Hollins was in a mood to draw blood.

'No – a ship, Mr Mayor.'

'Why a ship?' asked Hollins.

'Because it has to come from South Korea,' replied Benson, totally without emotion.

'You have to be joking,' roared Hollins, rolling his eyes towards the ceiling. 'Surely they can get a simple alloy flagpole a little closer than South Korea?'

'Apparently not, Mr Mayor, it seems that this kind of pole – which, incidentally, should last a good twenty-five years – isn't made in this country at all,' replied Benson.

'Twenty-five years?' rasped Tom Gaskell. 'It'll take that long to have the blessed thing erected as far as I can see, Mr Mayor. It's life span will be over before we put it up.'

'I do sympathise with what you say, Mr Gaskell,' replied the mayor, 'but sadly these things do happen – as they say. Hopefully, we'll soon take delivery of a new pole and it will be up there on top of the tower by the time we next meet.'

'I wouldn't back that with a lot of money,' muttered Jim Sparks.

'What I want to know, is why the defect in this flagpole wasn't discovered earlier?' said Mrs Beckett. 'After all, I would imagine, seeing as this job was supposed to be done months ago, that it's been in our possession for some considerable time.'

'Not in our possession,' interjected the works supervisor, rare urgency in his voice. 'No, it's never been in our possession. As the contractor, the obtaining of the flagpole like all the other materials – is the responsibility of Mr Matthews.'

'Well, how long has it been in his possession, then?' persisted Mrs Beckett.

'I don't really know,' replied Benson, 'but I think he's had it several months.'

'Then why didn't he discover this defect before?' Alison Beckett was not a woman to shirk her duty of ascertaining the truth when she suspected incompetence.

'I obviously can't say, Mr Mayor,' said Billy Benson, a little wearily. 'Perhaps it's only just developed this fault,' he added lamely.

'I can't accept that, Mr Mayor,' said the good lady. 'I'm no expert on metals, but I find it hard to believe that defects can suddenly appear in an unused alloy flagpole – just like that. It seems to me that this flagpole was delivered to Mr Matthews in a defective condition, and this fault was only discovered months later. Incompetence, that's what this is. I'm not at all sure that this contractor is the right one to be entrusted with the erection of a new flagpole on the town hall tower.'

'Mr Mayor, don't let us go over this ground again!' cried Jim Sparks. 'This entire business seems to be taking an eternity as it is, so for heaven's sake don't let us do anything which is going to drag it out even longer. I agree that this flagpole should have been checked months ago, but the fact is, it wasn't, so there's nothing we can do about that. The important thing now, though, is that a new one's on order and should be delivered in a fortnight. Then, with just a little bit of luck, the blasted thing will be erected on top of the tower and we can start flying flags again in a way which won't upset half the people of this town – and most of the visitors. So no more talk of getting a new contractor or anything like that; if we go along that road we'll all be in our dotage before the job's done.'

'Yes, I must agree with you, Mr Sparks,' said the mayor, nodding sagely. 'I think we must stick with Mr Matthews and hope that this new flagpole is soon delivered – and erected. Members agree?'

Members – or most of them – did, indeed, agree.

Frank Jackson looked at his watch; it was dragging on once again. He couldn't remember the last time he'd attended a brief council meeting. Here it was, nearly ten o'clock and there was still a good half hour left in it yet. It was Jack Dawson's fault this time – as it always was at the March meeting. Not habitually a man to mither on unless he really had something to say, Jack, nonetheless, always went to town about any expenditure on the bowling green; and March was when Cecil Conway always itemised the things which needed to be done to bring the green up to its traditionally excellent standard – and their cost.

Nobody knew why Dawson so resented any expenditure on the green – and consequent help to the bowling club – but throughout the fifteen years he'd been on the council, he'd stood up at every March meeting and made a verbose, almost passionate, appeal to his fellow councillors to cut back radically on the spending of public money on the green, and bowling club. This appeal usually led to a protracted debate, the statement from Sidney Bartlett that the bowling green was 'the jewel in the town's crown', and invariably, an overwhelming vote in favour of maintaining the green to the usual standard. And Jack Dawson would always demand of the town clerk that his name be recorded in the minutes as voting against it.

This night was no exception, although the debate went on even longer than usual. Perhaps 'debate' would be a rather inaccurate word to use, as it gives the impression of a number of people each contributing something different in the way of ideas and opinions to the discussion. Regarding the bowling green, however, it was a case of Jack Dawson on one side, the rest of the council on the other, with most members virtually repeating what had already been said. Still, Frank Jackson – probably the most patient mayor the town had had in years – rationalised it in his mind, as he sat in his imposing-looking chair gazing down at his verbally marauding fellow councillors, as being 'democracy at work.'

Jack Dawson's March madness was bad enough, but Mrs Gilbert had chosen this meeting as well to talk about trees – as she did at great length about four times a year. This time she suggested that an arboretum be created in a corner of the park, and painstakingly listed the twenty-five different species of tree which she felt should be bought by the council to fill it. And once again, she insisted on using the Latin names. Her monologue would have gone on even longer than it did, but Jim Sparks saved the day by interrupting her as she was about to list a dozen or so different varieties of shrub which she felt would look nice planted close to the arboretum.

'I'm sure there is much merit in Mrs Gilbert's ideas and suggestions, Mr Mayor,' said Sparks, 'but I feel that such matters should be looked at more closely and, perhaps, our entire policy towards tree planting brought up to date. With that in mind, I propose this matter be referred to the next meeting of the Properties Committee.' This wasn't the first time Jim Sparks had used such a ploy to stop Mrs Gilbert in full flood, nor was it the first time it had succeeded. Councillors wished to get home that night.

'I second Mr Spark's proposal,' interjected Tom Gaskell quickly.

'All those in favour, please show,' said the mayor, entering into the spirit of haste. 'Carried – the question of tree planting for this year, and future years, will be put on the agenda of the next Properties Committee.'

'Must make a point of missing that one,' muttered Jim Sparks to Tom Gaskell.

'Me as well,' agreed Gaskell.

For Billy Benson, it was the easiest meeting he'd known in a long time – largely because his report was almost positive. The town hall dry rot had largely been sorted out but there had been vandalism to the children's slide in the park. However, the youth who did it had fallen off the slide whilst trying to rip up the boards of the platform at the top, and broken a leg. He had been charged with criminal damage by the police, Benson reported with satisfaction to an irate council.

'Birch the bugger,' rasped Arthur Phillips, 'that's what they should do.'

'I beg your pardon, Mr Phillips?' inquired the mayor.

'Corporal punishment, Mr Mayor, that's the answer,' was Phillips modified comment. 'We're too soft with these young devils.'

The mayor had been that way before when the seemingly eternal problem of vandalism was discussed – seemingly eternally. 'We shall have to let the law take its course, Mr Phillips,' he said urbanely, and totally inadequately, something he was as aware of as the rest of the council.

Billy Benson further informed the council that although the town swimming pool contained a leak – as it had for the past ten years – thanks to the remedial work carried out during the autumn and winter, it was certainly leaking less than in previous years.

'I'm sure councillors will be pleased to hear this, Mr Mayor.' he said, almost with enthusiasm.

Members were, indeed, pleased to hear this. Any news, even minimally good, concerning the swimming pool was greeted with delight, it having a real rarity value. Members, though, didn't pursue any discussion on the continuing leaks – after all, the less said about the swimming pool, the better for all of them.

The works supervisor moved on to the last item on his list, and came close to smiling when he mentioned it – a rare thing indeed.

'The new flagpole has been erected, Mr Mayor, and is all ready to – to – well, to receive flags.'

'That is good news, Mr Benson,' said the mayor, stealing a further glance at his watch, and wincing as he saw the hands pointing to 10.35pm. 'I'm sure members will be very pleased to hear this.'

Members were, indeed, very pleased to hear such news.

Billy Benson gazed morosely out across the serried ranks of motley councillors from his seat to the left of the mayor. To think he had another three years of all this before he could retire on full pension. There might be a way, though, that he could go out through ill health. Scores seemed to do it and get away with it. And he'd felt a little 'peaky' lately. He had not the slightest doubt, though, that he'd feel more than 'peaky' before this evening was out.

As if he didn't have enough problems, for yet more dry rot had been discovered in the town hall – in the kitchens this time and the swimming pool was leaking like a colander again, with the water heating system on the blink for good measure; and somebody, somehow, had written graffiti on the walls of the mayor's parlour – how that had happened, when only official guests were ever admitted to that place, he really did not know. Still, at the end of the day, he felt he'd be able to talk his way out of it all – it wasn't, after all, directly his fault that these problems had arisen. It was the other thing which would really make him look an idiot; in fact, he could see some of the more vindictive members of the council – those who had little faith in him as works supervisor – really going to town on it. And he'd have to mention it in his report – that's if it wasn't mentioned by somebody before. After all, someone would have noticed, or been told about it, for sure. There'd certainly been enough phone calls to Cecil Conway concerning the matter.

Benson was right about his ability, like a veteran opening batsman to fend off the fast balls directed at him regarding town hall, swimming pool and mayor's parlour, all these issues being raised as Mrs Crosby, the chairman, read out the minutes of the Properties Committee. He was, though, taken by surprise by the 'bouncer' bowled by Douglas Denny. He knew such a ball had to come sometime during the course of the meeting, but was hoping that he'd be able to neutralise it by bringing the subject up himself whilst delivering his monthly report later in the meeting. Denny, though, who considered the works supervisor to be an overpaid incompetent, bowled for the head – and drew blood. As Mrs Crosby presented a minute concerning repair to the door at the foot of the town hall tower, Councillor Denny rose to his feet.

'Concerning the town hall tower, Mr Mayor,' he said evenly. 'If I might hang a hat, as the saying goes. It was pointed out to me this morning, by an irate elector, that a couple of days ago – the Queen's birthday – no flag was flying from our new flagpole. I did intend to take this up with the town clerk or the works supervisor before this meeting, but unfortunately business delayed me out of town until late afternoon, so I've only been able to get here just in time for the meeting. Mr Mayor, after much blood, sweat and tears we finally got a new flagpole erected on top of the tower because the previous one was rotten. We spent over a thousand pounds and a lot of council hours on the damned thing and what happens on one of the major – possibly, the major – flag raising days of the year? Why, simply, no sign of the Union Jack. This council and the tax payers of this town, demand an explanation.'

Cecil Conway slid down into his chair, glanced at the mayor, then at the works supervisor. Frank Jackson looked to his left – at Billy Benson.

'After all the problems we've had obtaining a new flagpole, then getting it erected, Mr Benson, the council does require some good explanation as to why the Union Jack was not raised on the Queen's Birthday,' said the mayor, rare authority in his voice. Billy Benson got to his feet and gazed wearily over the top of the council members towards the back wall of the chamber.

'Well, Mr Mayor, a – well, a slight – well, problem, has arisen,' he stuttered.

'You're not saying,' snapped Tom Gaskell, jumping to his feet, 'that the flagpole's defective already.'

'Well – no,' replied the hapless works supervisor 'the flagpole's all right.'

'What's the problem, then, for heaven's sake?' rasped the impatient Jim Sparks.

'The problem, Mr Mayor,' replied Benson slowly, still gazing, fixedly at the far wall, 'is quite simple really – though very annoying. . .' he cleared his throat noisily. 'The problem is that somebody has stolen our Union Jack!'

III

The Chapel of Rest

Alan Burton dropped his pen onto his notebook, sighed audibly, and leant back in his rather uncomfortable chair. A fine waste of time this was proving to be. It was somewhat unusual though, he had to admit that. Martin Mullins, editor of the *Bowminster Clarion*, had suggested to his deputy editor – and only full-time reporter – that he take in the monthly meeting of the Brendon Coombe Parish Council.

'It's worth a go, Alan,' he'd said that afternoon. 'There's usually something going on out at Brendon Coombe. In fact, the council out there has rescued more 'news drought' weeks than any other organisation I know. To be honest, I've usually had better and meatier stories from there than I've ever had from Bowminster Town Council meetings. Last night I didn't get a single real story from them – as you know. So we're desperate for something this week. If you can't get anything from Brendon Coombe tonight, then we'll have to lead with the story of the vicar breaking his leg when he fell off a ladder cleaning his windows, and fill up with pictures of Langham village carnival.'

'That'll take a bit of doing,' retorted Burton, with a laugh. 'They only had three floats and one of them couldn't parade through the village because it had a puncture right at the start.'

'True – but we can put in a picture of the carnival queen.'

'What – the one that's boss-eyed?'

'The very same. Well, she can't help that, can she? And to be fair, she's very pretty. But then we won't have to fill very much at all if you can bring in a good story or two from the meeting tonight. Always been a good place for a bit of scandal and jiggery pokery, has Brendon Coombe.'

Alan Burton looked blankly at the far wall of the ante-room of Brendon Coombe Parish Hall. Martin Mullins was usually right about things, but tonight was an exception. There appeared to be no sign of the slightest scandal or minutest dire deed at this meeting. In fact, he couldn't recall a more boring council meeting. It took a very protracted discussion – lasting over half an hour – during which all eleven members of the council spoke, for them to decide, on the casting vote of the chairman, to make a grant of fifty pounds to Brendon Coombe Hotspur to help them buy a new set of goalposts for the rapidly approaching season, the old set having been sawn up by vandals. That criminal activity had provided a neat little story for the *Clarion* – unlike the meandering discussions concerning the granting of a parsimonious fifty pounds.

The reporter had thought for a moment that there might have been a bit of mileage in an item on the agenda marked, 'obscene graffiti written on the walls of the Parish Hall: to determine a course of action.' Unfortunately for the *Clarion*, the course of action decided upon was to refer the matter to the next meeting of the parish hall sub-committee, for them to report to the full council at a later date. So although there could still be a good tale coming out of those proceedings, there would be nothing which would fill the columns of the paper that week. Another protracted discussion followed, concerning the buying of a new laptop and printer for the part-time clerk, George Miller, who was also the local postmaster. The council accepted that he needed a new one, the old machine being on its last legs, but they were concerned at the price, which was put at a thousand pounds or more. It was decided in the end – unanimously this time – to delay a decision until the clerk had had time to contact various office equipment companies and find out just what sort of discount could be had if the council paid cash, and if any of them would be willing to take back the old one in part exchange.

It was at this point that Alan Burton had thrown down his pen. Rarely had there been such a pointless evening in terms of news, and a glance at the remaining items on the agenda convinced him that there was nothing still to come which could possibly make his journey, and time, that evening, worthwhile. He looked at his watch, saw the time was past eight thirty and pondered whether or not it was time to call it a night – and go home.

To his surprise, however, the decision was made for him – and, in consequence, his innate curiosity and suspicion was roused.

'Item 7 – report of special meeting of the cemetery sub-committee,' read the council chairman, Henry Morris. 'Mr Miller, will you distribute copies of the report to the members, please.'

'Mr Chairman, before the clerk hands around the reports, could I ask that this item be taken in committee?' asked Gordon Long, the sub-committee chairman, an embarrassed expression upon his face.

Henry Morris made no attempt to conceal his surprise: 'Taken in committee, Mr Long? I don't recall anything to do with the cemetery being taken in committee before. I've always thought that excluding members of the public and press from any aspects of our proceedings is a course we should not lightly take. The grass roots democracy which we represent can only really flourish in the light of public scrutiny – not in the darkness of secrecy.' There were times when Morris tried to elevate proceedings and possibly his own image, by indulging in a somewhat flowery use of words. 'Can you give me the reason why you feel that this item should be taken in committee?' He gazed somewhat imperiously at the chairman of the cemetery sub-committee, rather proud of his stout defence of democracy!

'Well, it's a bit difficult really, Mr Chairman,' mumbled Gordon Long, now looking furtive rather than embarrassed. 'It's just that I feel the interests of the council tax payers would be best served if this report can be discussed in, well, in private, so that – so that we can reach the right decision for the people of this parish.'

'I'm still a little unhappy about this,' said the chairman, shaking his head.

'I can understand how you feel, and I apologise for not mentioning this matter before the meeting; I meant to but I was slightly delayed getting here and was not able to do so,' Long explained – rather excessively – 'however, I do feel that this item would be better taken in committee. Perhaps, Mr Chairman,' he added briskly, 'you might care to glance at the report first then possibly you'll see what I mean.'

The chairman looked puzzled, then shrugged his shoulders. 'Very well, Mr Long.' He took the sheet of paper proffered him by the Clerk, scanned it quickly, laid it down, and looked at the expectant faces before him – and none, now, more expectant, and interested, than Alan Burton. He'd been sitting at the back of draughty ante rooms and council chambers for almost twenty years, and he could always pick up the scent of a story wafting through the musty air. And there was certainly one here somewhere, of that he was sure – though whether he could ever really get hold of it was another matter. One thing for sure was that within the space of a couple of minutes his soporific boredom had changed to intense interest.

'Yes, I think possibly this item would be best taken in committee,' said the chairman softly. 'Do I have a seconder?' Councillor Mrs Myra Jenkins raised her hand to signify her seconding of the motion.

The chairman glanced around at the other members of the council. 'Members agree that we take this item in committee?' A series of 'ayes' and nods indicated their assent. Henry Morris gazed towards the back of the room at the two male parishioners and the single journalist present. 'Thank you for your attendance, gentlemen, but unfortunately I must ask you to leave the ante room as this item is to be taken in committee.'

The three observers got slowly to their feet and noisily trudged from the room, Alan Burton bringing up the rear, his curiosity intense and determined to be satisfied – though he was aware that it could take a while to do that. Martin Mullins would not have a good lead from this direction for this week's edition, but there were a few columns to come sometime, of that the deputy editor was certain.

As soon as Burton had closed the door behind him, Henry Morris restarted the proceedings. 'Perhaps you'll distribute copies of the report, Mr Miller,' he instructed the Clerk, 'then we can get down to discussing it – and the figures in it.'

'Yes, the figures in it,' said Gordon Long. 'That's the reason I felt it was vital this report be taken without the public being present.'

'I agree,' retorted Morris, his face looking almost ashen. 'Mind you, I do dislike any aspects of secrecy concerning council business, but I must say that at first glance it would be in nobody's interest for the contents of this report to be made public at present. Still, perhaps you'll take us through it, Mr Long, and explain to us the fearsome figures it seems to contain.'

'Certainly, Mr Chairman,' said Gordon Long, looking around at his colleagues, an uneasy combination of self importance and apprehension about him. 'Firstly, perhaps I ought to remind members of the background to this report.'

'Yes – good idea,' replied the chairman. 'I expect most of us could do with a recap on it. After all, it's many months since we asked Mr Markwell, the surveyor, to prepare a report on the Chapel of Rest.'

'Why did we go to Markwell, Mr Chairman?' asked Councillor Arnold Atkins. 'He's not a man I've got any faith in. He surveyed a house I was interested in buying and said it was in excellent condition. I bought it as a result of that report yet just over twelve months after we moved in, my missus went through the floorboards in the front room.'

'I'm not surprised seeing the size of his missus,' Councillor Sid Bowden muttered to the aged Stanley Cowling, sitting slumped down beside him.

'Rotten as a pear it was,' continued Atkins, becoming more irate by the minute. 'I wouldn't have Markwell in any house of mine ever again after that lot. Tried to sue him, but didn't get anywhere – you know how these buggers wriggle out of any responsibility for anything. I told my solicitor to take action but. . .'

'Yes, it must have been a most upsetting business, Mr Atkins,' interjected Henry Morris quickly – though using a sympathetic tone of voice. It was, he knew, important to stop Arnold Atkins before he really got going. 'Still, I don't think this council have ever had any reason to question Mr Markwell's professional abilities.'

'Quite so,' agreed the parish clerk.

'That doesn't altogether answer Mr Atkins' question though, does it Mr Chairman?' pointed out the astute Mrs Jenkins. 'He wanted to know why we go to Markwell and Company – and so do I. Speaking personally, I've nothing particular against Mr Markwell – though I have heard one or two stories, not exactly to his credit, concerning his private life.'

'Really Mrs Jenkins, the surveyor's private life is absolutely nothing to do with this council,' scolded Morris – quite severely.

'I agree, Mr Chairman,' replied the lady, a little contritely, 'but I've also heard criticism of his professional abilities – quite apart from Mr Atkins' this evening. It could be though that Mr Markwell is an excellent surveyor. All I'd like to know is why we go to him when there are others in the district we could use. Granted there is none practising in this parish, but there are two other companies providing surveying services in the area. Why do we always go to Markwell and Company and never to either of them?'

The clerk looked puzzled. 'Well, simply because we always have, Mr Chairman. We used to go to old Markwell years ago and when he retired, we naturally used the services of his son.'

'Old man Markwell didn't retire – he died,' rasped Stanley Cowling, not moving one inch from his semi-reclining position.

The clerk looked puzzled for a few seconds – as he often did – then nodded his head. 'I do believe Councillor Cowling is correct, Mr Chairman,' he said, a little pompously – as was his wont. 'However, with due respect, I feel this is all somewhat irrelevant. Both old Mr Markwell and the present one have generally served this council well over the years, and I can frankly see no reason to question the judgement of either. Obviously Mr Atkins has had an unsatisfactory personal experience regarding Mr Markwell but I feel that it's only fair for the council to speak as it finds, as the saying goes.'

'Yes, I agree,' said Gordon Lang impatiently. 'Markwell's always been reasonably efficient in my mind. He certainly did a good job in finding that leak in the parish hall wall a few years back when we called him in because of the fungus growing in the kitchen, so as far as I'm concerned, there's no need to question his conclusions in this report.'

'What are his conclusions in this report?' asked Sid Bowden rather irritably.

'Well, members have got them in black and white in front of them and, if I'm ever given a chance to, I'll explain them fully,' replied Long, tartly.

'Point of order, Mr Chairman.'

'Yes, Mr Cowling,' said Henry Morris, somewhat wearily.

'Well, it's the state of these reports. I don't know about everybody else, but I can hardly read mine. It's just as well Mr Long is going to go through it. They should be clearer than this, surely,' rasped the aged councillor. 'Why, we've only recently bought a new photocopier or printer or whatever they call them.'

'Actually it's almost ten years since we bought the copier, and even then it was second hand,' retorted the clerk, sharply. 'It's almost had its day, I'm afraid, but I'm willing to soldier on with it at present in order to save the council what would be quite considerable expenditure. The computer, however,' he added quickly, suddenly remembering the fight he'd made earlier in the meeting to get a new one, 'remains absolutely vital. The old one there really has had it.'

'So's the photocopier as far as I can see, Mr Chairman,' said Councillor Cyril Pellow, chairman of the Finance and General Purposes Committee. 'And I would suggest that the council receiving clear photocopies of various reports and minutes is more important than the parish clerk being able to save a few minutes knocking out a letter.' He glared at the clerk as he said it – no love had been lost between the two since George Miller had put too little in to the estimates a couple of years earlier to cover the cost of new play equipment for the children's play area in the park, then deftly passed the buck to Pellow when a group of irate parents called a public meeting over the matter.

'Perhaps we could form a small sub-committee to discuss all aspects of office equipment required by the parish clerk,' suggested Henry Morris, aware that if he didn't take some action then the meeting could meander on until midnight and still not get to the nitty gritty of what Gordon Long was trying to report.

'All right, I'll go along with that,' agreed Pellow, knowing that as Chairman of Finance he could probably, on a small sub-committee, block any moves to give the clerk a new computer.

George Miller was well aware of this. 'Mr Chairman, is it really necessary to waste members time with yet another sub-committee?' he cried.

'I don't think it'll be a waste of time, Mr Miller,' replied the chairman. 'No, I fancy it'll be a good idea. A sub-committee like this can really go into what is needed in the office and come up with a list of priorities. I don't suppose we'll be able to afford much on the list, mind you, but at least we'll know what is really needed, and in what sequence.'

'The usual members on the sub-committee I assume?,' asked Cyril Pellow innocently.

'Yes, I think so,' replied Morris. 'Chairman and vice chairman of the council, the chairmen of properties and finance committees. Members agree?'

Members appeared to agree.

'Right – now let's get on with this report. Mr Long, please.'

'Thank you, Mr Chairman. As I said just now, perhaps it would be best if I gave members the background, briefly, to this report – though I'm sure many will be aware of what it's all about anyway.'

'Carry on, Mr Long.'

'Thank you,' said the articulate, and very shrewd, Gordon Long. 'Now several years ago, after complaints from the vicar – and one or two from Harvey Hancock the undertaker – about the deteriorating condition of the Chapel of Rest at the cemetery, we asked Mr Markwell to prepare a report on the defects at the Chapel, and how much it would take to put it right.'

'Was that the present Mr Markwell, or his father?' asked Mrs Jenkins, who'd only come onto the council at the last election.

'Oh, the present one,' replied Long. 'The old chap's been dead these fifteen years or more, whilst the first report, which I'm referring to at present, was brought to us about five years ago. Now, in that report to the council, Markwell said that whilst the condition of the Chapel of Rest was not half as bad as the vicar and the undertaker made out, there were, nonetheless, things which needed doing, especially to the roof; and a certain amount of re-pointing of the stonework was also deemed advisable. Mr Markwell estimated the total cost of the work at not more than a couple of thousand pounds and, as I recall, advised the council to have the work done before the following winter. As his report was made to us in the early summer, there was adequate time in which the work could have been done before the short days came upon us, but sadly this did not happen. The council in its wisdom decided to shelve the report saying, as I recall, that whilst Markwell's advice would be kept in mind, there was no money, at that time, to put the work in hand.'

Arnold Atkins jumped to his feet. 'Mr Chairman, I refuse to sit here and listen to Mr Long implying that it was the council's fault that no action was taken,' he roared angrily. 'As I recall it, most of us were in favour of doing some of the work, if not all, but Mr Long himself talked us out of it. He was chairman of the finance committee at the time and said that we simply could not afford any expenditure on the Chapel of Rest seeing as we'd over-spent so heavily on improving the changing rooms up at the recreation field. I've got a good memory, and those are the facts – as you, yourself, might well recall.'

Gordon Long's face flushed with anger and embarrassment. 'Well, obviously we couldn't spend money we didn't have,' he retorted. 'But of course we would have had ample funds it we'd not spent a small fortune in refurbishing the playing field changing rooms – which, incidentally, was to the real advantage only of the football club of which Mr Atkins was, and I believe remains, the chairman.'

Arnold Atkins scrambled once again to his feet, his face brick red, his eyes bulging from their sockets – as they invariably did when anger was his master. 'Mr Chairman, Mr Chairman,' he spluttered. 'I will not have my integrity questioned in this manner. The improvements to those changing rooms were to the advantage of the entire village; the entire parish in fact – not just the football club. Scores of folk use them, all the year round, not just players in the village club. The cricket club use them through the summer because the changing rooms in their pavilion don't have running water. The scouts use them for. . .'

'Yes, yes, quite so, Mr Atkins,' soothed Henry Morris. 'I'm sure we all accept that the refurbishments made to the changing rooms were to the advantage of the entire parish – and I'm sure Mr Long was in no way questioning your integrity.'

'He damned well was,' retorted Atkins, still looking apoplectic, 'And he was doing so by implying that I should have declared an interest because I'm chairman of the football club – it's obvious to me what he means, and I'll not have it. As I said just now, so many in the parish have gained from those improvements, not just the football club. That's why I did not declare an interest – and that's why I say he was questioning my integrity.'

'In my opinion, he was not, Mr Atkins,' ruled the chairman, severely. 'So please let us have no more of this needless argument, gentlemen. The situation is that a previous report of Mr Markwell was not acted upon – five years ago or whatever it was – and now we have another report from him which Mr Long is about to take us through.'

Henry Morris was, generally, mild mannered, but when he had that certain look of annoyance about him, few would venture to argue with the man. Arnold Atkins had more sense, and respect for convention, than to directly confront the chairman. Yet he was a stubborn, tenacious fellow, and was determined to have the last word on the matter.

'I accept your ruling, Mr Chairman, of course,' he said evenly. 'However, I would like to point out before we move on, that if it had been deemed essential to have carried out this work on the Chapel of Rest at that time, then the money could quite easily have been raised by levying a higher council tax rate or by borrowing.'

'Mr Chairman, it's never been the policy of this council, except in the most dire emergencies, to raise money either by the levying of a supplementary rate – or council tax as it is now – or by borrowing,' retorted Long. 'There are occasions – albeit very few – when it is necessary to raise funds by levying an emergency charge on them, but it would have been difficult to have justified it on that occasion, even though it was important to have carried out the work on the Chapel of Rest – as we realise now. For if we had done the necessary repairs then, we wouldn't be having to face up to this report, with all its wide ranging implications, this evening. I submit that. . .'

Nobody was ever to know what Gordon Long was about to submit, for Henry Morris' patience suddenly snapped: 'Mr Long, I ruled some minutes ago that you should proceed to take us through the report which lies in front of us,' he snapped. 'I trust you will now do so without comment upon things long past – and that includes you as well, Mr Atkins.' The chairman fixed all about him with a glare which would still a marauding tiger.

'Very well, Mr Chairman,' acceded Long, demurely. Arnold Atkins said nothing at all.

'This report,' continued the chairman of the cemetery sub committee, 'was, as I said just now, compiled by Mr Markwell acting upon instructions from this council some months ago. We were concerned about the ever deteriorating state of the Chapel of Rest at the cemetery – as members no doubt remember.'

'Get on,' grunted Sid Bowden, 'that isn't the reason and Mr Long knows it. We asked for this report because the vicar and the undertaker kept on moaning about the state of the chapel – as they have for donkeys' years now. I opposed wasting our money on paying Markwell's excessive fees the last time, and, as members might well remember, I opposed it again a few months ago. These reports are a waste of time and money, because they forever tell us to spend money we haven't got on an old relic we should not be maintaining.'

'But the chapel is council property, Mr Bowden,' reasoned Henry Morris in the most accommodating tone of voice. He knew just how bloody-minded Sid Bowden could be when he got going

72

– and by how much he could lengthen a meeting. 'As such, we are obliged to maintain it to a reasonable standard – I'm sure you will agree.'

'And it's a listed building,' chipped in Councillor Mrs Lorna Higgins, who was always well up on such matters.

'Yes, that's a good point, Mrs Higgins,' agreed Henry Morris. 'We shall certainly be in trouble with the conservationists, not to mention the district council, if we let the place fall down. Their heritage officer will really take us to task.'

'If they want the chapel to be maintained in good order, Mr Chairman, then they should foot the bills,' persisted Bowden. 'Marvellous it is; this council gets not the slightest benefit from that chapel yet we've got to use our money to maintain it.'

'Not our money, Mr Chairman,' interjected Stan Cowling, 'the council tax payers' money.'

'All right, I accept that – the people's money,' agreed Bowden. 'And what good is the place to those good folk?' he asked aggressively.

'None, unless they're dead,' grunted Arnold Atkins.

'The only people who benefit from that chapel,' continued Bowden, 'are the vicar and Harvey Hancock, the undertaker. The vicar holds the occasional funeral service there if he knows hardly anybody is going to turn up, whilst Hancock uses it as his own personal Chapel of Rest which means he doesn't have to provide one of his own, like most undertakers do. They're the two who should be maintaining the chapel, not us.'

The parish clerk intervened hastily, 'Mr Hancock does pay a rental to this council for the right to use the Chapel of Rest for his – his. . .'

'Customers I suppose you could call them, Mr Miller,' said Henry Morris, with a rare attempt at humour.

'Quite, Mr Chairman,' said the parish clerk, with a sickly smile; George Miller had no sense of humour at all.

'How much does he pay?' asked Arnold Atkins.

'Fifty pounds a year,' replied the clerk.

'What?' roared Sid Bowden. 'Why, that's less than a pound a week. That's ridiculous. How long's he been paying that amount?'

73

d

George Miller shrugged his shoulders, 'I don't know. That's always been the amount he's paid during the, what is it now, sixteen or seventeen years I've been clerk to this council. He pays quarterly.'

'I don't believe this, Mr Chairman.' Sid Bowden was in full flood now. 'Are we being told that Harvey Hancock has been on a rental of one pound a week for more than seventeen years?'

'Well – yes, that's what I'm saying,' retorted the clerk. Bowden eyed the clerk belligerently, then lowered his voice. 'Are any other undertakers permitted to use the Chapel of Rest?' he asked.

'Well – no, not really, Mr Chairman,' replied George Miller, avoiding Bowden's eye. 'The Chapel of Rest can be used by other undertakers – which means undertakers from outside the parish seeing as Mr Hancock is the only one within it – when the actual burial service it to be held there, of course. On those occasions, the Chapel of Rest ceases to be that, but becomes a chapel in the normal sense, for the vicar to say words over the deceased, and for mourners to attend, and for hymns to be sung and so on. But when it is used in its normal capacity, as a Chapel of Rest for the accommodation of a corpse filled coffin until it is removed to the parish church, or to the United Reformed Chapel or perhaps to the Crematorium, for the full burial service, then Mr Hancock has the exclusive use of the Chapel of Rest.'

'For a pound a week,' rasped Sid Bowden. 'All those years ago when the rent was first fixed, a pound a week would have been peanuts. After all, even then he could never have rented a like building to lay a coffin for a trifling sum like that. But these days a pound a week will hardly cover the council's costs in collecting it.'

'Oh, it costs virtually nothing to collect, Mr Chairman,' interjected the clerk. 'I just send Mr Hancock a quarterly account and usually he sends a cheque by return – though sometimes he calls personally and pays.'

'You know what I mean,' snapped Bowden. 'What I want to know, though, is why his rent has never been increased. The parish clerk is as well aware as any of us – in fact, more aware by virtue of his position – of just how tight finances have been for this council over recent years, yet he's allowed a situation to carry on where a quite prosperous local businessman is paying what is nothing more than a peppercorn rent for a valuable piece of council property.'

'I resent Councillor Bowden's remarks!' cried George Miller jumping to his feet. 'As clerk to this council, I am but a paid employee. I have neither the power nor the right to adjust rents to council tenants. I am but a servant of the council, and act as I am bid. If the council had told me to put up Mr Hancock's rent, then it would have been done immediately. Of course, if we're to get technical about it, it's something which should have been looked into by the cemetery sub-committee. They could, and should, have proposed a new rental for Mr Hancock, and the full council would no doubt have approved it.'

'Mr Chairman, I must protest,' snapped Gordon Long. 'The cemetery sub-committee is a hard-working group, but we are an ever-changing body as are all sub-committees. At virtually every Annual General Meeting, the composition is changed as the parish clerk well knows. So it's down to him to keep us informed of what's happening and what needs looking into. Even though I'm chairman of the cemetery committee, this is the first time I've ever heard that Harvey Hancock only pays a pound a week in rent. I share Mr Bowden's shock and anger at this ludicrous rental and would ask that this issue be put on the agenda of the next meeting of the cemetery sub-committee, when a new and realistic rent can be fixed.'

'That sounds an excellent idea, Mr Long,' replied the chairman. 'Members agree?' There was universal assent. 'See that item is added to the agenda, Mr Miller, will you?'

'Very well, Mr Chairman,' replied the parish clerk in clipped tones. He didn't like being a whipping boy for council incompetence, and felt that it was happening increasingly often. And if they were talking about pittance rents, perhaps it was time they talked of the pittance they paid him for listening to their meandering deliberations, and carrying out their, so often, woolly-headed instructions. The time had come for him to seriously think about chucking it all in. If he resigned, then perhaps they'd realise just how much he'd done for them over the years. Still, if he did go, he'd miss the quarterly cheque he drew from the council – inadequate though it most certainly was. But they would push him too far one day, of that he was sure, and it could be that such a day was not that far distant.

'If a new rental's going to be fixed for Harvey Hancock at the next cemetery meeting, then surely we ought to fix a new amount for the vicar as well,' said Arnold Atkins. 'What does he pay at present?'

The chairman looked at the parish clerk. 'What does the vicar pay at present, Mr Miller?' he asked.

'I don't quite follow,' replied the clerk. 'Where does the vicar come into this?'

'He occasionally uses the Chapel of Rest doesn't he?' retorted Atkins, a little crossly. 'That's where he comes in. How much does he pay every time he actually holds a funeral service in our Chapel of Rest – that's all I want to know?'

The clerk's face assumed a puzzled expression – a not rare event. 'The vicar pays nothing. Why should he?'

'Why should he?' roared Arnold Atkins. 'Because he's using council property to make money for himself, that's why he should be paying a fee.'

'I don't quite follow,' commented the clerk, putting on what Stan Cowling always termed, his 'Stan Laurel' face.

'Well, he doesn't plant 'em for nothing,' rasped the exasperated Atkins. 'Every time he buries somebody, he charges a fee – and that includes those occasions when he holds the service in our Chapel of Rest and not the parish church. So whenever he uses our property when about his business – because, at the end of the day, that's what it is, his business and his living – he should pay the council a reasonable fee. I'm absolutely dumbfounded he doesn't already do so. This appears to me, Mr Chairman, and I hate to say this – but it appears to me to be another example of incompetence on the part of. . .'

'Yes, well, I don't think there's any need to get personal, Mr Atkins,' interjected Henry Morris before the acerbic Atkins could spit out the name – although everybody knew whose name was on his tongue. 'I think this issue should also be added to the agenda of the next cemetery sub-committee.'

'Very well,' said the parish clerk with unusual haste, not even giving the chairman the chance to get the formal approval of the council regarding his suggestion. The quicker deliberations moved on from their present inquisitional style enquiries concerning the undertaker and the vicar, the better for all concerned – especially himself. Henry Morris glanced at the parish clerk, an expression of mild annoyance on his face. He didn't like being hustled in this way, but with the slightest shrug of his shoulders, decided to let the matter go. After all, time was running on and they'd still not got down to the report.

'Now perhaps we can get into this report, ladies and gentlemen,' he said briskly. 'My glance at it before we went into committee suggests to me that there are financial problems and implications coming our way which will tend to make discussions concerning rents and fees paid by undertakers and vicars just a little irrelevant – though, I would agree that such matters do need discussing and updating as a matter of urgency,' he added quickly. 'Mr Long, would you take us into the real core of this report – and the reasons why you felt it should be taken in committee.'

'Yes, of course, Mr Chairman.' Gordon Long gazed, owl like, through his thick glasses, the expression on his face suitably grave. 'Perhaps members will ignore the preamble of this report and look at paragraph 6. As I said earlier, Mr Markwell was instructed to prepare this report some months ago following complaints as to the condition of the Chapel of Rest. In paragraph 6, he tells us exactly what's wrong with it and I'm sure you'll find it somewhat harrowing reading.'

'Get on, it can't be as bad as what he says,' snapped Stan Cowling. 'That Chapel of Rest was built about a hundred and fifty years ago when they knew how to build these kind of places. It'll be standing there when our grandchildren are dead and gone. Longer than that, I reckon.'

'Not according to this report, I'm afraid,' opined Gordon Long. 'Mr Markwell suggests that if we do not act immediately, there is a very real risk that the Chapel of Rest will deteriorate so much during the next six to twelve months that it will become impossible to use it. In fact, it could even become dangerous to use it. He says that the roof is in such a bad way, it urgently needs replacing, whilst any amount of work needs doing to the windows and general stonework. And he does stress that this work should be put in hand virtually right away if long term disaster is to be avoided.'

'Forty thousand pounds!' cried Mrs Higgins, glancing down the single sheet report to the final paragraph at the bottom. 'That's what he says it'll cost to put it right. Forty thousand pounds; where do we get money like that?'

'Nowhere, that's the simple answer to that question,' snapped Arnold Atkins. 'It might as well be forty million, Mr Chairman. There's no way we can find the sort of money Markwell's talking about here – and there's no way we should even try.'

'I feel we have to try,' replied the chairman. 'If we don't, then the Chapel of Rest will simply fall down.'

'Let it,' rasped Sid Bowden. 'If it does, all it'll mean is that the undertaker will have to find fresh premises to lay his coffins – and pay a realistic rental for them – whilst the vicar won't have a council sponsored chapel to hold funeral services in. I reckon that we would do the ratepayers of this parish a service if we let it fall down.'

'We can't,' insisted Mrs Higgins. 'As I said earlier, it's a listed building and it's part of our heritage; and we'll be in all sorts of trouble from so many groups, including probably the Department of the Environment, if we do nothing.'

'Then they can pay for it,' growled Bowden.

'Members will probably understand now why I felt this matter should be taken in committee,' said Gordon Long with an air of self-justification.

'I'm sure nobody disputes the wisdom of it, Mr Long,' replied Henry Morris rather curtly, seeing Long's comment as being totally superfluous.

'Good God, I should think it does need to be taken in committee!' cried Cyril Pellow. 'If Alan Burton of the *Clarion* was ever to get hold of this lot, then he'd crucify us.'

'It's not our fault,' grunted Stan Cowling.

'I'm not saying it is,' retorted Pellow. 'But if he puts in the *Clarion* that we refused to act on a report five years ago because it was going to cost just a couple of thousand pounds, and now it's going to cost forty, then I reckon we'd be made to look the biggest bunch of incompetent fools that ever sat on a council.'

'And it's elections next May. I don't think there'd be many of us get back on the council if the people of the parish heard a tale like that,' rasped Stan Cowling.

'But they must hear such a tale, Mr Chairman,' pleaded Mrs Higgins. 'There's no way around it. In fact I'm not at all sure it was a wise or necessary move to go into committee.'

'You didn't say that earlier when I suggested we should,' retorted Gordon Long.

'Well – no, it's true. But I was influenced by yourself and the reaction of the chairman after he'd glanced through the report. I see now though, with hindsight, that I should have voted against it. If it had been discussed in public then we couldn't be accused of trying to cover anything up.'

'But we're trying to cover something up – surely,' said Pellow.

'We're not covering anything up,' snapped Long, rather crossly. 'At present we're merely discussing this report.'

'Then we're going to do nothing about it,' persisted Pellow. 'It'll be discussed, then the clerk will be told to put it in the bottom of a file, and at the bottom of a cupboard somewhere. And we'll all hope that the Chapel of Rest doesn't fall down for the foreseeable future.'

'Not until after May, anyway,' grunted Stan Cowling, once again.

'Why all this insistence that we'll not act on this report, Mr Chairman?' the annoyed Mrs Higgins chipped in. 'As I see it, we have to act – we have no option.'

'I don't know about having no option,' retorted Pellow. 'The one certainty in my mind is that we have no money. That, simply, is the reason why we will take no action on this report.'

'Surely we have a reserve of money put by for emergencies,' said Mrs Jenkins.

'Well – yes, I believe we do, Mrs Jenkins. That is so, Mr Miller, isn't it?'

'Quite right,' replied the parish clerk. 'I always put a sum of money in the estimates to take care of any emergencies which might crop up regarding council property throughout the year.'

'How much?' asked Stan Cowling.

'Fifteen hundred pounds,' replied Miller, briskly.

'Fifteen hundred quid? That'll hardly settle Markwell's bill, let alone anything else,' rasped Cyril Pellow. 'The situation is as I said a moment ago – we have no money.'

'We can raise some,' persisted Mrs Higgins.

'How?'

'We can levy a charge. Or perhaps borrow the money. There must be some way we can raise it.' Mrs Higgins was a very persistent woman.

'How large a supplementary charge would we have to levy to raise forty thousand pounds?' asked Henry Morris of the clerk. George Miller looked nonplussed for a few seconds, then scribbled for a brief period on a pad in front of him. He looked up; 'I cannot really do this here and now, Mr Chairman – I will need time to work it out properly. It's only fair on everybody for me to get it exact, council and local tax payers alike. It will, though, be large – very large. In fact so great a charge that the district auditor might prevent us doing it.'

'Quite so,' agreed Cyril Pellow. 'There's no way we can levy a supplementary charge of such size, Mr Chairman. As I said just now, we must take no action on this report. File it and forget it, that's what I say.'

'But the place could collapse – possibly even kill somebody.' Mrs Higgins was not to be defeated that easily.

'If it collapses on somebody, the chances are he'll already be dead,' grunted Cowling.

'But we cannot have the place collapsing; it's – it's a listed building as I said just now.'

'Typical of the district council and the ministry, and so on, that is. They list a building as being of special architectural or historic interest or some old nonsense, tell parish councils like us we've

80

got to preserve them and suchlike, then don't give you a brass farthing to do it with,' grumbled Arnold Atkins. 'No, it's best for the council tax payers of this parish that we take no action whatsoever. I agree entirely with Mr Pellow on this point.'

'There are ways of getting a grant towards doing this work, Mr Chairman, seeing as it's a listed building,' chipped in the clerk, trying to sound helpful.

'The speed they put out these grants,' said Sid Bowden, 'the place'll be a pile of rubble long before we ever see a penny of it. And even then, we would only get a small percentage of the total cost – isn't that right?' Both his tone of voice and the expression on his face were somewhat belligerent as he turned his gaze upon the parish clerk, whom he'd long considered to be incompetent.

'Well, yes,' agreed the clerk, in a subdued voice. 'These things do tend to take some considerable time and we would only get a percentage of the total cost.'

'What size percentage?' asked Mrs Higgins.

'Well, I'm afraid I don't really know off hand,' muttered the clerk, in even more subdued tones.

'If he doesn't know something as important as that, then the parish clerk's not doing his job correctly,' snapped Cyril Pellow, never slow to have a dig at the hapless Miller.

'Mr Chairman, I resent that,' retorted the clerk. 'I can't be expected to know everything.'

'Perhaps not,' retorted Pellow, 'but I would suggest that the clerk, knowing the financial implications of the Chapel of Rest report to this council, should have come to this meeting with all details of how we could apply for any grants we'd be entitled to. The fact that it's unlikely we would pursue this path is irrelevant.'

Stan Cowling leant forward in his seat and opened his mouth to, probably, voice support for Pellow, but Henry Morris stilled him with a wave of his hand. George Miller didn't altogether deserve it, because Cyril Pellow was certainly correct, but Henry Morris felt obliged, as chairman, to come to his clerk's aid.

'I think we've had sufficient of this, Mr Pellow,' he said in his customarily calm way. 'It could be that the parish clerk might have overlooked information regarding grants we might have taken up, but even if he had, it's extremely unlikely we'd have availed ourselves of such a grant. It would almost certainly take far too long and produce far too little – as we said just now. So let's drop this – this interrogation – and try to reach a decision as to what we are going to do concerning this report.'

'Can we borrow the money?' asked Mrs Higgins, still not prepared to give up her fight to have something positive done towards restoring the Chapel of Rest.

'There's no way we can borrow any more money, Mr Chairman,' chimed in the clerk quickly. 'This council already owes more money than is wise, to be frank. The buying of the new tractor last year is the cause, of course; we had to borrow quite heavily to purchase it. I felt it was the wrong move at the time, and I feel the same way now; there was no reason why we had to have our own tractor. We could have continued to hire one on a daily basis from Mr Billings at Oakfield Farm as we'd done without any problems for years. But I wasn't listened to, I'm afraid, and as a result, we're in debt. I have to say. . .'

'Mr Miller, you made your feelings felt regarding this matter when it was discussed last year. Rightly or wrongly the decision was still made to purchase a tractor, and to borrow money to do so. That's an end to it,' admonished the chairman. 'I want to hear nothing more about it.'

'Very well,' replied the clerk huffily.

'That seems to settle it then,' said Gordon Long. 'We daren't try to raise the money to renovate the Chapel of Rest through the council tax, and we can't borrow. So the only thing we can do is to close it down.'

'But we can't just do that. We can't stand by and leave it to eventually fall apart,' pleaded Mrs Higgins. 'After all, it's a listed building.' This determined lady was not going to allow her fellow councillors to ignore their responsibilities regarding local heritage.

'There's no need to close the chapel, Mr Chairman,' said Arnold Atkins. 'All we need to do is get Harvey Hancock paying a realistic rent, and the vicar paying a fee every time he holds a funeral service there, and carry on as before.'

'But Mr Chairman, we can't carry on as before, we do not have that option,' retorted Gordon Long, exasperation in his voice. 'That's what the report is telling us. Forty thousand pounds is needed to put the Chapel of Rest into a reasonable state of repair. Sadly we don't have that kind of money, we can't raise it through an extra charge, and we can't borrow it. So the only thing we can do is to close the place down – as I've just said.'

'And be made to look a bunch of incompetents.' Arnold Atkins was on his feet again. 'Just imagine how the *Clarion* will go to town on us. A council who five years ago instructed their surveyor to prepare a report on the Chapel of Rest then refused to act on his findings because they were not willing to find the relatively small amount of money needed to carry out his recommendations. Then five years later, they pay the same surveyor another princely fee to prepare a similar report on the same building. In this one, the surveyor tells the council to do the same things as he did five years earlier but, due to the fact that all the defects have got worse, plus the ravages of inflation, the cost will now be twenty times as much. And the council don't act on this report either – simply because there's no way they can raise the money needed to carry out the recommendation. Instead, the council closes the Chapel of Rest which will mean, probably, that folk who were born, bred and lived all their lives in this parish, will probably be carted off to lie in a chapel miles away before being brought back here to be buried. Mr Chairman, Alan Burton's pen will cut us all up into little pieces – and we'll be fed to the local electors like bread to ducks. Councillor Cowling remarked a little earlier that there wouldn't be many of us returned at the elections next May if the people of this parish heard a tale the like of which I've just told – and he's right. And let's be honest, we wouldn't deserve to be re-elected. As it is now, I'm not sure any of us deserve to get on the council again, the way we've wasted time and money on this Chapel of Rest over the years.'

'So what is it you're saying exactly, Mr Atkins?'

'I'm saying this, Mr Chairman. I believe the best and wisest course now is for the council to carry on as if the report was never written. For sure we don't have the money to do anything about it, so it's best to ignore it altogether. We get Hancock and the vicar to pay realistically for using the chapel – which'll bring in a little more income to the council – and we carry on as before. It seems to me the only sensible thing to do. For if we just carry on then there's no real chance of any bad publicity. I would remind members we're in committee here, so no news of this report should go beyond this room. In fact, there's no real need for anybody to even know this report exists.'

'Mr Atkins, people are bound to know the report exists,' pointed out the chairman. 'Possibly more importantly, Alan Burton knows it exists. It is, if you care to glance at your agenda, written there for all to see. In fact, as I recall, I read out the item before Mr Long proposed we go into committee. Therefore I fancy it's a bit late to try and pretend the report does not exist.'

Arnold Atkins glanced at his agenda. 'With respect, all it says on the agenda is, "item 7 – report of special meeting of cemetery sub-committee" – and that's what you read out. That sentence doesn't tell anything. Certainly it doesn't tell anybody that there was anything contentious to discuss, like this report on the Chapel of Rest. I remember last year there was a special meeting of the sub-committee to discuss the cleaning of some of the old gravestones that had got green and slimy over the years. Nothing exactly earth shattering about that, Mr Chairman. So there's no reason why anybody who's even remotely interested should not think that this meeting was about something equally unimportant.' An expression of curiosity fluttered across his face. 'As a matter of interest, who exactly attended the special cemetery sub-committee meeting that discussed this report?' he asked.

'Well, in actual fact, nobody did,' replied Gordon Long, with a somewhat bleak smile. 'There seemed little point in the sub-committee discussing an important matter such as this when it obviously needed comprehensive discussion by the full council. Anyway, there are only three members on the sub-committee, and I knew the other two – yourself Mr Chairman, who was away on holiday, and Councillor Shaw, who was, and still is, indisposed –

would probably not be available for a meeting, until the full council met. So I thought it best – when receiving the report from the parish clerk – as chairman of the sub-committee, to bring it directly to the council for discussion. The formal entry on the agenda regarding "report of special meeting of the sub-committee" was only put there to keep our procedures in accordance with standing orders.'

'Fair enough,' said Atkins. 'So we know that the only people, except for Markwell and his staff, who know the report exists, are those in this room at present. I feel that is the way it should remain. So I formally move that this council takes no action on the report, and that the contents of it be not divulged to anybody not present in this ante room at this precise moment.'

'I second that,' said Stan Cowling.

'Just a minute, it's surely not that simple.' There was a pained expression on Gordon Long's face. 'This report pointed out several worrying structural defects at the Chapel of Rest, most serious of them being the state of the roof which, according to Mr Markwell, could collapse at almost any time. Mr Chairman, we simply cannot ignore a report of this kind. If we cannot afford to do the necessary work – and I accept we cannot at present – then the Chapel of Rest will have to be closed, and we will have to accept any criticism which comes our way. I cannot be party to a pretence that the report does not exist.'

'Stuff and nonsense,' rasped Sid Bowden. 'Every council of every size throughout the country suppresses reports now and again. It's all part of democracy at work. And governments – well they do it all the time. 'Not in the public interest', they say when covering something up. Well, it's not in the interests of the public of this parish that they be told the contents of this report. That's what Councillor Atkins has been saying, and I agree with him. Where ignorance is bliss, as the saying goes.'

'But Mr Long's point is surely the relevant one, Mr Chairman,' insisted Mrs Higgins. 'The Chapel of Rest, according to the report, is dangerous. Therefore it's dangerous to allow members of the public to enter it. I would agree with him that, in the short term, we close it, then take every possible step to raise sufficient funds to carry out the repairs. I would remind members that the Chapel of Rest is not just any old piece of council property – it's a listed building and part of our heritage. We have both a legal and moral duty to restore it as soon as possible.'

'Get on, it doesn't need "restoring" as Mrs Higgins puts it,' said Stan Cowling. 'There's nothing wrong with the place. That Chapel of Rest was there long before any of us were ever thought of and it'll be there, in good order, long after our grandchildren have passed on.'

'Not according to Mr Markwell's report,' retorted Mrs Higgins. 'For heaven's sake, Mr Chairman – he makes that very clear.' She made no attempt to disguise her frustration – even anger – at what she saw as a stupid comment.

'Get on, I don't take any notice of Markwell,' replied Cowling. 'He's like all these surveyors, and architects and suchlike, he's got to justify his fat fee. I dare say the Chapel of Rest could do with a bit of titivating, but structurally, I'm willing to bet the place is as sound as a bell.'

'It seems to me, ladies and gentlemen, that we've had a very full and frank discussion of this matter,' intervened the chairman quickly, aware that if he didn't take some sort of action the discussion could drag on half the night, with nothing fresh contributed.

'I feel it's time to put the issue to the vote. It's been proposed by Councillor Atkins, and seconded by Councillor Cowling, that no action be taken on the report prepared by Markwell and Company concerning the present condition of the Chapel of Rest at the Cemetery and, furthermore, that the contents of the report remain the knowledge solely of those present in this room at present. All those in favour, please show.' He counted the votes along with the parish clerk.

'Five in favour,' he said.

'Six, surely, Mr Chairman,' stated Miller.

'I don't think so. Still, perhaps members would show again. All those in favour?'

The chairman and the clerk counted once again.

'There, five,' said Henry Morris.

'Do you know, I made it six again, Mr Chairman.'

'Perhaps you'd state the names of the six. That's the only way to get this right.'

'Certainly. Councillors Atkins, Cowling, Bowden, Pellow, Mrs Jenkins and Mrs Higgins.'

'I've not voted for the motion, Mr Chairman!' cried out an angry Mrs Higgins. 'I should have thought by now that I had made my opposition to this motion more than apparent. This is the most scandalous action this council has ever considered taking during the seven years I've been on it.'

'But you put your arm up just now when the vote was held,' wailed George Miller.

'I did not. I was merely rearranging my hair, some of which had fallen down over my right ear.'

'Women,' muttered Stan Cowling, shaking his head sadly.

'Well, how was I supposed to know that,' snapped the clerk. 'It looked to me that . . .'

'I realised it, Mr Miller,' interjected Morris. 'In fact, it was clear to me that Mrs Higgins was not voting in favour of the motion. As she said, after the debate we've just had, it's obvious that she never could. So – there are five in favour of the motion. All those against?'

The chairman cast his eyes over the council. 'Two,' he said firmly.

'Yes – two,' said the clerk, authoritatively. 'Mr Long and Mrs Higgins. Other members, I assume, including yourself, Mr Chairman, are abstaining.'

'It would appear that way,' agreed the chairman. 'Anyway, the motion is carried. No action will be taken on this report; it will be filed and will not be spoken of outside this room. Will somebody please move 'open committee', then we can deal with the final two items on the agenda – and get away home.'

Councillor Stan Cowling's forecast that the Chapel of Rest would 'be there, in good order, long after our grandchildren have passed on' turned out to be somewhat inaccurate. For six weeks exactly after the meeting which decided the report should be shelved, and its contents not divulged, the storm broke – both literally and metaphorically.

The wind was rising towards gale force as Alan Burton made his way from his car to the bar of the 'Sportsman's Inn', a pub on the edge of the village. When he left two hours later, the wind was shrieking like a demented demon, though Burton didn't really notice it; his mind was trying to assess how best to handle the exceedingly interesting news he'd just been given. It had certainly been a profitable session at the bar, he mused, as he clambered into his car, the, by now, heavy rain slanting searchingly into, and through, his lightweight suit. He'd a feeling that if he dug around just a bit the following day, then he could well have a splendid lead story for the weekly edition of the *Clarion* due out, as always, on Friday.

During the time since he'd been asked to leave the meeting of the Brendon Coombe Parish Council, Burton had asked a few questions to a few folk here and there but had made little headway as to what the report contained and what action the council had taken on it. He had learnt though, that Markwell and Company had prepared the report, and had tried the direct approach of asking Markwell himself what the report contained. The surveyor, naturally, pointed out that the report was confidential and could only be made public by the council. Burton went through the motions of contacting the Parish Clerk of Brendon Coombe Parish Council, then the chairman, then, finally, the chairman of the sub-committee and got nothing out of any of them – as he'd expected. He would have pursued the matter with his customary zeal – as he was convinced that the council was behaving, at best, deviously, at worst, scurrilously – but the *Clarion* had run into a rich seam of good stories during recent weeks and he had been so busy filling columns with the local headline-making news which was constantly snapping at his heels, that he'd had no real time to probe for the story which, his instinct told him, very much surrounded the report concerning some aspect of Brendon Coombe's cemetery.

That evening though, as he'd leant against the public bar of the

Sportsman's, he'd got into conversation with a young fellow whom he only knew vaguely by sight. It transpired, however, that the young man was a trainee surveyor with Markwell, a factor which made him a most interesting drinking companion indeed as far as Alan Burton was concerned – and one to be cultivated. So he saw that the young surveyor's glass was not allowed to remain empty, and was rewarded by an ever more voluble and careless tongue, one, which under subtle questioning from Burton, told him the full contents, and the full significance, of the report compiled by Markwell's, on the Chapel of Rest in Brendon Coombe Churchyard.

'The place could collapse like a house of cards at any time,' concluded the slightly tipsy trainee surveyor, with a touch of exaggeration. Those words were very much in Burton's mind as he started up his car and wended his way home through the dark, wet, stormy night. The next morning he would delve and dig amongst the councillors of Brendon Coombe until he had his news item – and it would most certainly be a lead story.

Alan Burton, that night, could not know that the following morning his story would be strewn around Brendon Coombe Cemetery. When he arrived at the *Clarion*'s offices, he made a pot of tea, as usual, and took a cup out to the front office where sat the ancient Beryl, a lady who'd been with the paper apparently since the dawn of history, and, virtually, always at the reception desk.

As the deputy editor dropped the cup of tea onto her desk, the main door, leading into the street, opened and a woman came in. 'Morning,' she said brightly, 'I've come to collect the photo I ordered a couple of weeks ago – the one of the Brendon Coombe Church Sunday School outing. Mrs Wooley's the name.'

At the mention of Brendon Coombe, Alan Burton took some interest in the proceedings.

'Morning, Mrs Wooley,' he said affably. 'How're things at Brendon Coombe?'

'Well, not too good today,' she replied, a serious expression on her face. 'The terrible wind through the night has blown the roof off the Chapel of Rest.'

Burton was stunned – and excited. 'Are you sure?' he asked abruptly.

'Oh yes,' she replied, 'the postman told me first of all, then I saw it myself as I walked past the cemetery to catch the bus. Not all the roof's come off, but about half has gone, with slates and wood and suchlike scattered all over the cemetery. It's a shame, isn't it? Hundreds of years old that Chapel of Rest, you know.'

'It is a shame – it is indeed,' agreed Burton, with almost manic glee. He spun on his heels and almost ran to his tiny office at the rear of the building. He had his lead story all right – and he wouldn't have to dig and delve. Yet he needed a quote or two to toss into the columns to give them extra spice. So he phoned Henry Morris, Chairman of the Brendon Coombe Parish Council. Sadly, according to Mrs Morris, her husband was not at home; in fact, he would not be back until late that evening. A likely tale he thought to himself as he dropped the phone onto the receiver.

Next he tried George Miller, the parish clerk. He had no trouble getting hold of the man, but it did him little good. 'No comment,' said the clerk when asked what the council were going to do about the roofless Chapel of Rest – and why they had not acted on the surveyor's report. 'I'm merely an employee of the council, and do no more, nor less, than what I am told to do by them. The chairman's the one.'

'I've already tried to speak to him,' replied Burton, 'but he's away until late tonight – according to his wife.'

'Then you should speak to the chairman of the cemetery sub-committee, Gordon Long,' snapped the parish clerk before putting down the phone.

So Alan Burton did as he suggested, and telephoned Gordon Long. The sub-committee chairman answered the phone himself – mainly because he appeared to be just about the only person in Brendon Coombe Parish not to have heard about the disaster which had struck the Chapel of Rest.

The news shocked him immensely, a fact made apparent by the faltering nature of his voice over the phone. So with his defences in disarray, Alan Burton fired at him the question which was central to his entire projected front page spread.

90

'Mr Long,' he said sternly, 'would you not accept that the council has acted very badly in this matter and that it is down to council incompetence and deceit that the Chapel of Rest – which is, I believe, a listed building – is now largely wrecked?'

'No, no no. It's not the council's fault at all,' stuttered Long, well aware that although he felt the report should have been made public and the Chapel of Rest closed, going along with the majority decision of the council made him as much responsible – and vulnerable – as all the other members.

'Then whose fault is it?' persisted the deputy editor.

'Well – well, I suppose, when you get down to it,' spluttered the chairman of the cemetery sub-committee, 'it's – well, really, nothing more or less than – well, simply an act of God.'

IV

The Tree

If there were two things in this world which councillor Albert Bingley detested, they were rain and site meetings. And the trouble was, they usually came together.

He glanced up at the sky as he clambered stiffly from his car; it was going to happen again today. The sky was as black as an undertaker's hat, and the wind was freshening from the west. Still, it wasn't raining yet so with a bit of luck – and unusual brevity from the committee – they might be able to finish before it did, though he would not put any money on such.

He walked towards the wide, ornate, black painted gate, checked the name, 'Fresh Winds', emblazoned in white upon it, considered it most apt as the rising westerly tousled his whitening hair, opened the gate and went inside. A group of councillors and officials stood to the left of the house in a large garden which consisted of a wide expanse of grass, with a few shrubs dotted about and a large copper beech tree almost in the middle. One of their number, David Nisbet, the chief planning officer, left the group having seen his chairman come into the garden.

'Morning, Mr Bingley,' he said brightly. 'Rain's holding off – but not for long I'm afraid.'

'No, not for long, David. That's why I think we should get this meeting over and done with as soon as possible,' replied Councillor Bingley, Chairman of the District Council Planning Committee.

'It shouldn't take long. There aren't many members present actually.'

'There never are when the weather doesn't look too good.'

They joined the group, standing on the lawn, amidst a flurry of 'mornings' and 'going to be a dirty day' and so on. Albert Bingley positioned himself in the middle of them, pulled a bundle of papers from his abused pocket, and eyed the group which surrounded him.

'Well, ladies and gentlemen, I think perhaps we'd best make a start. You can just about touch the rain with a stick, so the quicker we get on with this meeting – and get it over – the better. Mr Nisbet, please.'

'Thank you, Mr Chairman. As members will be aware, this site meeting has been called in order to be able to forward a recommendation to the next full meeting of the planning committee as to whether the planning application in question should be allowed or refused.'

'Perhaps you would remind members of the nature of the application, and of course objections, and so forth,' said the chairman, keen for the able, amiable, but often long winded Nisbet, to get to the point.

'Yes, of course,' replied Nisbet, in his un-ruffled way. 'As members will be aware, the application has been put in by Mr and Mrs Carter, who, of course, own this house to our left here, the garden of which we are now standing in. They have submitted plans for a four-bedroomed house to be built here in this garden. Now whilst we as a planning authority have no objection to the plans as such – size, lay out, materials and so on – there are considerable numbers of objections from other bodies and individuals.'

'County highways for one, no doubt,' snapped Councillor Ivor Ogden.

'Well, yes, that's correct, Mr Chairman,' agreed Nisbet. 'They object on the grounds that it is inadvisable to have any more outlets onto this road at present.' He indicated the busy Victoria Road, which lay on the other side of the garden hedge, with a rather theatrical wave of his hand.

'They always object on those grounds when it comes to this road, Mr Chairman,' said Ogden, his voice dripping with cynicism.

'That is so,' agreed the planning officer. 'And I fancy they'll continue to do so until a bypass is built, which will take away much of the traffic that at present uses Victoria Road, and indeed, clutters up the town.'

'Bypass? We'll all be dead by the time that's built,' snorted Councillor Mrs Ethel Nugent.

'Oh, I do think Mrs Nugent's being just a little pessimistic, Mr Chairman,' said Nisbet, stoically. 'After all, we are down on the forward planning list for a bypass in the foreseeable future.'

Helen Nugent snorted: 'Foreseeable future? Foreseeable for our great grandchildren perhaps – we'll never see it, that's for sure. There's not enough money available to maintain the roads we've got, let alone build any more.'

'Sadly, I do tend to agree with you,' said Albert Bingley.

'Point of order, Mr Chairman,' said Councillor Jim Jennings, in his husky, rather croaking voice.

At eighty, the old fellow was 'father' of the council in terms of age, though two members had actually served for longer.

'Yes, Mr Jennings,' replied the chairman, in a deferential tone of voice. A great respecter of age and experience was Albert Bingley.

'It's just that my old legs are playing me up a bit – they don't like all the wet weather, you know. I wonder if it would be all right if I sat down on this low wall here to my left.' He indicated an ornamental wall, some two feet high and about eighteen inches wide, which ran for about ten yards across part of the garden, but appeared to serve no useful purpose at all.

'Yes, of course, Mr Jennings,' agreed the chairman instantly. As the old fellow slumped down onto the wall, the chairman glanced at the chief planning officer.

'If you'd continue, Mr Nisbet, please.'

'Thank you, Mr Chairman. To continue with the letters of opposition to this application. There is one from the next door neighbours, on both sides, claiming that the proposed house would overlook them and take their light.'

94

'That's plain daft,' stormed Councillor Joe Davidson. 'It can't overlook both of them. If the house was to be built roughly where we're standing now – which is what the plan suggests – then it can only overlook the house over the fence facing us, which is thirty feet away. The other neighbour though, is on the other side of the applicants' house. There's no way they'll ever even see this building – if ever it's put up – from over there. Overlook them? Take their light? Rubbish – mischievous rubbish as well. A clear case of somebody in a nice comfortable position in life trying to stop somebody else building a decent home for folk to live in. Makes me sick.'

'I agree with Mr Davidson,' croaked Jim Jennings from his low, stone perch. 'There are too many people in this town trying to stop others building decent homes. And that's something we've all got a right to, you know – a decent home. That was one of the things we fought the last war for as well – "homes fit for heroes." Well, perhaps we didn't actually fight for that,' he said, an expression of doubt flitting momentarily across his face, 'but it was promised nonetheless. Yet here we are with scores of homeless people about and the council has waiting lists getting longer every day. It's a poor show, Mr Chairman, and no mistake. The only way we're ever going to sort it out is to build more homes – and I can see no reason why they shouldn't go ahead and build here. After all, it'll get somebody's name off the waiting list. . .'

'Mr Chairman, with respect,' interjected David Nisbet, 'I feel that Councillor Jennings is being perhaps a little premature in saying that the building of this house should go ahead. After all, councillors have not yet heard all the objections to the passing of this planning application – and there are many. Also, I do feel I ought to point out that the house here will cost, I would estimate, somewhere in the region of £400,000, so it won't be occupied by somebody whose name is on the public sector waiting list.'

'That's not the point, Mr Chairman,' argued Jennings, doggedly. 'If a house is built, then it's going to be lived in by somebody. That person will probably move from a cheaper, smaller house they're already living in which will leave that one empty for somebody else to move into – and so it goes on, right down through the line, with, at the bottom, somebody moving out of a pubic sector house and somebody else coming off the list and going into that empty house.'

There was a brief silence as the small assembly tried to come to terms with the old fellow's devastating logic.

'Well – yes. There could be something in what you say, Mr Jennings,' opined the chairman, at last. 'However, as Mr Nisbet pointed out, there are several other objections to the plans, I believe, due to a number of other aspects of the situation, so we really should hear from them before we try to come to any conclusions on the matter.'

The elderly councillor shrugged his shoulders in acquiescence, and tried to make himself more comfortable on his hard seat.

Albert Bingley, meanwhile, nodded at the chief planning officer. 'Carry on Mr Nisbet.'

'Thank you, Mr Chairman,' he said, urbanely. 'There is a letter of objection from the Water Authority saying that until the larger main planned for this road is put in, then there should be no further development.'

'That's a new one,' snorted Ivor Ogden. 'Just like the Water Authority to think of something to stop us using water.'

'They're a disgrace, the Water Authority,' snapped Mrs Nugent, quickly astride another of her favourite hobby horses. 'The only time they ever seem able to supply water is when it's raining. A few dry days and there's a hosepipe ban – a couple of dry weeks and they turn if off altogether. I think, Mr Chairman, we should write to the Water Authority in no uncertain terms and complain about the way they treat us in this area – and about their general incompetence. Furthermore, I feel we should demand. . .'

'Yes, yes, yes, Mrs Nugent,' interjected the chairman hastily – aware that if urgent action were not taken, then the able, but voluble lady would flood them with a deluge of words – 'What you say has some truth in it, although in the past few years they have improved very considerably – after all, is it not some time since we had any real problems with water supplies? This, though is not directly a matter for this site meeting. Our brief, at the moment, is simply to note the objection from the Water Authority regarding the plan under discussion today.'

'Yes, but. . .'

'Thank you, Mrs Nugent,' interjected Albert Bingley once again – forcibly this time. 'Carry on Mr Nisbet,' he said, in a tone of voice which silenced even the valiant Ethel Nugent – though she did continue to mutter in the background.

'Thank you, Mr Chairman,' said Nisbet, a touch wearily now. 'We also have letters of complaint from the Civic Society, the Men of the Trees, the Council for the Preservation of Rural England, Friends of the Earth and the Willfell Trust, all objecting to the application on the grounds that to grant it would mean the chopping down of the copper beach just behind us.'

He turned and indicated a fine, sturdy tree close to the middle of the lawn, its copper coloured leaves twisting frantically in the rising wind.

'Did I hear you say the Wildfowl Trust?' enquired Ivor Ogden, a look of surprise on his face. 'I mean to say – what has a copper beech tree, at least twenty miles from the coast, got to do with the Wildfowl Trust?'

'I suppose ducks perch in the tree on their way south – or north perhaps; or whichever way they happen to be going at the time,' said Jim Jennings.

'Rubbish, ducks don't perch in trees,' rasped Councillor Miss Helen Hinton. 'Water is what they like – obviously.'

David Nisbet looked puzzled regarding the conversation for a few seconds, but then his face brightened as he understood what had happened. 'I'm sorry, Mr Chairman, but members seem to have misunderstood what I said. I did not refer to the Wildfowl Trust, but to the Willfell Trust, which is, I believe, a recently formed organisation in the town – funded by the estate of the late Mr Henry Willfell of Langley Manor – dedicated to the preservation of all aspects of the countryside locally, which includes trees, naturally. In fact, in this town, trees more than anything else.' The "tree lobby', as he termed them, had over the years caused him immense aggravation as a planning officer, the

e

downing of the most puny of saplings being seen by some 'zealots' as being an act of desecration.

'Thank you for that clarification, Mr Nisbet,' said the chairman, gazing at the threatening sky. 'Now, if we can get on, the rain's going to be upon us fairly soon, I would say.'

'Well, as I was saying,' continued Nisbet, 'we've had all these objections from these various organisations concerning the inevitable chopping down of the copper beech should we grant planning permission. It must be said that, as you can see, it is a very fine specimen and is, in the opinion of the planning department, the one real element regarding the application which might cause the committee to refuse the application. The other objections – highway problems, water and overlooking neighbours and so on – are not really sufficient, in our estimation, for us to recommend the application be refused. But that tree is a different matter. The outcry there would be should it be cut down leads us, in the planning department, towards the opinion that possibly the application should be refused.'

'Trees, trees, trees – that's all we ever hear about in this town,' rasped Joe Davidson. A pragmatic man who, whilst having some respect for fauna and flora, would rarely allow its preservation to influence him greatly. 'I reckon if half the people around here had to choose between chopping down a man or a tree, they'd cut down the man.'

'Trees are important, Mr Chairman,' chipped in Helen Hinton. 'They're out heritage. They were planted by our forebears to improve the world in which we live, so it's our duty to protect them. Certainly this lovely copper beech must be protected. Ultimately, its continued presence is more important – far more – than the erection of a dwelling.'

'That's all very well,' argued Davidson, 'but we've got to let just a little bit of reality come into our judgement. Let's face it, if our forebears, as Miss Hinton calls them, had refused to chop down every tree that got in their way, then this town now wouldn't even be the size of a hamlet. There wouldn't be half a dozen houses here. This copper beech is a nice enough tree, but there's scores more like it about. In fact, there's a couple down there at the bottom of the garden.' He indicated two rather insignificant trees close to the far hedge of the large garden, both puny in comparison to the fine specimen which was the subject of discussion.

'Is there a tree preservation order on it?' wheezed Jim Jennings from his stone seat.

Albert Bingley looked at a tallish young woman standing beside the chief planning officer. 'Your department, Miss Clarke, I think.'

'Thank you, Mr Chairman,' replied Myra Clarke, who spent most of her working life gazing at trees on behalf of the council. 'In actual fact, surprising as it might seem when one looks at such a splendid copper beech, there isn't a TPO on it. That's obviously something which should be rectified – in my opinion.'

'If there's no preservation order on it, then chop the blasted thing down,' said Jim Jennings. 'Then there can be a decent house built here in a proper manner. I propose we recommend to the full committee that these plans be passed.'

'I second that,' snapped Joe Davidson.

'I don't know, Mr Chairman; I fancy we'll be in trouble if we chop this tree down.' Ivor Ogden shook his head as he said the words. 'You know what people around here are like when it comes to trees. I mean – we've got more than our share of nutters when it comes to trees. Having said that, I'm sympathetic to Mr Jennings feelings that the house should be built. Perhaps we could compromise in some way. Perhaps we could – perhaps we could. . .' 'His face suddenly lit up. 'Perhaps we could dig it up and plant it somewhere else!' he cried triumphantly.

Albert Bingley looked perplexed. He was no expert on trees – one of the few who would, in fact, admit to such a deficiency in a town which appeared to abound with 'tree experts' – but he had a feeling that Ivor Ogden's suggestion was plain daft. He glanced across at Myra Clarke. 'I wouldn't have thought such an operation possible, Miss Clarke,' he said tentatively. 'Would I be correct?'

'Perfectly correct, Mr Chairman,' she stated authoritatively but respectfully, even though she felt that it was amongst the daftest suggestions she had heard in many a long year. 'It would be impossible to transplant a tree of that size and age. Even if we could lift it with all its roots intact – which is highly unlikely as they will have spread a great distance on all sides of it – the tree would almost certainly die if put elsewhere.'

'With such confirmation from our expert, Mr Ogden, I fear your idea is a nonstarter,' said the chairman gravely.

'With that in mind, I propose the plan be rejected,' said Helen Hinton, 'I feel. . .'

'Just a minute, Miss Hinton,' interjected Albert Bingley, 'we've already got a proposition from Mr Jennings, seconded by Mr Davidson, that we pass the plan.'

'That means the tree would have to be chopped down, Mr Chairman, which is intolerable,' persisted the rather strident Councillor Hinton.

'Obviously the tree would have to be chopped down if the plans are passed,' retorted the chairman rather testily, 'but you're jumping the gun – we haven't had a vote yet.'

'Move the vote be taken,' intoned Jim Jennings.

'Yes, good idea,' agreed Bingley. 'The proposition is, ladies and gentlemen, that the plan be passed. All those in favour please show.'

Councillors Jennings and Davidson raised their hands in unison. 'Two,' droned the chairman. 'Against?'

Councillors Mrs Nugent and Miss Hinton quickly thrust their arms into the air, whilst Ivor Ogden sheepishly and falteringly did likewise.

'Three,' said the chairman. 'The motion is defeated.'

'Which means the plans are rejected,' said Helen Hinton brightly. 'The house will not be built.'

'Not necessarily,' retorted Ivor Ogden. 'All that vote means is that the plans can't be passed if it means chopping down the copper beech. If there's any way the house can be built with the tree remaining where it is, then the plans could still be passed – that's correct Mr Chairman, isn't it?'

'Well, yes – yes, I suppose it is.' The chairman glanced at David Nisbet for confirmation.

'As I see it, Mr Ogden is correct,' replied Nisbet. 'We would appear to have established that the tree must not be cut down – that's the first thing. Oh, and on that point, is it the wish of the sub-committee that a recommendation go forward to the full committee that a tree preservation order be put on this copper beech?'

'Members agree?' asked the chairman.

Councillors Nugent and Hinton did, Councillors Jennings and Davidson did not, and Councillor Ogden didn't really know whether he agreed or not. Albert Bingley glanced at the angry looking sky; he was sure he felt rain on his face. It was time to hurry this meeting along. 'I shall vote in favour of the motion, so it is carried,' he snapped. 'Recommendation to go forward to the full committee that a TPO be put on this tree. Carry on Mr Nisbet.'

'Thank you, Mr Chairman. As I said just now, we have established that the tree must not be touched. We have not, though, necessarily decided that the plans be rejected. However, having said that, I don't really see how the proposed house can be built if the copper beech is to remain where it is.'

'If we've got to keep the blasted tree,' grunted Jim Jennings, 'why don't we allow them to build the house in front of the tree? That seems to be a reasonable compromise to me.'

Nisbet looked aghast. 'That's impossible, Mr Chairman – absolutely impossible,' he rasped. 'That would bring the house almost up to the road, and well in front of the building line. We can't allow that. It would open the floodgates the length of Victoria Road. There'd be planning applications coming in left, right and centre to extend homes in all directions, to put bungalows on the front lawns and all sorts. No, we cannot allow any building forward of the existing line on this road.'

'Well, how about building it behind the damned tree then?' persisted Jennings. 'Can't see anything wrong with that.'

'Not on, Mr Chairman, I'm afraid,' retorted the chief planning officer quickly. 'To start with it would be most unwise of this committee to allow building well to the rear of the great majority of houses on this road. Once again it would set an unfortunate –

perhaps even dangerous – precedent. Quite apart from that, though, the main sewer goes underneath the back garden here, as it does for most of the length of the road; so obviously we can't have a house built over the main sewer. Against all building regulations and planning laws that would be.'

'No – quite so,' agreed Albert Bingley, wearily, wishing there was a way in which he could bring the meeting to a conclusion. It looked as if it could hammer down at any moment. 'In actual fact, Mr Chairman, if I may be permitted to say so, I really don't think there's any way in which this plan can be permitted to go ahead. It is this sub-committee's view – quite rightly in my opinion – that the copper beach must be preserved. So if that is the case, the house obviously cannot be built, as the only spot where it can be put is where the tree stands.'

'Quite so, Mr Nisbet,' said the chairman quickly, seeing a way of bringing this tiresome meeting to a close before they all got soaked. 'As the chief planning officer says, ladies and gentlemen, there's no possible way this plan can be allowed to go forward, so can I have a formal proposition it be rejected?' He looked expectantly at his committee.

Helen Hinton began to raise her arm, but before she could say anything, Ivor Ogden proposed an idea. 'I agree that the tree should stay, Mr Chairman, as you know, but surely there's a way a compromise can be reached. Surely the plan can be revised for the house to be built – well, sort of – well sort of around the tree.' The final words were said without conviction.

'Yes, that's a good idea,' agreed Jim Jennings enthusiastically. 'As I've said, I believe this house should be built. A structure of the size envisaged will be an asset to this road – and to the town. This committee though, have already decided we've got to keep the copper beach; so the only solution is to plan the house in such a way that it sort of curves around the tree – sort of banana-shaped.'

'You can't have a banana-shaped house,' rasped Joe Davidson. 'That'll look absolutely daft.'

'Well, I don't know that it should be built banana-shaped, Mr Chairman,' said Ivor Ogden brightly, pleased that somebody else felt the co-existence of both the tree and the new house was possible. 'But I do feel that Mr Jennings' idea does have merit. For instance, there must be some way that this house can be designed so that the bulk of it lies each side of the tree, whilst these two halves – for want of a better description – could be joined together by a narrow portion which lies behind the copper beech; if you see what I mean.'

'I'm not sure I do Mr Ogden,' retorted the chairman, testily. 'This sounds like a most peculiar house to me.' A raindrop splattered onto the middle of his agenda. He glanced quickly at the sky; there were a lot more to come, and very soon. He returned his gaze to the gathering of councillors and officials. 'Still, if the committee wants to pursue the possibility of getting the applicants to submit fresh plans which will accommodate both the tree and a re-shaped house, then so be it. All I ask is that such a resolution is proposed right away – before we get wet through.' The committee knew Albert Bingley very well; he'd been on the council for almost twenty years and chairman of planning for the past six. He was an amiable, courteous man, and generally very patient. But when he spoke in that certain, clipped fashion, they knew he was in no mood to be argued with; he wanted a proposition, and that was what he would get.

'I propose that the planning department liaise with the applicant and get him to submit plans which will ensure that the copper beech remains,' said Jim Jennings authoritatively.

'Seconded, Mr Chairman,' snapped Helen Hinton. 'Not that I'm convinced that this is a good idea – or even a feasible one. I frankly don't believe it's possible to come up with a design which doesn't look ludicrous, whilst retaining the tree. Still, that's a problem for the applicants and the planning department, not for us. The only important thing, to my mind, is that the copper beech remains in all its splendour.'

'There are one or two problems here as I see it Mr Chairman,' opined Ivor Ogden. 'To start with. . .'

'Thank you, Mr Ogden,' interjected Albert Bingley, 'but I feel we've had ample discussion on this matter, and I'm not prepared

103

to allow any more. We have a proposition and I shall now put it to the vote. Those in favour, please show.'

Jim Jennings right arm shot into the air, Helen Hinton's was raised sluggishly, whilst Ethel Nugent raised hers somewhat sheepishly, not terribly keen to be seen supporting such a silly idea, but aware that if they didn't reach some conclusion then they'd all end up wet through. As her hand reached its zenith, she assuaged her conscience by convincing herself that the bizarre plan would never go through the full planning committee.

'Three,' said the chairman. 'And against?'

He looked at Joe Davidson and Ivor Ogden. The former, though, stood gazing morosely into the distance; thinking the entire business was daft, he refused to vote at all. In fact, he began to wonder whether it wasn't time for him to come off a committee that could vote for a tree instead of a decent house, and then decide to build some absurd contraption around it. The latter gazed back at the chairman for a few seconds, then looked away. He was so confused with the entire business that he didn't know whether he was for it or against.

'None. The proposal is carried.'

'I accept the decision of the committee, naturally, Mr Chairman,' said David Nisbet, considerable disquiet evident in his normally soft, level voice. 'However, I must say that this is all very irregular. I really don't see how it's possible to retain the copper beech and build the house. To construct such a building would mean the breaking of half a dozen basic planning laws – perhaps more – I feel the entire idea's a non-starter – I have to say that.'

'Well, that's for you to decide in liaison with the applicants,' snapped the chairman. 'We have merely passed a resolution that an attempt should be made to accommodate both the tree and the new house on this site – with the tree taking priority, of course.'

The chief planning officer shrugged his shoulders. 'Very well,' he acquiesced.

'Good – that's settled then,' said Albert Bingley, almost jovially. They had finished the meeting without getting soaked – though the rain was now falling quite heavily. 'I declare the meeting closed, and thank you for your attendance, ladies and gentlemen.'

The words had scarce passed his lips before the assembled throng galloped for the road, and their parked cars, even the ancient Jim Jennings showing a fair turn of speed despite his ailing legs.

As Albert Bingley reached his car – which was parked farthest away because he was last to arrive – the rain began to fall heavily, carried on a south-west wind little short of gale force. He clambered quickly inside, put the key into the ignition, and started up.

He glanced to his left, at the garden where they had just spent the last half hour, then to the open road on his right, pulled the car onto it, and shook his head sadly. He had known greater wastes of time, but he couldn't really remember when. Their proposal of the morning would be put to the full planning committee and would be rejected as a whole; the copper beech would be retained, a preservation order would be put on it, but plans for the house – no matter in what shape it was presented – would not be passed. The applicants would then appeal to the Ministry, where their appeal would probably be upheld, the tree condemned to the chainsaw, and within twelve months a fine, new house of traditional style would stand where they had stood that morning. The owners of the existing house, who were the applicants, would be a good deal richer and would surely by then be living somewhere else. Almost certainly there would be no way they would remain in a dwelling where a goodly part of the garden had been devoured by a large building.

'Oh, well,' he muttered to himself as he steered his car towards home, 'that's grass-root democracy at work, I suppose.'

V

The Emergency Committee

Over a period of some fifteen years, Henry Morris had been chairman of the parish council on five occasions and not once during that time had he ever used a gavel to call a meeting to order. Blessed with a loud and penetrating voice, and, at almost twenty stones in weight, a considerable presence, a thunderous clearing of the throat and a booming, 'Let us make a start, ladies and gentlemen, please,' or an even louder 'Quiet, please,' when the council was gripped with excitement, always restored order to proceedings. So it was on this evening when the 'special meeting' was about to commence.

'Let's have a bit of quiet, please, ladies and gentlemen,' he rasped. 'It's time we made a start. We don't want to be late finishing this evening.'

'As far as I'm concerned, Mr Chairman, I don't know why we're starting at all,' grumbled Councillor Arnold Atkins. 'Why can't this business, whatever it is, be put on the agenda of the normal monthly meeting? There's nothing that urgent, surely?'

'Well, Mr Atkins,' replied the chairman, 'I'm not really sure myself how urgent the matter is. The point is, though, that the clerk has received a letter from the district council advising us to call a special meeting of this parish council to set up an emergency committee – and it's got to be done before the end of the month. And that, of course, means that our next scheduled meeting would be too late by more than a fortnight. Still, Mr Miller will explain the situation more fully.'

The parish clerk got hastily to his feet, scattering papers like confetti – as was his custom – and immediately launched into an explanation in his fast talking, staccato way. 'Thank you, Mr Chairman,' he gabbled. 'As you so rightly say, this meeting has been called in accordance with advice given us by the district council. The facts of the matter are these. The district has received instructions from the Home Office that every parish in the district – in fact, every parish in the entire country, for that matter – must form an emergency committee. Of course, our district council won't be responsible for the rest of the country, but merely for the parishes in this district. I only mentioned the rest of the country to show that we in this parish, and in this district, are not being singled out.'

'We know that,' snapped Councillor Gordon Long. 'We're not daft. And we've not got all night either – or, at least, I haven't. I've got a snooker match on at half past eight down the club – and I'm not going to be late for it,' he added aggressively. 'Please ask the clerk to get to the point.'

'I was about to come to the point, Mr Chairman,' whined George Miller in aggrieved tones, 'when Mr Long interrupted me. However, the facts are these: firstly, as I said just now, every parish and town council throughout the land has to appoint an emergency committee; secondly, it should have not less than six members and not more than ten – and at least half should be members of the council with the others co-opted; thirdly, these committees have to be set up before the end of this month – hence the calling of this special meeting, as I said just now.'

'Why?' asked Councillor Lorna Higgins.

'Why what, Mr Chairman?' asked the clerk.

'Why does this emergency committee have to be set up before the end of the month?'

'Because it says so in the letter from the district council,' retorted the parish clerk, the tone of his voice suggesting that he considered he was conversing with an idiot. 'To be fair, many parishes locally – throughout the county and, in fact, the country have had emergency committees for years. It's just that now it's being made mandatory everywhere.'

'I know it says so in the letter, Mr Chairman – I'm not stupid,' rasped Mrs Higgins. 'What I want to know is why there should be such a rush to set the committee up and what the committee is supposed to do.'

'Well, Mr Chairman, I don't really know why there should be such a rush to set up this committee,' replied the clerk. 'The letter doesn't really give a reason, but ours is not to reason why, as the saying goes. I suppose that if anybody has to do it then there has to be a specific date by which – well – by which they have to do it.' Such seemed, to the clerk, totally logical, although he doubted it would be to the council. 'As to what the committee's duties are, I would have thought that was obvious, Mr Chairman. It will be a committee to deal with emergencies.'

'What's that supposed to mean?' asked Councillor Cyril Pellow. 'Are we supposed to run around and help the fire brigade fight fires, mop up floods and suchlike? If we are, then I for one don't want to be a member of this committee.'

'No – no – no, Mr Chairman, it's nothing like that!' cried a rather exasperated Miller. 'All emergencies will be taken care of by the fire brigade, police, ambulance service and so on, just as they always have been. No, the committee will be there to supervise other kinds of emergencies – or that's as I understand the purpose of it after having spoken to the chief executive of the district council about it. Although, I must admit he seemed a bit vague about it all himself.'

'I was speaking to the chairman of the policy and resources committee of the district council myself yesterday – on another matter,' said the chairman, 'but did happen to mention this business about an emergency committee being set up. I naturally asked him what the purpose of it was and he seemed to feel that each parish had to have one to co-ordinate things if the area had drought, floods, that sort of thing. It's all down to this global warming nonsense – business,' he corrected himself, aware this was not the time to air his scepticism on the matter. 'He and the chairman of the district council plus their chief executive, of course, will be the leading organisers of things in the event of such emergencies, but each parish committee will be responsible for the actual running of things in their specific area or that's how he sees it, anyway.'

'You might see that lot if there's a drought or a flood about, but not see sight nor sign of them if there's a nuclear attack, Mr Chairman,' opined Councillor Sam Bowden, with a grin. 'They'd all be in the bunker.'

'What bunker's that?' asked Cyril Pellow.

'What bunker?' Bowden's voice was full of incredulity. 'I thought everybody knew about the bunker. It's the secret one built underneath Ferndown Hill. You must have heard about it. Derek Allen's Plant Hire – just up the road here – supplied all manner of plant to excavate it; I do know that – he told me long ago. What it is, they built a nice snug little place there so if a nuclear attack ever came, they'd be safe whilst the rest of us would be fried.'

'I don't think it was quite like that,' admonished the chairman, gently. 'As I understand it, the bunker was for those leading citizens of the district, responsible for the organising of all emergency and basic services in the district, to be able to go into so that they could continue to maintain some semblance of administration over the area – so that total anarchy would be avoided. It's difficult to see how they can do that locked in a bunker, but that's ever been the basic idea as far as I'm aware. Still, we shouldn't be discussing this – it's still secret even now, decades later.'

'Secret, Mr Chairman?' snorted Larry Parson. 'I reckon the football results of a Saturday afternoon are more secret than this. Oh yes, I know it's supposed to be secret, but the daftness of that was really shown up when all those years ago the district council publicly invited tenders from builders to construct a secret bunker. Classic one, that was. Most local folk have known about it for years.'

The chairman smiled. 'Yes, that's true enough,' he agreed, 'but still, I fancy we've spent long enough talking about something which isn't the responsibility or business of this council. The formation of an emergency committee is what we're here to discuss – and set up. Mr Miller, please.'

'Thank you, Mr Chairman. As I see it, we have, tonight, to decide who should be on the emergency committee. . .'

'Shouldn't we first decide how many we want on it?' interjected Gordon Long.

'I was about to come to that, Mr Chairman,' snapped the clerk. 'Yes, we have to decide just how many we have on the committee.'

'None, Mr Chairman, that's what I'd have on the committee – none,' snorted Arnold Atkins. 'This is the biggest load of nonsense I've ever heard in my life. If the bomb ever fell we'd all be blown to kingdom come. Not that it's ever going to happen now we live in a different world to when they built the bunker. Where floods are concerned, this parish is so high above sea and river level that if we're flooded it's the Judgement come; and as to drought, that's for the Water Board to sort out, not us. I propose we have nothing whatsoever to do with any of it. I'm sick and tired of all this nonsense about global warming and suchlike.'

'But, Mr Chairman, with due respect, Mr Atkins is talking rubbish!' cried an exasperated parish clerk. 'The point is. . .'

'Hang on mister – nobody speaks about me like that,' roared Atkins, his face the colour of raw liver. 'I've been on this council for over twenty years and no councillor has spoken to me like that before, let alone a parish clerk. I demand an apology.'

'Damned right, Mr Chairman,' snorted the elderly Stanley Cowling, Father of the Council. 'We give our time for no reward, except that we know we're serving the people of this parish. We certainly don't do it, though, for the paid servants of this council to insult elected members. The parish clerk should apologise to Mr Atkins immediately.'

'Yes – yes, I do agree,' said the chairman evenly, hoping to take the sting out of the situation. 'However, I'm sure the parish clerk has spoken in haste and frustration. Certainly I'm sure he meant no offence to Councillor Atkins – is that not correct Mr Miller?'

'Yes, indeed, Mr Chairman,' replied the clerk hastily. 'I most definitely meant no offence to Mr Atkins, and if I've given it then I apologise unreservedly. It was just that I got a touch exasperated when Mr Atkins proposed the one course of action that's not open to us. You see, Mr Chairman, the point is that this is not a directive from the district council. If it were then there might be ways we could take – well, take minimal action on it. The reality, though, is that this instruction only comes through the district council; they're not the authors of it. The Home Office is the power behind this and so we've no option but to do what they instruct. After all, a parish council such as we cannot fly in the face of the Home Office.'

'No, quite, quite,' agreed the chairman. 'Obviously, we have to do what they say. So we must decide as to who's going to be on the committee – and how many, as Mr Long said just now. Also, we have to decide who we wish to co-opt onto the committee.'

'I reckon we should have the minimum number, Mr Chairman,' opined Cyril Pellow. 'The more members of any committee there are, the more yap and the less action.'

'Yes, that's true enough,' agreed Edwina Compton. 'Although I wouldn't expect much action from such a committee, no matter how many members it has. Especially if there are members – and sadly I fear there are several – of the negative mind set which constantly denies the reality of global warming and climate change despite the overwhelming evidence of it taking place. At last even the Government are waking up to the reality and, probably too late, trying to do something about it; and we should also, urgently, if belatedly. Let's face it, we as a council aren't exactly noted for action. I mean, we all sit here and talk about things, around things and from time to time, through things – but we never seem to do anything.'

'But we're not here to do things, Mr Chairman,' snapped Arnold Atkins. 'That's not the purpose of this council – or of any local authority for that matter. My father was a member of this council for over thirty years and he always said that if you didn't do anything, then you couldn't get anything wrong. And he was right. We're here to keep the council tax down – that's our main purpose. And, of course, we're here to listen to the local voters' complaints. But, having said that, they don't really expect us to do anything about them; just as long as we listen. I've seen these men and women of action over the years; they never last. Either they burn themselves out, or the electors throw them out. No, I never trust action, Mr Chairman.'

'No – no – quite, quite,' muttered the chairman. 'There's much in what you say. However, our purpose at the moment, is to decide just how many members the emergency committee should have. You said just now, Mr Pellow, that you thought the committee should have the minimum number of members,' he continued, looking vaguely in the general direction of that councillor. 'Was that a proposal?'

The man shrugged his shoulders. 'If you like, Mr Chairman,' he replied.

'Thank you. Do I have a seconder?'

'Yes – I second that,' said Gordon Long, briskly. 'Anything to get this silly meeting over and done with.'

'That's hardly the spirit, Mr Chairman,' complained Councillor Mrs Myra Jenkins. 'I'm sure Mr Long would be the first to welcome the efforts of an emergency committee if he were flooded out.'

'If I was flooded out, I reckon I'd welcome the efforts of St Peter,' he snorted. 'Seeing as I live on possibly the highest spot in this generally very high parish; the day flood waters lap at my door will certainly be the Judgement Day.'

'Well, you know what I mean,' she snapped. 'I believe it's important for us to have an emergency committee. It's rare I agree with the Home Office, but I think they're right – for once.'

'If Mrs Jenkin's so much in favour of this committee, Mr Chairman, perhaps she ought to serve on it,' retorted Long. 'I certainly don't want to.'

'I would be pleased to serve on such a committee if nominated, Mr Chairman,' replied Councillor Jenkins. 'It sounds to be like the sort of committee which might actually do something constructive – something to help the council tax payers of the parish when they really need it. I can't think of any other sub-committee of this council that ever really helps anybody at any time. In fact, I can't think of any other committee which actually ever does anything at all,' she concluded, with spirit. Her acerbic remarks failed to provoke a response – largely because the chairman, keen to bring the entire business to some conclusion, quickly came in with a question to the parish clerk.

'It's been proposed and seconded that we have the minimum number possible on the emergency committee,' he boomed, even louder than usual. 'Perhaps you could tell us how many the minimum number are, Mr Miller.'

'Six, Mr Chairman – as I said a little earlier.'

'Six, so that means we appoint three councillors and co-opt three others from the parish.'

'That's quite correct, Mr Chairman,' agreed the clerk in his at times somewhat pompous way.

'I thought the clerk said earlier, Mr Chairman, that *at least half* the committee should be made up of councillors,' argued Arnold Atkins, 'not, just half. The way he put in then, suggests that more than half of the committee can be made up of councillors – is that right?'

The parish clerk cleared his throat, studied the paper in front of him intently, then looked at the chairman. 'Well – yes, I suppose it does mean that more than half of the committee can be made up of councillors. However, I feel that the spirit of the directive of the Home Office is that there be an equal partnership between the council and the local community. With that in mind, I do feel that it would be fairest if the council have just the three on the committee, with the other three members being co-opted from the community.'

'I don't give a damn what the parish clerk feels, Mr Chairman,' rasped Atkins. 'It's the elected members of this council who make the decisions here – not the paid officials. The fact is, if we've got to appoint such a daft committee as this, then for heaven's sake let's keep control of it. Four members of the council, with two co-opted from the parish – that's my proposal. If we have equal numbers, then the co-opted members will be trying to run things. I've been on these sort of committees before – they come up with all sorts of tomfool ideas and the whole thing becomes a farce. Anyway, it's not democratic for non-elected folk to have too much say. After all, we've got to answer to the voters every four years – so it's only right that we make all the decisions.'

'I agree entirely with Councillor Atkins,' said Gordon Long, 'and I second his proposal.'

'Well, I disagree with Mr Atkins,' snapped Mrs Jenkins. 'I would have thought that democracy was all about people having their say and putting forward new ideas. We could certainly do with it on this parish council. I've been on it for two years now, and I've not heard a really positive idea or comment put forward yet on any subject whatsoever. This is a thoroughly moribund body.'

'I object to that, Mr Chairman,' stormed Cyril Pellow, an angry, almost malevolent expression on his face. 'There's been no lack of good and positive ideas and proposals put forward to this council by the members over the years. And I'm talking about many years as well – over twenty in my case. I take particular exception to somebody like Mrs Jenkins, who's only been on a dog's watch, accusing us of not doing our job – because that's what she's saying in effect. And I object to being called mor – mor – mor. . .'

'Moribund,' assisted the chairman.

'Yes – exactly,' he rasped. 'I object to being called that.'

'So do I, Mr Chairman,' said Sam Bowden. 'There's nothing moribund about this council. Just the opposite, in fact; we're always involving ourselves in schemes to help the people of the parish.'

'Such as?' questioned Councillor Jenkins, somewhat aggressively.

'Well – well – well, there's scores of things, really,' stuttered Bowden. 'I can't call them all to mind at the moment, of course, but there's been all sorts of things over the years.' He didn't like the way this debate was developing. He needed to attack quickly, or else the quick witted Myra Jenkins would have him in trouble.

'Still, instead of Mrs Jenkins finding fault – unfairly – with the rest of us, perhaps she should make an effort to be constructive herself,' bellowed the councillor, his voice suddenly strident with the confidence of having, to his mind, launched a first class counter offensive. Whether his verbal missile would have sunk Councillor Jenkins would never be known, for Henry Morris, aware that such an acerbic debate could go on for hours and get ever more bitter – and pointless – decided to intervene in order to return it to the rails along which it should be running.

'I'm sure Mrs Jenkins, like the rest of us, makes every effort to be constructive, Mr Bowden,' he said soothingly. 'However, we're straying somewhat from the subject under discussion, which, may I remind you, is the setting up of an emergency committee in this parish. Now, I've had a proposal from Mr Atkins, and seconded, that the committee consist of six members, four of whom should be serving councillors, the remaining two members being co-opted from amongst the ratepayers of the parish. All those in favour?'

He noted the wavering raised arms, then called, 'against?'

Only Myra Jenkin's arm went up and stayed there. 'I'm voting against it because I believe there should be, at least, equal representation from the people of the parish,' said she. 'Perhaps even greater representation – we, after all, are in a sense, their servants.'

Lorna Higgins put her hand up to start with, but then thought better of it and settled for the anonymity of abstention.

'The proposal is carried,' said the chairman. 'Now we have to decide who is going to serve on the committee. Perhaps we could decide on the four council members first.'

'May I propose yourself, Mr Chairman,' suggested Stanley Cowling, 'and, perhaps, the chairman of the finance committee and of the properties committee – and one other member.'

'Yes, that sounds fair enough,' agreed Councillor Atkins. 'That is, of course, if you and the other two proposed members are willing to serve, Mr Chairman. I second it, on that condition.'

Henry Morris shrugged his shoulders. 'Well, I'm willing to serve. After all, I can't imagine us having to meet very often. Floods, famines, droughts and the like aren't exactly regular occurrences locally. Nor nuclear attacks for that matter. Mr Jarvis, the chairman of the properties committee isn't present this evening, unfortunately, but I would imaging he'd be willing to serve on the committee. He is always keen to serve on committees, as we all know,' said he gently, greatly understating

Councillor Murray Jarvis' enthusiasm for involvement in everything. The chairman of finance, Mr Bowden is with us, though, so can answer for himself as to whether he's willing to be a member.'

The chairman of finance grimaced, then nodded slowly. 'All right, Mr Chairman, I'll serve on it,' he replied slowly. 'It's all a total waste of time, of course, but as you said just now, I doubt we'll meet very often. And I assume we are only appointed until the next AGM of the council?'

The chairman looked at the parish clerk, who responded with unusual alacrity. 'Naturally, Mr Chairman,' he said confidently. 'This is just a sub-committee of the council like any other, and has to be re-appointed at every Annual General Meeting. Which means, of course, you can change the constitution of the emergency committee entirely then should you wish to. Of course, it could be that you might not want to do so, but if you did then. . .'

'Yes, thank you,' interjected the chairman quickly. The clerk, in this mood, could witter on forever.

'So, we're agreed that Councillors Jarvis, Bowden and myself should make up the emergency committee?'

There were myriad murmurings from about the chamber, from which the chairman assumed that members were, indeed, agreed.

'I would remind you, Mr Chairman,' said the clerk sternly, 'that it has been agreed that the committee have four members. You have only appointed three so far.'

'Yes – yes, I know; I am well aware of that,' retorted the chairman, untruthfully. 'I was about to ask for proposals for the last position on the committee.'

'As she's so keen on it, then I propose Mrs Jenkins, Mr Chairman – as I suggested a little earlier,' said Atkins.

'Councillor Jenkins has been proposed. Do I have a seconder?'

'Seconded,' grunted Stanley Cowling.

'Thank you. All in favour – carried,' droned the chairman without even glancing at the councillors spread around the chamber before him.

'Well, that would appear to conclude the business of the

116

evening, ladies and gentlemen,' continued Henry Morris, enthusi-astically, 'so I. . .'

'Mr Chairman, we have two further members to appoint before the meeting can be closed – surely!' cried the parish clerk. 'We've appointed the four members from the council, so now we've got to decide who we wish to co-opt. Two people we're looking for.'

'Yes – yes, of course, Mr Miller,' muttered the chairman, an expression mingling annoyance and resignation on his face – there were times when meetings were a total pain. 'Do I have any proposals as to who should be co-opted onto this committee?'

'How about the vicar?' opined Cyril Pellow. 'If there's a lot of emergency about, a vicar's essential I would think.'

'I disagree, Mr Chairman,' snorted Lorna Higgins. 'At such times, we need practical men and women, people of action. With all due respect to the vicar, I don't see him in that role; I very much doubt he'd see himself in that role, come to that. He'd be useful if we had to bury folk, but I would think that the purpose of an emergency committee was to save people, not bury them. No, I can't agree with having the vicar on the committee.'

'Frank Donnelly, in charge of the fire brigade – he should be on it, Mr Chairman,' said Gordon Long. 'I mean, they are the emergency service aren't they? And trained men. It's obvious one of them must be on the committee, and as he's in charge of the local fire engine, Donnelly's obviously the man.'

'Trained men, be damned,' stormed Atkins. 'Have you ever seen them in action? Well, I have,' he ranted on, without waiting for an answer to his question. 'Never forget it as long as I live. We called them out last year when our chimney was on fire; I wish I'd let it burn. They took a quarter of an hour to turn out to start with – and the station's only a quarter mile up the road from our place. And when they arrived they only had three men aboard – and there's about a dozen on the payroll so I'm told. Then another one turned up on a bike a couple of minutes after they'd arrived. Fine effort that was too; he came hammering down the road, braked too quickly outside our house, went flying over the handlebars, and knocked himself out. So, when they should have been putting out our chimney, the fire crew were organising an ambulance to take this fellow to hospital. Shambles it was. And when they did get round to putting out the fire they got more water on our front room carpet than they did onto the flames. And who was in charge of it all? Why, Frank Donnelly, of course. The man was worse than useless. Why, if I had my way, I'd. . .'

'Mr Atkins, I must remind you, we're in open committee,' admonished the chairman. 'I really can't allow such comments about a respected member of this community.'

'Respected be damned,' muttered the councillor, largely to himself. 'I'll certainly oppose him being on the committee,' he continued, his voice, this time, carrying to the far corners of the chamber.

'How about Mrs Moss, over at Oakways Cottage, Mr Chairman? I think she'd be ideal,' stated Myra Jenkins. 'She's a very efficient, level-headed woman – and highly practical. Also, as chairperson of the local Women's Institute, she is used to organising events and people, which has to be an important consideration when deciding who we're going to appoint to such a committee as this.'

'I reckon we'll have plenty enough trying to organise things, Mr Chairman,' snorted Stanley Cowling. 'It's workers we want – doers, not organisers and talkers. Anyway, I know Mrs Moss, typical school teacher – too bossy by half.'

'That's grossly unfair, Mr Chairman,' stormed Mrs Jenkins. 'She's a splendid person, dedicated to helping others, and a tireless worker. Mr Cowling is talking prejudiced nonsense about somebody he scarcely knows.'

'I take exception to that,' retorted the veteran councillor. 'How can Mrs Jenkins state who I know or don't know. I've a good knowledge of this parish and the people who live in it – having been born and bred here, and lived here all my life, which is more than can be said for some members of this council. In fact, it's more than can be said for most members of this council. As for Mrs Moss, it will no doubt surprise Mrs Jenkins to learn that I served on a parish hall committee with her a few years back – and it was not an enjoyable experience.'

'Mr Chairman, I do object to the councillor's comments,

rasped an angry Myra Jenkins. 'Surely he's out of order making such spiteful comments about a respected member of this community, at a public meeting like this?'

'You're quite correct, Councillor,' agreed the chairman. 'As I pointed out to Mr Atkins just now, Mr Cowling, comments of a personal nature should not be made in open council. I do trust we'll hear no more of it – from anybody.'

'A doctor's what we need,' opined Sam Bowden. 'A committee like this dealing with emergencies will definitely need a doctor on it. Old Doctor Strange is the man. He's lived and practised in this parish for nigh on forty years. He'd be an ideal man.'

'Get on, he'd never be sober,' snorted Arnold Atkins. 'You know what he's like – liquored up half his time.'

'Mr Atkins, please,' remonstrated the chairman. 'These personal attacks and criticisms of leading citizens of this parish are intolerable in open council – as I've already said on two occasions. Let us please have a little more dignity, and thought for others, in our discussions.'

'You keep saying about open council, Mr Chairman, but there's nobody here but councillors and the clerk. No voters, not even the press reporter tonight; unusual that, mind you. But as I say, there's nobody here to get upset or suchlike over what we say.' Councillor Atkins was visibly unhappy at being admonished by the chairman in a such a way.

'There's something in the idea of having a doctor on the committee,' interjected Lorna Higgins before the chairman could make reply – in spirited tones – to what he saw as disrespect from the opinionated Councillor Atkins, 'but I wouldn't support the nomination of Dr Strange – simply because of his age. I would have thought that somebody much younger was needed for a committee which, by its very nature, will only be called into operation when some disaster has occurred. I would have thought Dr Strange's junior partner, Dr Anthony, would be the ideal man.'

'Get on, the fellow knows nothing,' snorted the irrepressible Atkins. 'When my missus went down with 'flu a few weeks back he swore blind it was glandular fever. I never heard such nonsense in my life. I. . .' He stopped abruptly as he saw the

119

chairman's angry eyes upon him, and the gavel raised to hammer him into silence. As Morris returned the gavel to the desk top before him, Councillor Atkins cleared his throat noisily, and contented himself with an innocuous, 'he's not got a lot of experience.'

'That's true,' agreed Gordon Long. 'But even if he had it wouldn't do us a lot of good to ask him to join the committee.'

'Why not?' asked the chairman.

'Because he's left the area. Moved out about a week back. I know because I tried to book an appointment with him yesterday, for him to have a look at my back – playing me up again,' he added for the benefit of anybody who might have been interested. Nobody was. 'He's moved to a big practice in the London area. I always knew a sharp, progressive fellow like him wouldn't stay around here long.'

'Why have we not been told of this, Mr Chairman?' asked an aggrieved Lorna Higgins.

'Well, I don't think a local doctor has an obligation to tell the council of his intentions, or the direction of his future career,' said Henry Morris as soothingly as he could – upsetting the somewhat volatile Mrs Higgins was something to be avoided when the object was to finish a meeting as soon as possible.

'How about Colonel Marquand over at the Grange, Mr Chairman?' suggested Long. 'An ex-military man of his rank would be ideal for an emergency committee.'

'Nonsense,' snorted Councillor Mrs Jenkins, 'the man's senile.'

'Mrs Jenkins,' growled the chairman in his best warning tones.

'I'm not being disrespectful, Mr Chairman,' opined the persistent lady, 'merely factual. The Colonel is very elderly – well into his eighties I should think – and shows all the signs of advanced senile dementia. It's nothing to be ashamed of; it happens to so many people in advanced old age. In fact, it can happen to people when they're merely in middle age.'

'Several suffering from it on this council if you ask me,' said Arnold Atkins in a loud whisper which was heard in the far corners of the chamber.

Myra Jenkins fixed him with a withering glare, then continued in her positive, somewhat strident way.

'All I'm saying, Mr Chairman, is that Colonel Marquand, though undoubtedly a fine servant to the country in his time, is now far too old to render any useful assistance to an emergency committee.'

' 'Course he's no good on a committee,' agreed Stanley Cowling. 'I reckon everybody who knows him realises that. As Mrs Jenkins says, he's half daft these days, and would be a liability. But I doubt he'd have ever been much use; men like him aren't. All they're good at is giving orders and leaving somebody else to do the work. We've got plenty enough like him about already. Workers are what we want – folk who'll take their coats off and get stuck in.'

'I disagree, Mr Chairman,' retorted Gordon Long. 'Councillor Cowling makes it sound as if we're looking for people to dig latrines or some such thing. We're not. We're looking for sound, sensible people who can bring qualities of leadership at a time of crisis. With that in mind, Colonel Marquand would be an excellent man to be co-opted onto this committee. After all, he had a long and distinguished war service and, no doubt, came through many crises and dangers whilst leading his troops.'

'Stuff and nonsense,' rasped Cyril Pellow. 'He never knew any dangers in the War – or at any other time for that matter. He was in the Pay Corps; I know that for a fact because his wife once told me. He's a qualified accountant; she told me that as well. She's dead now, of course, but she was always a friendly, outgoing woman, and I remember she told me all about the Colonel's military career when I talked to her at a fete, or something or other, which he opened – what, it must be twenty years ago now. He wasn't a career soldier, but was called up at the beginning of the War, and because of his financial qualifications, was put in the Pay Corps. How he ever made it to Colonel, God only knows – but he did, and he was demobbed in 1946. Nice enough old boy in his way, of course, but absolutely useless to have on such a committee as is proposed.'

'Ladies and gentlemen, we do seem to be getting nowhere at

f

an alarming rate,' said the chairman, somewhat testily. This meeting had, in his estimation, threatened to be a time wasting bore and was most certainly living up to that promise. 'We really must make a decision as to whom exactly we wish to co-opt onto the committee or else we shall be here all night.'

'Well, I propose George Maunder, Mr Chairman,' said Cyril Pellow. 'As a butcher it's obvious he knows all about food and feeding people – which, of course, has to be an advantage at a time of emergency. But even more important than that, he's sergeant of the specials in the parish – which makes him a man of authority well used to keeping public order and so on.'

'What, George Maunder – keep order?' Arnold Atkin's voice was pregnant with incredulity. 'That's news to me, Mr Chairman. Why, it's common knowledge he's to be found in the snug of the King's Arms well after hours almost every night of the week. And another thing is. . .'

'Councillor Atkins!' thundered the chairman. 'I've warned you incessantly throughout this meeting about your – your – well, the only word I can use is 'slanderous' remarks about various members of our local community. I remind you once again, that we're in open council and even though there's nobody here, such remarks are just not acceptable. In fact they'd not be acceptable even if we were in committee. If it happens again,' – he lent forward menacingly and fixed the sinning councillor with a stare which would have curled the hair of a more nervous man – 'If it happens again,' he repeated, 'I shall have no option but to order you from the chamber.'

Arnold Atkins had served on this council with Henry Morris for very many years – and he'd known him for a lot longer than that. They weren't really friends, but, generally speaking, they'd always got on well both inside and outside the chamber, each having a healthy respect for the other. Atkins certainly knew the chairman to be a man of his word. If he threatened banishment from the chamber for further misdemeanour, then he meant it. A portion of humble pie lay before the councillor, and he knew he had no option but to eat it.

'I apologise, Mr Chairman, if I've stepped out of line,' he said

122

meekly. 'I've certainly not intended to upset you or anybody else, but I am concerned that if we are to appoint people to this committee – though, as I said just now, I think it's a daft committee before it even starts – we appoint the right people. As I say, if I've gone a bit too far then I apologise most sincerely. Still, all I've really done, Mr Chairman, is to use my background personal knowledge of local folk in the interests of the parish as a whole. You, yourself, have often said that it's essential for a local councillor to have wide-ranging knowledge of the place and the people he represents. I am merely falling into line with that sound opinion.'

A flicker of a smile played around the chairman's lips, before being pushed away to be replaced by the habitual firm, uncompromising set of the jaw. This was Arnold Atkins at his best, and the chairman had enjoyed every word.

'Thank you, Mr Atkins,' he said mildly. 'I'm sure you'll not go too far along those lines again. Now, where were we? Oh, yes, we'd had a proposal from Councillor Pellow, that George Maunder be asked to join the emergency committee. Do I have a seconder?'

'Much as I deplore Mr Atkin's attack on the reputation of a man not here to defend himself, Mr Chairman,' stated Lorna Higgins, judiciously, 'I do feel there is some relevance in what he has to say. I do know that Mr Maunder's name is often bandied around in the parish for activities not exactly to his credit. Certainly, he has been named in connection with liaisons with – well, two or three ladies in the village – and whilst it could well be that such stories are not entirely true, I do believe it to be common knowledge that they are not entirely without foundation. With that in mind, I feel bound to support Mr Atkin's broad thrust that Mr Maunder is not entirely suitable to be a member of the emergency committee.'

'I've never heard such bigoted, narrow-minded, puritanical codswallop in all my life,' stormed Cyril Pellow. 'What, for heaven's sake, has this man's private life to do with his being appointed to an emergency committee? What if he does spend half his life chasing the women of the parish; what if he does spend the other half drinking after hours at the pub. . .'

'Councillor, please,' interjected the chairman. 'You're going along the same road as Mr Atkins; I would remind you we're in open council here.'

'With respect, Mr Chairman, all this talk about being in open committee is nonsense,' retorted the angry councillor. 'I mean, even if we went into secret sessions on this issue, nobody in this chamber at present would have to leave. There are no members of the public present, no press, as Mr Atkins has said – nobody except elected councillors. So we can say the same things in open council as we'd say if we went in secret sessions, without hurting a soul.'

'That's not the point,' persisted the chairman. 'Things have to be done properly, and in accordance with standing orders. It's our rule book – our law if you like – and we must abide by it.'

'Get on,' snorted Pellow, 'three quarters of this council don't even know what it says in standing orders – myself included.'

'Then I must be a member of the single quarter, councillor,' snapped the chairman, his face flushed with anger, 'because I am very well aware of what it says in standing orders concerning all aspects of conducting meetings. That includes the demeanour of members, Mr Pellow, and the automatic respect they show the chair. Should such respect be lacking, then the chairman has the right to order the offending member – or members – to leave the chamber. And, should it prove necessary, the chairman has the right to call the police and have the member – or members – forcibly ejected.'

'Seeing as we've not got a full-time copper ourselves,' muttered Sam Bowden to his 'neighbour', Gordon Long, 'We'll have to get George Maunder around to throw Cyril out of the chamber simply for wanting George Maunder to be on the emergency committee. A right classic this one is.'

'Do I make myself clear, Mr Pellow?' asked the chairman, in a tone of voice which did nothing to disguise his very real anger with the erring councillor.

Cyril Pellow had rarely seen the chairman as angry as this, and decided not to tempt fate any further. 'Yes, you make yourself perfectly clear, Mr Chairman,' he said as casually as he was able.

'I'll not pursue the matter any further, except to ask that you seek a seconder to my proposition that Mr Maunder be asked to join the emergency committee.'

'Certainly,' replied the chairman. He cast his eyes about the chamber. 'Do I have a seconder to Mr Pellow's proposal?'

Not an arm, hand, or even as much as a finger moved into the air in support. Mr Sergeant of Specials might well have been an ideal man to be on the committee, but the proposal that he should be had caused such a furore that members of the council felt that discretion being the better part of valour, less contentious persons than the hapless George Maunder should be appointed.

'There being no seconder, then obviously Mr Maunder's name cannot go forward for the committee,' said the chairman evenly, most of his previous anger having evaporated. 'Are there any more proposals as to whom should be on this committee? Although I doubt there's many left in the parish who've not already been proposed,' he added, wearily. 'It seems to be. . .'

'Point of order, Mr Chairman,' interjected Sam Bowden.

'Yes?'

'Well, I feel that we, as a full council, shouldn't be appointing co-opted members of a sub-committee at all. I may be wrong of course, but I seem to remember that a few years back when we had to appoint another committee for some purpose or other – I can't remember what it was now – we left the co-opting of people from the parish to the sub-committee itself. I would have mentioned this earlier, before we ever got into this debate on who should be on the committee, but it's only just occurred to me. Perhaps the parish clerk can give a ruling on this.'

'I'm sure you're right,' retorted the chairman enthusiastically – and quickly, before George Miller had a chance to speak. Henry Morris was only too well aware that the parish clerk would spend half an hour burrowing into papers and making notes, before coming up with an answer – and that reply would be so vague as to be useless. If this interminable, pointless meeting was ever to be brought to a close, then the bull of prevarication had to be taken by the horns.

'I do seem to recall that members of sub-committees have in

the past, been responsible for co-opting folk onto those sub-committees,' he continued, hastily. 'So, with that being established, there's obviously no need for this council to deliberate any longer as to who should be co-opted onto the emergency committee.'

'Are you quite sure that's the correct procedure, Mr Chairman?' asked Lorna Higgins, a pugnacious expression on her face. 'Personally, I'm not at all happy about it. I feel. . .'

'Quite sure, Mrs Higgins,' thundered the chairman, a 'don't dare argue with me' expression on his face.

'Very well,' retorted the lady, tersely.

'Good – that appears to be settled then. The emergency committee will consist of Mrs Jenkins, Mr Bowden, Mr Jarvis and myself, with two further members – not councillors – to be co-opted when we have our first meeting. When will that be, Mr Miller?'

'When will what be, Mr Chairman?'

'The first meeting of the emergency committee, of course.'

The clerk could be so obtuse at times, mused an ever increasingly impatient chairman.

The parish clerk looked surprised. 'Well, obviously, when we have our first emergency,' he retorted.

'But that's plain daft,' snorted Councillor Pellow.

'The whole thing's plain daft, from start to finish,' opined Arnold Atkins.

'But there's got to be meetings of this committee to set the thing up, co-opt members onto it and so on. It would be totally stupid to wait until there was an emergency before having a meeting. I've never heard such nonsense in my life,' Pellow continued.

'Well, it says nothing in the directive from the district council about holding a preliminary meeting. It just says we should form a committee,' stated the clerk, doggedly.

'That's beside the point,' stormed an ever more exasperated Councillor Pellow. 'Surely we've enough common sense on this council to be able to proceed to act without being expressly told to do so by the district council. If we haven't then it seems to be we're all wasting our time here – and everybody else's as well. We must fix a date for an early meeting of the emergency committee, Mr Chairman.'

'Yes, yes, I quite agree, Councillor,' said the chairman nodding vehemently. 'However, seeing as Mr Jarvis isn't here, may I suggest that this be put on the agenda for our next full council meeting, next month, when hopefully all four of us appointed to the emergency committee will be here and we can therefore settle on a mutually acceptable date. Members agree?'

A series of grunts indicated that members did agree, though Pellow looked none too pleased about it all. 'I see your point, Mr Chairman,' he acknowledged grudgingly, 'but I feel that a date should really be fixed this evening. Not that I'm convinced there's any real need for an emergency committee – we've survived quite adequately over the years without one. But if we've got to appoint one then let's do it properly and fix a time for its first meeting, instead of leaving those loose ends as we always seem to do. After all, it's this seemingly constant lack of action which gives us a bad image in the eyes of the council tax payers. Still, the council's decided not to fix a date until our next full meeting, so naturally I go along with that.'

'Thank you,' muttered the chairman.

'It's all very well Councillor Pellow going on about taking action now and tying up loose ends and suchlike Mr Chairman,' Arnold Atkins opined, 'but I've long believed that the worst thing any council can do is to rush into things. "Look before you leap" as the saying goes.'

'Yes, indeed, thank you Mr Atkins.' Henry Morris glanced quickly at his watch, then glanced around the gathered councillors before him.

'Well, that would appear to bring the business to a close, ladies and gentlemen,' he said briskly. 'We've certainly given the subject considerable airing, and I doubt there's anything else can be added at this stage.'

Myra Jenkins, however, had other ideas. 'I don't wish to prolong the meeting, Mr Chairman,' she said, doing just that, 'but I do feel the parish clerk should read out to us just what the duties of the emergency committee are. It would be helpful to know now so that we can give it all some thought before we actually meet.'

George Miller looked perplexed. 'Well, I should have thought that the duties of an emergency committee would have been obvious, Mr Chairman,' he replied. 'Such a committee is there to handle emergencies in the parish.'

'I know that,' she snapped. 'I'm not stupid. What I want to know is what are the precise duties as laid down in the directive from the district council. I would have thought the parish clerk would have been well aware of what I meant.'

Miller looked even more perplexed. 'Duties? In the directive? But there's nothing along those lines in the directive. It simply says that we must form an emergency committee. It doesn't say what that committee should do, Mr Chairman, naturally.'

'What does the parish clerk mean, Mr Chairman? How can it be natural to be told to form a committee and then not be told what the committee is for and what it has to do. I've never heard anything so absurd – so – so – so mind-bendingly stupid, in all my life!' roared Councillor Jenkins, her face now almost purple with combined rage and frustration. The parish clerk took no notice of her outburst – he'd seen her like this before. In fact, he'd seen most members of the council – and numerous previous ones over the years – in similar rages. He merely shook his head sadly, shrugged his shoulders, glanced at the chairman and delivered a verdict half a lifetime in the making.

'There's nothing stupid about it, Mr Chairman,' he said simply. 'It's the way we do things in this country, isn't it? I mean it's one thing for the Home Office, through the district council, to tell us to form a committee, but it's a very different thing for them to try to tell us what we should discuss on it – and what we should do. That, after all, is up to us. That's what we're all here for; that, Mr Chairman, is grass root democracy.'

VI

The Curtains

Sandra Miles was pleased. When first looking at the agenda for the monthly meeting of the properties committee, she had anticipated a long session – perhaps right through to ten o'clock or even beyond; but the reality had been so very different. Of course, 'apologies for absence' held the key to the unexpected brevity of the meeting. For the one apology for non-attendance had come from Edward Hancock, a man only elected in a by-election a couple of years earlier, who had a rare talent for making the obvious, obscure, the simple, complicated and who could add an hour to any meeting. However, his had not been a full apology; rather he had said he would definitely be late because he had to attend the Annual General Meeting of the bowling club, but hoped to get to the properties meeting before it finished.

Sandra Miles was convinced that it was this threat of his probable arrival at some time or other which had led to an unusually brisk and well-disciplined contribution from the other members of the committee, all of them desiring to finish the gathering before he came. She glanced at her watch; only five minutes past nine and they'd almost achieved it.

'We come to the last item on the agenda, any other business,' she said quickly, 'I believe there is one item, Mr Conway.'

'Thank you, Mr Chairman,' replied Cecil Conway, the town clerk. 'I've received a letter from the town's Gilbert and Sullivan Society concerning problems they had with the stage curtains in the town hall during their show which took place last week.'

'What show was that?' asked Councillor Jim Sparks, slouched in his seat towards the back of the council chamber.

The town clerk looked a trifle nonplussed. 'Well – I don't really know, Mr Chairman. I'm not into Gilbert and Sullivan to be quite honest. Having said that, I must admit that I should know, seeing as I received the customary invitation to the mayor and council to attend on Civic night. Unfortunately I was unable to go, and the mayor's not here this evening. I don't know if any other councillor went to the show?'

'I went,' replied the veteran Sidney Bartlett, wheezing away enthusiastically. 'It was very good as well. Thoroughly enjoyed it, the missus and me.'

'That's splendid, Mr Bartlett,' said the chairman in a respectful tone. 'Perhaps you could tell us which Gilbert and Sullivan operetta they put on this year.'

'The Importance of Being Ernest,' replied the old councillor instantly. 'One of my favourites that – and the missus's as well.'

'That's not Gilbert and Sullivan,' rasped Jim Sparks. 'That's Oscar Wilde – and that's a play not an opera.'

'I think perhaps Councillor Bartlett is thinking of the dramatic society's recent production, Mr Chairman,' explained the town clerk, trying to be helpful. 'I remember he, and Mrs Bartlett, attending that, along with the mayor, myself, and a few other councillors. About two months ago, I fancy.'

'Yes, that's what he's thinking of,' agreed councillor Arthur Phillips, a long, beanpole of a man, he seemed to entwine himself around his chair rather than sit on it. 'A load of rubbish it was, as well. Never been so bored in my life; the acting was shocking, hardly anybody on the stage could remember their lines, and it was freezing cold,'

'It's always cold in the town hall,' snapped Councillor Sparks. 'I've been freezing in there in June. It beats me how anybody ever hires the damned place. It's time the heating was sorted out.'

'Actually the heating problems of the town hall are on the agenda for the next meeting of the forward planning committee,' said the town clerk quickly. 'Hopefully we'll then be able to formulate some future policy to solve the problem once and for all.'

'When's that?' asked Sparks.

'When's what?' retorted the clerk.

'The next meeting of the forward planning committee, for heaven's sake,' snapped an exasperated Councillor Sparks; he was never a man to whom patience came easily.

'Well, we haven't fixed a date yet, Mr Chairman,' replied Cecil Conway, somewhat uncomfortably. 'We just seem to have had too much to do recently.'

'He'll have me in tears in a minute,' muttered Tom Gaskell to his near neighbour, Sidney Bartlett. The veteran councillor didn't hear, though, his entire concentration centred on trying to remember what Gilbert and Sullivan production he had seen the previous week.

'It seems to me that this forward planning committee is a farce,' ranted Sparks. 'I mean it's been formed for several years – five at least – yet how often has it met? I can't remember the last time there was a meeting. Certainly there's not been one since I've been on it – and that's a couple of years. So, when was the last time it met? When did the forward planning committee ever actually forward plan?'

The chairman looked searchingly at the clerk. 'Well, Mr Conway?'

He cleared his throat nervously. 'Well, Mr Chairman,' he said slowly, his voice very soft, 'I do believe that, in actual fact, despite many wide ranging ideas for the future having come from the council, and indeed, having been put to the council from several outside bodies, ideas of considerable relevance to the town and the charge-payers. . .'

'For heaven's sake, get to the point,' roared an angry Sparks, 'we've not got all night.'

'I was about to, Mr Chairman,' retorted the town clerk, rare annoyance in his voice. 'The fact, as far as I'm aware, is that the forward planning committee has never met.'

'Never?'

'As far as I'm aware,' retorted the town clerk, his voice returning to its normal urbanity.

'Then why, Mr Chairman,' continued Sparks, in his terrier-like way, 'do we go through the time wasting farce every May at the Annual Meeting of appointing members to a committee that never meets? Why does the town clerk speak of putting things on an agenda which will never be discussed? I've been on this council fifteen years and seen some pretty stupid things, but I've never come across anything as daft as this.'

'Well, obviously, if we appoint a committee then it can meet should the council wish it to; and if we draw up an agenda then we're prepared should the council decide to call a meeting of the committee,' retorted the town clerk, defensively. 'The fact that it hasn't met as yet over – over the years – is, with respect, irrelevant. It's like having a fire extinguisher isn't it, Mr Chairman? I mean, we've got fire extinguishers in this chamber, and in this building, but we never use them – and hopefully we'll never have to. But. . .'

'We did once,' interjected Arthur Phillips. 'Remember it well.'

'Remember what, Mr Phillips?' asked the chairman sharply; she was getting somewhat frustrated at the way the meeting was degenerating into a rambling squabble.

'When we used a fire extinguisher, Mr Chairman,' retorted Phillips in exasperated fashion, as if amazed that his meaning had not been understood.

'I don't ever recall this,' said the town clerk.

'Oh, it was before your time,' said the councillor. 'Years ago it was. A car caught fire outside in the street whilst we were in the middle of a sub-committee. The chairman then – poor old Harry Daniels, dead and gone now – grabbed an extinguisher and rushed out into the road.' He stopped suddenly, and shook his head, a wry smile playing around his lips.

'What happened then?' asked Councillor Mrs Julia Beckett, who had just dragged her attention away from the agenda of the following evening's planning committee, which lay before her.

'The car burnt out, that's what happened,' snorted Phillips. 'The extinguisher didn't work.'

132

'That's extraordinary,' said a bemused Cecil Conway. 'Those extinguishers are checked every year. In fact, I. . .'

'Mr Chairman, what are we doing talking about fire extinguishers?' snapped Jim Sparks. 'I thought we were discussing the fact that the forward planning committee has never met.'

'Well, yes, that's correct,' replied the town clerk somewhat wearily. 'However, I brought the purchasing of fire extinguishers into the debate to provide an analogy as to the wisdom of looking to the future.'

'Then it's a poor analogy,' retorted Sparks. 'What, after all, is the similarity between the purchasing of fire extinguishers and the fact that the forward planning committee has never met? And – and another thing,' continued the councillor quite excitedly, a new train of though having suddenly come to him, 'the town clerk talks about the appointment of this committee being an act of wisdom in looking to the future, yet the committee itself, which is all about planning for the future, never actually meets. I've never heard anything as daft in all my life.'

'The reason why this committee has never been convened,' retorted the town clerk sternly, 'is simply because the council has never instructed me to do so.'

'But that's not the point,' persisted Councillor Sparks. 'What I want to know is. . .'

'You're quite right, Mr Sparks, that is not the point,' interjected the chairman, rather crossly. 'In fact the point we should be discussing was lost several minutes ago. We should be discussing the letter which we have received from the Gilbert and Sullivan Society – and that is what we shall do, without going off at any more tangents. Mr Conway, please.'

'Thank you, Mr Chairman. Well, as I said just now, the letter concerns problems which the society experienced with the stage curtains during their final show last Saturday night. It says. . .'

'Macbeth!' cried Sidney Bartlett. 'Macbeth, that was the name of the Gilbert and Sullivan show we saw last week. I knew it would come to me if I pondered long enough.'

Sandra Miles smiled wanly, quickly decided that to disagree

133

with the aged councillor would prolong the meeting possibly well into the night if he was to return to his pondering, so nodded gravely. 'Yes – quite. Thank you, Mr Bartlett,' she replied gently, 'carry on Mr Conway, please.'

'Thank you, Mr Chairman. Well, regarding these curtains; it appears that something went wrong with the smooth running of the left hand one along the – the – well, the sort of runners they run on. One of the cast grabbed hold of the curtain to pull it to the centre and so screen the stage, and the entire curtain came down on him. It caused quite a bit of alarm at the time and, according to the letter, ruined the final curtain call of the show. So the society are demanding that the entire curtains around the stage area be renewed, as they are, according to them, rotten beyond repair.' He coughed somewhat nervously, then continued, 'They are also demanding a reduction in the hire charges for the hall because of the incident.'

'I was waiting for that,' came a voice from the back of the chamber. Depression instantly engulfed the gathering as the chairman and town clerk looked towards the far end of the room and the members of the committee turned to gaze behind them to see who had caused the interruption to their deliberations. Not that they needed to look; they knew that raucous voice all right.

'Good evening, Mr Hancock,' said the chairman, rather icily, a note of despair, also, entering her intonation.

'Good evening, Mr Chairman,' replied the late arrival, politely. 'I apologise for being so late, but I did tell the clerk that I would never be able to get here for the beginning of this meeting. I'm glad to see, though, that I'm not too late to make some contribution to the proceedings.' All the time he had been talking, he had been moving forward towards his usual seat on the right of the chamber. He reached it, dropped his agenda and minutes on the desk in front of him, sat down, and immediately had his say.

'I repeat my comment of a couple of minutes ago, Mr Chairman,' he trumpeted in his usual confident, not to say, bombastic fashion. 'I was waiting for a demand from the Gilbert and Sullivan Society for a reduction in the hire charges for the town hall. I'd have almost been disappointed if they'd not made one; after all they've done so on some pretext or another for the past few years. Something I've noted – checked out in fact – even though I've only been on the council a relatively short time. Last year they wanted a reduction because just a tiny bit of the stage collapsed with dry rot; the year before that they were complaining, and demanding a discount, because a fuse blew in the kitchen and they couldn't make tea one evening; and I believe, or, at least, I've been told, the year before that they tried to get out of paying the full amount because the caretaker was in a hurry to go home at the end of the show and inadvertently locked some of the performers in the hall. Now, I reckon. . .'

'Point of order, Mr Chairman!' cried Julia Beckett.

'Yes, Mrs Beckett?' asked Sandra Miles, somewhat surprised. The admirable Mrs Beckett, although a regular adversary of Hancock's, was not usually very much to the fore in the 'point of order' stakes.

'Well,' she continued, 'is it in order for Mr Hancock to go on about this business when he was not here when the town clerk described the contents of the letter from the Gilbert and Sullivan Society? After all, he's talking about something he knows nothing about.'

'Rubbish,' retorted Hancock. 'I heard every word the town clerk said regarding the curtains. I was standing inside the door of the chamber, taking off my coat, and listening for at least a couple of minutes before I spoke. It seems to me that Mrs Beckett is just trying to stifle free speech – and I've a good idea I know why.'

'What's that meant to mean?' snapped Councillor Beckett, her thinnish face white with anger. One day, thought the chairman to herself, Julia Beckett would go through a meeting without getting angry with Edward Hancock – but she doubted she would ever live to see it.

'I fancy she knows what I mean, Mr Chairman,' insisted Hancock. 'It's simply that her husband is a stalwart member of the local Gilbert and Sullivan Society. Is that not correct, Councillor Beckett?'

'Mr Hancock, I don't think that this form of debate is right or proper,' reproached the chairman. 'The fact that Mr Beckett is a member of the society is nothing whatever to do with this committee. Mrs Beckett is perfectly within her rights to enter into debate on this matter just as she is obviously within her rights to raise her point of order as she did just now. Having said that, you also, Mr Hancock, have a right to express your views on any matter which comes up for discussion in this chamber whether or not you are in full possession of all the facts. So, with that in mind, I reject Mrs Beckett's point of order. I mean, if we only spoke when in possession of all the facts or had completely thought matters through, then I fancy debates would be exceedingly short.' There was a certain acidity to her tone when she articulated the last sentence.

'Thank you, Mr Chairman,' replied Hancock, a rare tone of meekness in his voice.

'Surely she should declare an interest,' snapped Jim Sparks, slumped down in his seat, as was his way.

'I beg your pardon, Mr Sparks?'

'Mrs Beckett – she should declare an interest. If her husband is a member of the Gilbert and Sullivan Society – and I must admit, I hadn't realised it until Mr Hancock said – then she must declare an interest, and then withdraw from the chamber before we discuss the matter of the curtains. That would seem to be the proper thing to do in my view.'

Sandra Miles looked perplexed; she always hated any discussions on the possible declaring of interest.

'I wouldn't have thought Mrs Beckett needed to declare an interest on this matter, Councillor,' replied the chairman, the tone of her voice not nearly as confident as the words she used.

'Of course not,' retorted Councillor Beckett. 'After all, pecuniary interest is the basis of declaring an interest – and there's no way I can gain financially from this business.'

'Yes there is,' persisted Sparks.

'How?' Mrs Beckett managed to make the single syllabled word pregnant with hostility and anger. Such things, though, were lost on Jim Sparks.

'Because you live with your husband, so you're his partner; therefore, any financial benefits he gets naturally come to you as well – is that not so, Mr Chairman?'

'This is absolute nonsense,' rasped Councillor Beckett. 'I mean, my husband's not seeking any financial gain from this council. Merely, the Gilbert and Sullivan Society, of which he's a member, is asking for a rebate because of the problems they had with the curtains. No matter how much the council decides to refund on the hire charges, there's no way it can benefit him by even a penny. So therefore, there's no way it can benefit me. Mr Spark's objection is absolute nonsense.'

'I'm not so sure, Mr Chairman,' said Arthur Phillips, thoughtfully. 'I'm not saying, of course, that Mrs Beckett will take personal gain in any way from anything this committee might recommend; there's no possibility of that happening, I'm, well aware of that. But the fact remains that although Mrs Beckett's husband doesn't have a direct financial interest in the Gilbert and Sullivan Society, he is still deeply involved with them. So any gain, financial or otherwise, which comes the way of the society, must in some way benefit them – perhaps by way of hiring a better quality costume in the next production or a more professional orchestra to sing to, and that sort of thing. As I say, no direct financial gain to Mr Beckett, but benefit nonetheless and, as Councillor Beckett is his wife, then anything which benefits him must indirectly benefit her. So I feel she should declare an interest and leave the chamber before we discuss the problem of the curtains. I'm being a bit pedantic perhaps, but we're custodians of the public purse so we have always to do things correctly – to dot I's and cross T's.'

Sandra Miles still looked perplexed. 'Well, I still don't feel that Mrs Beckett needs to declare an interest – but perhaps you can give us some guidance on this, Mr Conway.'

The town clerk appeared more than perplexed – he looked as if a nervous breakdown was heading his way. Eventually he stuttered: 'It's a little difficult, Mr Chairman. The law always seems to me to be somewhat vague regarding declaring an interest. It's couched in such ambiguous terms that I really wouldn't like to hazard an opinion as to whether Mrs Beckett should declare an interest or not.'

The chairman now looked exasperated. A typical, ambivalent Cecil Conway reply, she mused. Suddenly, she made a decision; there was only one way to sort it out, and she would put it into operation immediately. 'We will take a vote on the matter,' she snapped. 'Mrs Beckett not to vote, of course. All those in favour of Mrs Beckett declaring an interest and leaving the meeting; three. Now, all those opposed to her having to declare an interest.' She immediately thrust her right arm into the air. 'Three again,' she said. 'So the vote is tied. I therefore use my casting vote – a vote in favour or Mrs Beckett not having to declare an interest. Now perhaps we can get on.'

Jim Sparks was not so easily thrust aside. 'Point of order, Mr Chairman,' he barked.

'What is it, Mr Sparks?' retorted Sandra Miles, testily.

'Well, with respect,' he said firmly. 'I'm not at all sure you had the right to a casting vote in this instance.'

'What do you mean, I hadn't the right? That's absolute nonsense. A chairman of any committee always has the right to a casting vote should the initial vote be tied. This vote was tied, so I broke the deadlock with my casting vote – which is as it should be.'

'With respect, Mr Chairman, I think you're wrong. We had such a situation as this many years ago – before you were on the council, I fancy,' he added, somewhat acidly. 'We established then, as I recall, that the chairman of the committee could not vote, then have the casting vote. Or, in other words, the chairman of a committee can only vote once. Only the mayor, when chairing the full council, can use a casting vote as you did just now. But you don't have to take my word for it, it's all in standing orders.'

'Then we shall consult them,' rasped Sandra Miles, her face white and taut with anger. An efficient woman, she did not take kindly to anybody questioning her decisions. Those who had the little booklet with them (a minority), turned to the relevant clause, whilst those who didn't waited to be informed. The chairman gazed at the wordy paragraph which covered voting, and casting votes, and so on, but found that she was so annoyed with the entire business in general – and with Councillor Sparks in particular – that she was unable to concentrate on the words before her eyes. She looked quickly at the town clerk.

'This is your province, Mr Conway. Please tell us exactly what standing orders say in terms of 'casting votes',' she snapped.

The town clerk did not look happy. Deciphering standing orders, as far as he was concerned had all the joy of having a tooth extracted without anaesthetic. Not for the first time, he was to claim ignorance because the rules of the council had been drafted long before he had appeared upon the scene as clerk and, possibly more unfortunately, because they were couched in jargon which would have tested the translation powers of a pre-war solicitor. Thus, from him, for several seconds, there was silence, his eyes riveted upon the jumble of words laying on the desk before him. He then, at length, cleared his throat and gazed at Sandra Miles.

'There are problems in deciding what the standing order on 'casting votes' actually says Mr Chairman,' he said, most hesitantly. 'The way it's written, and the somewhat antiquated language used, makes it all somewhat ambiguous. Frankly, it could possibly be argued that Mr Spark's interpretation is correct; on the other hand, though, it is possible that your action in voting twice is also perfectly correct. It's all so very difficult – and of course, was drafted long before I came to this authority.'

'That's no end of help,' muttered a frustrated Councillor Phillips to nobody in particular.

'Well, as I read this standing order, Mr Sparks is right,' opined Edward Hancock in his stentorian way. 'You shouldn't have used your vote twice. It might not have been your intention, but in actual fact it seems to me that you have abused your position somewhat.'

Sandra Miles was reasonably patient – some might even say, long suffering – but there was a limit to her forbearance. She was totally fed up with the nit-picking nonsense coming from many members, their time wasting, their trivial approach and, now, from Hancock, this as she saw it, attack on her character. She showed a rare flash of intense anger.

'Mr Hancock, how dare you accuse me of abusing my position. I have been a member of this council much longer than you have, and have occupied the chair of various committees on several occasions,' she rasped. 'I have always approached my duties with a total honesty of intention and what decisions I have been called upon to make have always been arrived at after careful and deep thought. How dare you question my integrity and even-handedness.'

'I meant no offence, Mr Chairman,' replied the slightly chastened Hancock, 'but. . .

'You might not have meant offence, Mr Hancock, but you've certainly given it,' retorted the chairman. 'Still, enough of all this. We have discussed this nonsense long enough. As everybody seems to be interpreting the standing order in a different way, I shall make my own interpretation – which will also be my ruling from the chair. As far as I'm concerned, standing orders state that I'm justified in using my casting vote in the way I did – so that's an end to the matter. The vote that Mrs Bartlett be allowed to remain and take part in any debate on the town hall curtains, is valid – and that's an end to it. Do I make myself clear?'

She gazed belligerently at, firstly, Edward Hancock, then Jim Sparks. They said not a word; she had, indeed, made herself clear.

'Right, Mr Conway, let us get on, for heaven's sake,' she snapped.

'Thank you, Mr Chairman,' said the town clerk, urbanely. 'As I was saying just now, the Gilbert and Sullivan Society want a reduction in the hire charge of the town hall because of the problems with the curtains. Also, of course, we have to decide what we're going to do about the curtains. According to the town hall supervisor, the curtains are, to use his phrase, "rotten as a pear", and will have to be replaced. That will cost a lot of money, and. . .'

'Where is the town hall supervisor this evening, Mr Chairman?' interjected Edward Hancock, clearly not abashed for long by his tongue lashing from Sandra Miles. He indicated the empty chair where Douglas Rawson, town hall supervisor, usually sat during meetings; 'he should be here tonight to give us a report on these damned curtains.'

'Unfortunately Mr Rawson's on holiday this week,' explained Conway. 'However, he has left me a few notes regarding the matter.'

'What's the use of notes?' snapped Hancock, scornfully. 'You can't ask questions of notes. And there are questions to be asked – many of them. What's the cost of new curtains, for one? Can the old ones be repaired? What caused them to rip in the first place? These things need to be asked, Mr Chairman – and probably much more besides. And there's obviously no way these questions can be asked if Mr Rawson isn't here.'

'So what are you suggesting, Mr Hancock?' asked the chairman, again icily.

'Simply that we defer discussions of this business until our meeting next month, when hopefully, Mr Rawson will be here to tell us exactly what the problems are and what he feels should be done to put things right.'

'I agree with Mr Hancock,' said Sparks. 'We've got to have the full facts before we can discuss this – and take decisions.'

'Nonsense Mr Chairman,' snapped Julia Beckett. 'Mr Conway says he's got notes regarding these curtains – which is surely all we need. Once he's given us the information he's got, then we can decide what to do about it. And I do feel we should decide something this evening – and get something done. After all, winter's almost here now and the town hall – and the stage of course – will be used quite a bit. There's the dramatic society, the Boy Scout Gang Show, the – er – the Gilbert and Sullivan Society Christmas Carol Concert and many more things. So the stage – and curtains to draw across it – is going to be essential during the next three months or so. That's why it's so important we do something about the curtains right away.'

'That's all very well,' retorted Edward Hancock, 'but I reckon it's more important to ensure that we spend council tax payers money wisely, than it is to rush things just to help the dramatic society – and the Gilbert and Sullivan Society,' he added pointedly. 'Not having stage curtains might cause them a touch of inconvenience, but that's all – it's something which can easily be overcome. After all, there's nothing vital in having stage curtains.'

'Mr Chairman, Mr Hancock is talking absolute tripe!' cried Councillor Beckett angrily. 'He obviously knows not the slightest thing about stage work, because if he did he'd be well aware that it's impossible to put on a play or show, or even a concert for that matter, without stage curtains. I do feel. . .'

'Move next business, Mr Chairman,' interjected Arthur Phillips, totally fed up with the entire business. Sandra Miles was likewise fed up, frustrated and exasperated with it all, but she was well aware that they couldn't just move on to the next business – which was to declare the meeting closed – until some decision was taken as to what they were going to do about the stage curtains.

'Sadly, Mr Phillips, it's not quite that simple,' she explained in a tone which lay somewhere between exasperation and exhaustion. 'We've got to decide what we're going to do concerning these curtains.'

'Propose the matter be referred back to the next meeting of this committee for a full verbal report by the town hall supervisor,' said Jim Sparks quickly.

'Seconded!' roared Edward Hancock.

'It's been proposed and seconded that the matter be referred back,' droned Sandra Miles. 'All those in favour, please show. Three. Against – two.'

The chairman did not vote this time. She had some sympathy with Julia Beckett, there was no doubt about that; the curtains needed to be replaced – or repaired – as a matter of urgency, not left for at least another month; but she was tired of the whole business, fed up with the trivial bickering of people who really ought to know better, and partially relieved to see it all put off for another month. At least she'd be able to get home at a reasonable hour.

'The motion is carried,' she said wearily. 'The matter of the town hall stage curtains will be referred back to next month's meeting of this committee.'

She glanced at the town clerk sitting to her right. 'Are there any other matters, Mr Conway?'

'None that I'm aware of, Mr Chairman.'

'Then I declare the meeting closed,' the chairman said with an audible sigh of relief. She rapidly picked up her papers, pushed them into the small attache case which she habitually carried, bade everybody a brusque 'good night' and speedily left the chamber, most of the committee following closely in her wake.

Edward Hancock and Jim Sparks were the last to leave, each helping the other on with his coat as they stood just inside the door. Whilst Hancock was somewhat unpopular with many members of the council, mainly because of his inability to desist from making comment on virtually every item on the agenda, he and the long serving Sparks got on quite well, the latter admiring the relative newcomer's independence of mind and spirit and his constant pursuance of what he thought was right and fair, even though it riled colleagues – and, indeed, himself on occasions.

'You know, Jim,' said Hancock, flicking up the switches and plunging the chamber into darkness, 'I can't see us having new curtains in the town hall for a very long time to come.'

They passed through the door into the vestibule, and closed the door behind them.

'Why do you say that?'

'Simply because we've got no money to do it. After all, we're talking about a fair bit of money here you know; thousands I reckon, at the end of the day. And we've not got it.'

'No, I suppose not. There's no way the council tax can be kept down – as it has been for the past two years – and the council have money for replacing stage curtains as well,' replied Sparks. 'There was only about twenty thousand pounds put by for emergencies for the entire year and most of that was used up months ago, as I recall, when the gang mower had to be replaced and also a new van bought.'

'Exactly,' said Edward Hancock, as they went out into the street. 'Which means that there'll be no money until we fix the new charge in May – after the elections.'

'We certainly don't want to levy any supplementary charge or spend any of our little remaining reserves, before the election,' muttered Councillor Sparks. 'That'll not look good at all.'

'Exactly,' said Hancock once again. 'Which is why we'll have to make sure no real action is taken on this curtain business until May at the earliest.'

'That's no problem, is it? I mean it would probably take until May, well beyond, in fact, even if we were in a hurry to get the curtains replaced.'

Hancock laughed. 'Quite so.'

They walked to the end of the street, turned the corner and entered the lounge of 'The King's Head' for their customary after-meeting nightcap – or two.

VII

Reynard

Henry Morris, pleased at the way the meeting had gone – it had been brisker than normal which was always a bonus – noted the last item on the agenda; any other business. 'I've not been informed of any, Mr Clerk, have you?'

The parish council's long-serving clerk, George Miller (who was also the local postmaster), shook his head. 'Nothing that I'm aware of, Mr Chairman – which is probably good news for us all. We had a long session last month as you'll recall – what colour to paint the ceiling of the parish hall. The time it took to decide, two or three of the younger, fitter members of this council could probably have done it – though as I'm only the clerk, and not an elected member, it's not really my place to say so.' Clearly this was right, clearly he knew it – and clearly he was trying to make the point, which he had tried to do time and time again to councillors, eternally without success, that if they would only show some discipline, talk less and when they did so, to the point and, crucially, only go into serious debate about serious issues (not such trivialities as the colour of paint), then they could all get home to their firesides, or TV viewing, or simply bed, so much earlier.

Councillor Mrs Myra Jenkins, who taught the infant class at the village school, was no fan of the parish clerk – whilst having confidence in his efficiency and wide knowledge – as she felt he, as essentially an employee of the council, had too much to say for

g

himself, and was allowed to get away with it, especially by the chairman, as they had both lived their entire lives in the village, and were friends of very long-standing. 'It's not for the parish clerk to criticise this council for taking its time to ensure the colour of the parish hall ceiling is suitable and in-keeping with its surrounds. I recall there being a very fair, full and informed debate, and a sensible decision. Why, if. . .'

'As you say, Mrs Jenkins, there was a full debate – and a decision was made,' interjected Morris, aware that, good councillor though she was, she could certainly 'go on a bit'. Also she had a tendency to talk to fellow councillors in similar tones she would use to her five year olds at school. 'I believe work is about to start on the painting within the next couple of weeks – is that not right, Mr Clerk?'

'In theory, yes it is, Mr Chairman,' agreed Miller. 'Trouble is that Cedric Blowey who usually does such work for this council fell over a few days ago on his way home in the dark from the Tamar View Inn – had, well, probably, knowing Cedric, one or two too many; hurt his back. He hopes to start at the beginning of next month – just over a fortnight away – as long as he's better, of course.'

'This is no way to proceed, Mr Chairman – we need a firm date here, not a hope. If this fellow drinks in the way he appears to, and cannot be relied on, then it seems to me he should not be given valuable council work. We should. . .'

'Mrs Jenkins, the decision has been made,' rasped the chairman. 'If Mr Blowey is unable to proceed with the painting in the near future, then no doubt Mr Miller will bring the matter to our attention and we will have to put the work elsewhere. All I want to know now is whether you, or anybody else, has urgent business which needs to be brought to the attention of the council. Seeing as nobody has followed the usual procedure of mentioning it to me before the meeting, I assume there is none.' He spoke the final sentence in tones which suggested he would be exceedingly unsympathetic to anybody who did now raise an issue, beyond the 'eleventh hour'.

'Well – well yes, I do, Mr Chairman.' Sid Bowden was rarely

reticent, but even he sounded a touch embarrassed. 'I'm sorry I didn't speak to you before the meeting, but you'll note I was a bit late getting here. You were on apologies for absence when I came. Got held up – cow calving. If it hadn't come when it did, I'd not have been here at all. That old cow usually has problems calving for some reason. Good cow though, and turns out good stock. She's just had a fine, healthy bull calf. Anyway, I feel there's something that needs to be brought up here and now – it's over a month before the next meeting.'

'I hope it's urgent, Councillor Bowden,' stated the chairman in a tone which suggested the farmer would be suspended by his thumbs were it not.

'It's urgent all right; it's foxes – on council property – and they're killing good laying hens on mine.'

Henry Morris was, unusually for him, nonplussed. 'I'm not with you – what council property?'

'The playing fields – in the high hedge beside the football pitch to be exact; and as you know, the other side of that hedge is our place, Enid and me. It was Enid that put me wise to it; smelt them she did – about three days ago. I've never known anybody like my missus – can smell a fox a quarter mile away. They're there all right – and last night they proved it. Four of our hens this morning when we went to collect the eggs – three dead, one with a wing ripped off, poor creature. I had to finish her off. Wicked things foxes; vicious. They don't kill just to live – they'll kill, wound, maim as many as possible, then take just one for food. Loathe them – always have. I'd kill every one in England if I could. Anyway, there it is. There's two foxes living in that hedge in the playing fields – a dog fox and a vixen that looks heavy with young. It's crucial they be killed as soon as possible – and the vixen before she can give birth. Don't want three or four more in the world with their vicious ways.'

The chairman's initial ire at having the meeting extended had evaporated. Although a newsagent, not a farmer, he was a country man, having lived within sight of the fields and woods of this parish his entire life. 'Reynard' was as much his enemy as it was that of Sid Bowden and his hapless hens; action needed to be taken. 'Well, Sid – er, Councillor Bowden – you're right to bring the matter up – and under urgent business, 'cause that's what it is. Action has to be taken, and right away, to get rid of this – this vermin. Shoot them, perhaps – that would be the best way.'

'It would Mr Chairman,' agreed Bowden, 'and I know just the man to do it. Me. I've got a shotgun – two, in fact – and I could be round there first thing in the morning to put them down. In fact, this afternoon it was my intention to do just that; but it struck me that being on the council I ought to do things in a proper fashion. They're on parish property, not mine, so I ought really to get the council's permission before I shoot them. So that's what I'm asking for – your agreement that I go round in the morning and get rid of the murdering devils.'

Morris nodded. 'Quite so, Councillor. Well I cannot imagine anybody on this council could possibly object to you killing foxes – especially as they're a threat to your poultry; and they'll be a threat to anybody keeping chickens, lambs too. They have to be kept down, foxes – there's always been a lot on this peninsula and my feeling is they're increasing. I fancy that I'm speaking for the entire council when I say the quicker you shoot these pests the better.'

'I'm sorry, Mr Chairman, but you're not speaking for me.' The voice was female, sharp and uncompromising. Miss Mary Barrett, daughter of a former Minister of the Congregational Chapel – who also had lived in the parish her entire life – glared firstly at the chairman, then at her fellow councillors. 'I'm shocked and – and – outraged at such a suggestion. That we can officially agree to the slaughter in such callous fashion of wild animals just doing what is instinctive – just getting their every day food and the suggestion that the vixen, heavy with her pups, be destroyed so her progeny also are eliminated, disgusts me more than I can say. I can understand Councillor Bowden being upset that his hens have been attacked in such a way, and certainly if he caught the fox in the act of attacking them, then it could be said he would be justified in taking immediate action to defend them – perhaps even the shooting of the fox could be justified in such a situation. But such cold blooded killing as he suggests is utterly wrong – contrary to all decency and what is right. Why – why,' she cried, another argument coming her way, 'It might be that the fox – or foxes – in the recreation grounds are not responsible for the attack on the hens. It, or they, could have come from further afield.'

'So what are you suggesting,' cried an outraged Bowden, 'I get PC Barton to go round to them and ask questions – ask them if it was them that killed my chickens? All right, it might have been some other blasted fox, but the two in that hedge next to us will certainly kill somebody's fowls and livestock – that's the nature of them.' The councillor's face was plum coloured with rage.

'Comments through the Chair, Councillor, please – you know the rules.' Henry Morris had much sympathy with the farmer – total, if truth be told – but he had been on councils long enough to know that proper procedure had to be maintained at all times if indiscipline – indeed, anarchy – was not to rule.

'Sorry, Mr Chairman,' spluttered a slightly repentant Bowden, 'but Miss Barrett is talking nonsense, there's no other word I can use; and absolute nonsense, as well. There's hardly a farmer in this land who will not see a fox as anything other than an enemy and a menace – and do something to get rid of them, to destroy them. The hunt, with their 'osses and 'ounds never did come through here, even before the ban, so we've always had to shoot them.'

'That's a point, Mr Chairman,' interjected Councillor Mrs Lorna Higgins. 'The hunt. There are two hunts in the area, one very near Tavistock, the other up close to Okehampton. I like seeing huntsmen and women on their horses, with a fine pack of hounds – it's a good spectacle. Why don't we get them to come here, to this parish?'

'I don't want to see them, Mr Chairman,' stormed Miss Barrett, in no way abashed by Sid Bowden's recent tirade. 'It's the very last thing I want to see in this parish. I know they are banned from catching foxes now, but just the idea of poor creatures being chased, harried to exhaustion then ripped to death by savage hounds. It's better they be shot than that.'

'It will be amongst the last things you'll see in this parish, 'osses and 'ounds,' retorted Councillor Sid Bowden. 'The hunt doesn't come here ever – it never has and never will, 'cause the mainline railway runs through a large part of the peninsula. It's too dangerous for 'osses, riders and 'ounds alike. They could easily be mown down by an express. Fair point – 'ounds chasing a fox, riders too to some extent, wouldn't worry too much about a railway line until it was too late. Anyway, if Miss Barrett doesn't want them laid hold of by 'ounds, then she should be happy that I'm prepared to get rid of them in a quick, humane way, by shooting them. I can see no logic to her objection.'

'Well, could I ask Councillor Bowden, Mr Chairman, if he'd shoot a fox because it killed a rabbit in one of his fields. I doubt it – he'd be pleased to see one rabbit less, creatures which forever nibble away at his crops. It's just because the animal has killed something in his ownership – bluntly put, it's cost him money.'

Sid Bowden, momentarily, was stunned by the comments of his fellow councillor – and before he could muster his response, which would have been one of controlled anger (though he would not have been able to guarantee full control) he was forestalled by Councillor Jim Fulton, also a farmer – a good, deep thinking man, who said not a lot but who, when he did speak, selected his words carefully, ever able to state his case with clarity, brevity, accuracy and, if he was in disagreement with the views of a fellow councillor – torpedo like.

'Mr Chairman,' said he, 'I am surprised an intelligent lady like Miss Barrett, also a country woman, can make such comments – how she cannot distinguish the huge difference between a fox killing a rabbit in a field and it butchering a fowl in a henhouse is beyond my understanding. A rabbit, like a fox, is a wild animal, free to wander where it will. If a fox catches it, then that is the law of nature. A hen, though, like a lamb, is totally different. The hen is in its pen or henhouse because that's where the farmer has put it. The lamb, likewise, is in a field due to the whim of the shepherd. Both are there to provide its owner with food and income – eggs from the chicken, wool and ultimately meat from the lamb, and probably the chicken as well at some stage. Both are owned by the farmer – and, in the case of hens, very often by people who keep a few in their back garden to provide them with fresh eggs. Therefore, Mr Chairman, the owners of these birds, these animals, have a responsibility to ensure their welfare – a duty of care, if you like. It's not about profit, Miss Barrett, the loss of a few hens will not put Councillor Bowden in the Bankruptcy Court. No it's about what is right, about protecting the defenceless, the vulnerable. If Mr Bowden as a farmer, fails to take action to defend his fowls then he is failing in this, and failing badly. By asking permission to destroy the predators in the recreation ground, he is merely seeking to do this – to do what is right, fair and humane. I am surprised and saddened that Miss Barrett, who is, I know, a devout Christian lady – something I much respect, being a man of strong faith myself – seems unable to appreciate this. Mr Bowden could easily have taken his shotgun this morning, gone into the playing fields and destroyed this vermin. To be frank, that's what I might well have done. He chose, though, to act very honourably, with a high level of respect for the fact that these fields are not his property, and brought the matter to the attention of this council whose property it is. All he seeks is our permission to dispose of these foxes – and all he's getting is prevarication and opposition. Let us quite simply give him our agreement that he be able to shoot these pests whenever he has the opportunity.'

Councillor Miss Barrett put her hand up to speak, but clearly was a touch shell-shocked by Jim Fulton's uncompromising assault. 'Mr Chairman – Mr Chairman,' she stuttered. 'I really must – well, well, defend myself against Mr Fulton's – well, very harsh, unfair words. He – he – he has misunderstood my position in a sense, I feel, he has. . .'

'Mr Chairman,' cried Councillor Murray Jarvis, suddenly coming to life – and drowning out Mary Barrett with his loudish, rather shrill voice (from most, such a sudden intervention without warning or invitation would be seen as rudeness; from Murray though, such an intervention was motivated almost invariably by a burst of enthusiasm. This occasion was no exception.) 'Surely we as a council should give a lead here. Councillor Bowden is having serious problems with foxes at present, and we know he's not alone in this. There are far too many foxes on this peninsula – they're taking hens from coops in people's gardens, and are a danger to livestock. Perhaps we do need to organise a shoot. We've had them in the past, so why don't we do it again, and soon. I'd be very willing to be involved in organising it.' Nobody doubted Murray Jarvis's last words, for he was a man of almost constant action, enthusiasm and involvement – a Church Warden, member of the choir, Scout Master, Special Constable, Chairman of the Carnival Committee and charity fund raiser, amongst other things – always seeking new ways to use up his seemingly inexhaustible supplies of energy (remarkable in a man now in his sixties).

The chairman nodded. 'Thank you, Councillor Jarvis for that – and for offering to organise a shoot. That sounds to me like a reasonable idea, though I'm not sure it's really a matter for the council to be involved in.'

'Definitely not, Mr Chairman,' came the instant agreement of the parish clerk. He had plenty to do, he reasoned, without having to be involved with a motley bunch of farmers and others in the area let loose with shotguns pursuing foxes. Not that he was unsympathetic to the idea – he'd lost hens from his large back garden in recent months to predatory Reynard, so the hunting down of this merciless foe had appeal. Quick thinking as always, he made a suggestion to Henry Morris. 'I would point out, though, Mr Chairman, that whilst it's certainly not council business, there's no reason why a councillor – or councillors – cannot be involved in organising such an event, in a private capacity, of course. Councillor Jarvis has volunteered to be involved in arranging a shoot – so perhaps that would be a way forward.' There were times when Murray Jarvis's boundless energy was little less than a menace to colleagues on the council and in the manifold other organisations with which he was involved – no man to have about if one wanted a quiet life – but this, reasoned the clerk, could be one occasion where he could be put to good use.

'Yes – yes, Mr Miller; That could be a way forward,' agreed the chairman with a touch of enthusiasm himself (not a common occurrence). 'It doesn't address the immediate issue, of course, of the two foxes in the recreation field. We have to make a decision on that seeing as Councillor Bowden had the courtesy to bring the matter to us even though, to be frank, he could easily have gone in there and destroyed the pests without us knowing about it as Mr Fulton observed just now – and I'm sure there are those amongst us who would have done just that. As to whether or not there is a parish-wide organised fox shoot is a matter for members as individuals and for the community in general, of course. It cannot, as both I and the parish clerk have said, officially be the business of this council.' He paused, then was about to try to guide a session of any urgent business which threatened to stretch into eternity to a speedy conclusion; but was forestalled by Mary Barrett, clearly having recovered her second wind – and re-grouped.

'It most certainly cannot be an issue for this council, Mr Chairman,' she rasped. 'It would be outrageous for us, an elected body, to be instrumental in organising a – a – a ritual slaughter of innocent creatures just following their instincts, just foraging for food. Equally it will be disgraceful if we grant Mr Bowden permission to kill foxes on our property. Also, I feel that if this dreadful shoot is organised, we as a council should ban those taking part in killing any creatures on council owned property. The idea, though, of a group of men, armed with guns, running wild over our lovely local countryside, shooting lovely animals who just live by the laws of nature, is utterly repugnant. I would imagine the reality would be that hardly anyone would wish to be involved.'

'What – nobody involved?' snorted Councillor Arnold Atkins, who earned his living as a plumber and usually, both within and without the council chamber, was a man of many words. 'Mr Chairman, Miss Barrett clearly doesn't know – which surprises me as she has lived in the parish all her life – that back in the fifties, before as well, they used to have regular shoots; probably every three years or so. They used to bag a lot of foxes too. Since then, though, there's hardly been any. I can remember one – probably ten years ago, but none since. I don't know why – there's plenty of foxes out there still, all causing mischief.'

153

'The wounding, isn't it,' stated Councillor Cyril Pellow, who made his living from sizeable market gardens close to the banks of the Tamar. 'I expect you remember that, Mr Chairman – I imagine virtually everybody here will remember it. Councillor Atkins is right – there's not been a shoot in seven or eight years now; and the reason has to be that people still remember that day and are staying away from organising such an event again even though I agree it's needed. And there's no reason why a shoot shouldn't go ahead – after all, that day, whilst it was a nasty accident, nobody was killed or, in truth, terribly wounded.'

'Well, I suppose it could possibly be described as an accident, Mr Chairman,' opined Sid Bowden, 'but it was on the verge of being criminal. As I said just now, you probably remember it – as I'm sure many here will.'

'Yes – of course,' said Morris, 'old Howard Higgins wasn't it? Shot Seb Symons in the backside – cowman, isn't he, out at Highfield Park, or at least I think he's still there.'

'Yes, he is – and Howard's still around, of course, though he's got to be eighty now – always had poor sight,' continued Bowden. 'Even then he wore pebble glasses with lenses that thick you could probably walk on them. He turned out on the shoot along with forty, fifty others – and had his shotgun with him. Well, as I recall, they were out in some woods on Harry Martin's place, when Seb Symons put down his gun and bent over to do something to one of his boots. The trouble is, he was wearing light brown breeches – now Seb then, as now, was not a thin man, so there was a fair bit of light brown rump exposed for all to see. Trouble is, Howard with his awful sight caught a glimpse of something roughly the same colour as a fox, so aimed his gun and fired. Fortunately, he only let off one barrel, and, also fortunately, many of the cartridge pellets he did fire missed the target. Enough hit poor old Seb though to put him in hospital for several days. It could have been worse, of course – he could have killed him. But it was a bad business, nonetheless. So bad, in fact, even Claude Barton took some action.'

'I don't remember that,' said Atkins, 'though I remember everything else – I was there. Always enjoyed a bit of sport; if there's another shoot in the future, I'll be there again. But PC Barton, I don't remember him being involved. What did he do, take him to court? – I'm surprised I don't remember if he did.'

'What, Claude Barton take somebody to Court.' Sid Bowden laughed. 'No, Mr Chairman – that's not Claude's style. I reckon if a serial killer had fled to the parish, Claude would not have prosecuted him – too much paperwork. No, what he did was to confiscate his shotgun – and Howard had enough sense not to argue about it. I reckon he must have been relieved he wasn't called to court. He would have been in a fair bit of trouble had he been summoned. Anyway, that was the last time there was an organised fox shoot in the parish; and I fancy it's a good idea for there to be another one.'

'It is, Mr Chairman,' enthused Murray Jarvis. 'And as I said, I'd be perfectly willing to help organise such an event.'

'I like the "help" bit,' Cyril Pellow murmured to Jim Fulton, sitting beside him. 'When did Murray ever help in any way. He'll do the organising from start to finish – a few could well help him, but it will be his show, all right, that's for certain. Mind you, he'll do a good job – he always does.'

'Thank you, Councillor Jarvis,' said the chairman, urbanely. 'I'm sure you'll have much support amongst the farmers and, come to that, the wider community. There are a lot of people in a parish such as this who, whilst having no direct involvement with farming or the countryside, have no love for foxes – and many, like Councillor Atkins, who just like some sport. Still, as we've already decided, this is not directly a council matter, so I cannot allow it to take up any more of our time. We have already seen what should have been a brief meeting turn into an unnecessarily long one. I must move matters on – bring them to a conclusion – or we'll still be here at breakfast time.'

'Quite so, Mr Chairman,' replied Jarvis, awash with positive contentment as, out of the blue, a new exciting project had appeared – a challenge for a man whose entire being craved, eternally, constant endeavour. 'Just to say, though, I will call a public meeting and do so within the next few days. I'll put up notices around the village – I'm sure there will be a good response. Also, I. . .'

'Thank you, Councillor,' interjected the chairman – softly but firmly. 'I'm sure the matter is in good hands, but as I've just said, this is not a council matter so we really must get on and come to a decision on what is – the problem of the foxes in the recreation field and the request from Councillor Bowden that he be permitted to shoot them, they having slaughtered some of his poor hens.' The final words were spoken in a tone which suggested he would happily, and rapidly, go around and eliminate the pests himself.

'I repeat, Mr Chairman,' said Mary Barrett, shrilly and angrily, 'that such behaviour would be barbaric. I feel. . .'

'Seeing as, by your own admission, Councillor Miss Barrett,' said the chairman strongly, and very formally, 'you have already stated such views, you have no need to state them again. Also, by the rules of council, you have spoken once on the matter and do not have the right to speak again. Do I make myself plain?'

Henry Morris, in this mood, was not a man to tangle with, but Mary Barrett – who really should have known better as she had been on the council many years, some of them under Morris's chairmanship – could be a pedantic, blinkered and uncompromising woman. 'Mr Chairman, I feel you are denying me free speech – and I protest. This is to me a matter of principle and – and moral code. What is being proposed in this chamber – what Councillor Bowden wishes to do is – is – is murder. He should be ashamed to even propose such a thing, he should. . .'

Mary Barrett had chosen her words badly. Anger swept across the chamber like a bush fire, with raised voices coming from all sides. Quick to see a chance to bring this interminable debate to a close, the wily clerk interjected with alacrity – 'I must point out, Mr Chairman, that we are at present attempting to make bricks without straw. There is no proposal on the table. Nothing, at present, on which we can make a decision.'

'Quite right, Mr Clerk,' snapped Morris. 'It really is time we brought this matter to a close – may I have from the floor, a proposal regarding whether or not Councillor Bowden be allowed to go into the playing fields owned by this council and shoot the foxes he believes are responsible for killing his hens.'

'I move he be given the permission, Mr Chairman;' Cyril Pellow spoke instantly.

'Seconded.' Arnold Atkins's support was also forthcoming with some rapidity.

'Thank you, members,' responded the chairman. 'We have spent a great amount of time on this matter, especially seeing as it was not an agenda item. So I will put it to the vote, immediately. All those in favour, please show.'

'Mr Chairman, I must protest,' came the cry from Mary Barrett – part anguish, part outrage. 'You have given us no time to debate the matter – not since the proposals have been formally put before us, at any rate. By standing orders, we have the right to debate the matter before a vote is taken.'

She was right – and all, certainly the experienced councillors that most were, knew she was right. Also, the chairman knew she was but he had had enough of Mary Barrett. He always found her difficult, but this evening she had, in his view, been beyond awkward – she had been obnoxious and offensive. Some members – though probably not sympathetic to her views – would have supported her simply because she was right. This time they said nothing, thereby in effect supporting the chairman in his decision to put the matter to the vote.

'I must rule you out of order, Councillor Miss Barrett,' said he, the tone of his voice bleak – even icy. 'There has been more than enough debate on this item – more than enough time wasted. As I said just now, I will accept no more argument. I put the matter to the vote – all those in favour?' Ten arms shot into the air – including the chairman (he did not always vote, but he was so incensed this time, he felt he had to make a point). Probably as many as three or four other members would either have abstained or, in a couple of instances, voted against the proposal – not entirely easy with the prospect of foxes being, in effect, sentenced to imminent death – especially a vixen in pup. Mary Barrett, though, with her unbending, self-regarding righteous indignation, had alienated them. Thus they punished her by their failure to give her support or, even, an abstention.

'Those against.'

Councillor Miss Barrett's right arm shot into the air – in solitary splendour. Determined to the very end to give no ground, she said in clipped, angry tones, 'I wish to be recorded in the minutes as voting against this – this – this monstrous and inhumane motion.'

'That is your right, Councillor Miss Barrett – so it will be done,' stated the chairman, his normal equanimity slowing returning. 'You will see that's done, Mr Miller?'

'I will, Mr Chairman.'

'Thank you.' Morris looked towards the potential hunter. 'Clearly Councillor Bowden, you have the permission of this council to enter the playing fields and destroy the foxes when convenient to yourself.'

'Thank you, Mr Chairman – I shall do so very soon,' said he, thinking that had he not taken what he felt, as a councillor, the correct, responsible path of seeking formal permission from his peers, then the butchers of his hens would already be dead. One thing of which he was certain – never again would he bring such a matter to the council chamber. He would take instant action and give explanations at a later date – if they were sought, which, he felt, was unlikely.

The following morning, he regretted even more his failure to take the law into his own hands. For at first light, after swallowing, quickly, a cup of tea, he had put on a warm coat, his wellington boots, picked up his shotgun, strode rapidly away from the dwelling house across a couple of fields, scrambled over a high Devon hedge into the playing fields, crept to where he knew the foxes had their den, took the safety catch off, then, after a few seconds – put it back on again. For there was nothing to aim at – no quarry. He was too late. It was as if Reynard had listened to the council debate; or, perhaps, somewhat more likely, Mary Barrett had gone around to the playing fields even earlier than him that morning and driven them off. Their scent was still very strong – clearly they had been in that den until very, very recently. It was possible they had been there even half an hour before – but would the single minded Miss Barrett do such a thing? The farmer's view was that whilst 99 percent of folk would not carry their convictions to such lengths, she would – and he convinced himself she had. Something, clearly, which could never be proved.

He still thought he would have them, though – he would avenge his slaughtered hens, and do it by courtesy of Murray Jarvis when that man of action fixed a date for the shoot. Clearly the one – or two – who had visited their destruction upon his layers could not be identified with any certainty but the elimination of any would be of satisfaction to him. So, it was with that he comforted himself – but he rued the fact that he had not acted 24 hours before. Reynard – and Mary Barrett – had triumphed.

VIII
The Twinning

Basil Parfitt banged his gavel, and called for order. They were a bit boisterous tonight, he thought, but he'd known them worse. And they had at least moved along at a reasonable pace. That, of course, was largely due to the fact that Denzil Dillow wasn't there. He'd gone down with the 'flu that very morning and, although at the beginning of the meeting Parfitt had wished him a speedy recovery, there was probably nobody in the chamber who was sorry Denzil was absent. For with his constant points of order, his frequent referrals to standing orders and his remarkable ability to make even the most simple issues complicated, he could add an hour to the length of any meeting.

Basil glanced at his watch, then down at the agenda. Only one more item, which shouldn't take long, then he'd be away home – hopefully just in time for the *Midsomer Murders* on TV which he always enjoyed.

'Item 8 – Any other business,' he droned. 'I believe Mr Wilson, you've got something you wish to bring before the council.'

'Yes, thank you Mr Mayor.' Ken Wilson was a tall, well-dressed man, who carried a certain amount of authority with some members of the council by virtue of his impressive bearing. 'It concerns a recent holiday I had in France, Mr Mayor. We stayed in a town in Southern Brittany called Guipapont and had a wonderful time there. It's a delightful place, clean, prosperous, and the people are extremely friendly and courteous.'

'He'll be showing us the holiday slides next,' muttered Councillor Dick Conway to this elderly 'neighbour', Councillor Jim Bennett – who didn't hear him for the simple reason he was in the midst of one of his occasional dozes – though perhaps regular would have been a better description.

'The town is of similar size to ours – though probably a touch bigger – and, also, like ours, it has a mixture of light industry side by side with an important cattle market and a number of agricultural merchants. Also, near the town, there are. . .'

'Mr Mayor,' thundered Councillor Roland Smith. 'I didn't come along here tonight to listen to Mr Wilson's holiday experiences, pleasant though they might well be. So he had a nice holiday in France; well me and my missus had quite a nice one in London – except we were robbed left, right and centre with the prices up there – but I don't intend to waste the valuable time of this council giving a detailed description of it. I move next business.'

'I think your proposal's a little premature, Mr Smith,' replied the mayor, rather gently. 'After all, Mr Wilson's not really got to the point he wishes to raise, yet. However, I would concede that your statement, Mr Wilson, does seem to be rambling on somewhat. I'm sure we'd all be obliged if you would get to the point.' He gave Ken Wilson a somewhat old-fashioned look as he spoke the words.

'I was about to, Mr Mayor,' he retorted in his rather imperious fashion, 'and would have done so already if I'd not been interrupted by Councillor Smith.'

'Saucy bugger,' muttered Roland Smith.

'The point of my description of the town of Guipapont is merely to paint a rough picture of the place in the minds of members of the council, for it's important that everyone here has some idea of the kind of town which it is. You see. . .'

'He's at it again!' rasped Smith, jumping to his feet with unusual alacrity. 'Tell him to get on with it or we'll be here all night. I just want to get home to have a cup of tea, though I fancy I'll have a Scotch if this goes on much longer.'

'I don't need you to instruct me on how to chair this meeting,

Mr Smith, thank you very much,' retorted the mayor, rare acidity in his tone. 'Still,' he continued, shifting his gaze to Ken Wilson, 'I trust you will not beat about the bush any longer.'

'I wasn't aware that I was beating about the bush,' retorted Wilson, huffily. 'It's not my style to procrastinate and it never has been. However, I feel it's important for members of the council to be aware of the background to the idea I wish to put forward. You see, whilst I was in. . .'

'Mr Mayor, I've had enough of this,' stormed Roland Smith, his face as red as a pillar box. 'If Mr Wilson doesn't state exactly what his proposition is, then I shall walk out of this meeting.'

There had been little love lost between Smith and Wilson, since Ken had publicly criticised Roland's handling, as chairman of the finance committee, of a debate on whether or not to give a grant to the local amateur dramatic society. As Wilson was, and remained, a staunch member of the society, Smith's description of the amateur actors as a 'bunch which should be doing something better with their time', offended him deeply. The chairman's stubborn resistance to the paying of a grant, and his subsequent use of his casting vote to prevent it, created a gulf between the two men which would never be bridged – largely because neither would ever seek to bridge it.

'Mr Smith,' replied the mayor, his voice a little shorter than previously, 'you are at liberty to leave this meeting, or stay, as you see fit. I, however, will conduct it and decide when a proposition is due. Having said this, I think it time, Mr Wilson, for you to state exactly what you wish to bring before this council. Should you fail to do so, then I shall formally move 'next business' from the chair. Do I make myself clear?'

'Perfectly, Mr Mayor,' replied Wilson, evenly, 'and I shall, of course, abide by your ruling. With that in mind, I would like to bring before the council, for their consideration, the idea that we might form a twinning link with the town of Guipapont. The reason why I took a couple of minutes actually getting to the point was simply because I felt the council would like some background information regarding the type of town Guipapont is, its size and so on. No doubt councillors will want to know quite a bit more about the place, and I am, of course, very willing to provide such information. However, I felt, because of impatience by certain members of the council who seem unable to lift their minds above the parochial' – he glared at Roland Smith as he said the words – 'and because of your ruling, Mr Mayor, that I should put forward the suggestion immediately.'

'Point of order, Mr Mayor!' cried Councillor Mrs Harper in her somewhat pedantic way.

'Yes, Mrs Harper,' replied Basil Parfitt, a tone of weariness about his voice. He might have known that Vera Harper would interrupt somewhere along the line.

'It's just that I wouldn't have thought that the question of twinning was one for this council to discuss; I really don't see it as being a council matter.'

'Of course it's a council matter,' rasped Councillor Sam Simmonds, impatiently. 'I mean, if we don't discuss it, who's going to – Toc H?'

'Yes, obviously it has to be a council matter,' agreed the mayor. 'That's if we're talking about an official twinning, of course. Any organisation is at liberty to arrange their own exchange with people of like interests in foreign countries on their own initiative. I know that the football club did this a few years back when they went to Italy for a week. I think they played a few games there and made a lot of good contacts. Then, the following year, the football club of the Italian town visited here. Mind you, it doesn't seem to have continued. I've heard of no further exchanges between the two clubs since.'

'I'm not surprised, Mr Mayor,' rasped Roland Smith, 'they were a shocking lot those Italians when they visited here – filthiest footballers I ever saw. In fact, one of them broke our centre forward's leg – dirty devil. And off the football field all they did was to drink the pubs dry and chase women.'

'Caught one of two as well from what I heard,' interjected Councillor Monty Bell, grinning broadly.

'Too damned right,' agreed Smith. 'We don't want them back again – nor any others like them either.'

'I seem to remember there was a bit of trouble when they were here,' agreed Basil Parfitt, 'but I'm sure that this was not necessarily a good example of twinning, Mr Smith.'

'Of course it wasn't, Mr Mayor,' snorted Ken Wilson. 'In fact this wasn't really twinning at all; this was merely an exchange between the football clubs of two towns in two separate countries. Nothing wrong with that, of course; in fact such exchanges are a part of twinning. But an official twinning, which is what I'm talking about, is the joining together of two towns at the very top – meaning at council and civic level – and from that other exchanges and associations arise. So if we twin officially with Guipapont, then we sign a twinning charter, we have official twinning visits and everything springs from that. There would be exchanges of school children, sports clubs, probably police and firemen, perhaps Rotary clubs and folk dance groups and so on. I do believe that such an official link could only bring advantages to the people of this town.'

'Aren't we twinned with somebody already?' asked Jim Bennett, who had been woken from his doze by Roland Smith's tirade a few minutes earlier.

'Not that I know of, Mr Bennett.'

'I could have sworn we were twinned with some town in France,' continued the aged councillor, doggedly. 'Surely we are. Didn't the town's British Legion Club make an official visit?'

The mayor's face looked blank, as did those of all the other members of the council. The town clerk, Bernard Dalton, came to the rescue.

'I think, Mr Mayor, that Councillor Bennett is referring to the visit by members of the local Royal British Legion to the battlefields and war graves of Normandy,' he said in his customary quiet, respectful, yet efficient manner. 'About two years ago that was. It was a private visit, of course, nothing to do with any twinning. Very successful though, I'm told.'

'Yes, I remember it now,' agreed the mayor. 'That's the explanation, Mr Bennett. No twinning involved there.'

Jim Bennett refused to give in. 'But the Morris Dancers went as well. I remember that because my nephew's one of them. As I recall, they had to come home early when their chairman, poor old Frank Hammond, dropped dead, in the middle of a dance. Heart. Remember it well. That was something to do with twinning, surely?'

Again the mayor and the members were at a loss – and once more the town clerk stepped into the breach.

'I do believe that there was a visit of the local Morris Dancers to Holland to take part in a folk dance festival. That again was probably about two years ago – or it might have been a little longer. As Mr Bennett says, Mr Hammond died during the visit – I certainly remember that. Still, it wasn't anything to do with a twinning.'

'Can't understand it,' persisted Bennett. 'I could have sworn we're twinned with somebody, somewhere. Perhaps the clerk can look back through the minutes to see if we are.'

'Surely we can't be twinned with somebody and not know it, Mr Mayor,' said Councillor Miss Dorothy Parsons, a touch of exasperation in her voice.

'Most unlikely, I would say,' agreed the mayor, urbanely.

'Still, assuming we're not twinned with anyone, it's time we were,' continued Dorothy Parsons. 'Everybody else seems to be. It's virtually impossible to drive into a city, town or even village now without passing signs giving the name of the place they've twinned with. In fact, some places are twinned with two or three overseas towns.'

'Exactly,' chimed in Ken Wilson. 'Miss Parsons is right. Some towns and, indeed, villages, much smaller than ours, are twinned with more than one continental place of usually similar size. It is most unusual in this day and age for any town as large as ours not to be twinned with somebody.'

'I can't say that I feel deprived in any way that we're not twinned with anybody,' opined Roland Smith. 'In fact, I'm pleased we're not if truth be told. Contacts with foreign countries – especially European ones – have never brought any benefits to this country at all. We're an island race, Mr Mayor, and should remember that. The good Lord in his infinite wisdom surrounded us with water to set us aside from other nations; he didn't mean us to fraternise with people on the Continent and suchlike. Our strength has always lain in our isolation and that should never be forgotten. It's sadly significant that since this twinning nonsense has taken hold throughout the country during the past fifty years or so, this country has gone downhill faster than a horse can gallop. I give fair warning, Mr Mayor, that I shall oppose any move towards officially twinning this town with the Frogs – or anybody else for that matter – with all the energy I can muster. And I'll go as far as to say that should this council decide to have an official twinning, then I shall resign – after serving this town in this chamber for over twenty years. I won't be part of any council who betray the interests of the people of this town.'

As Roland Smith's ample rear hit his seat, the full significance of what he had said overwhelmed him. Where had resignation come from? He'd not had anything like that in mind when he'd stood up to speak. It was that fool Wilson – he was to blame. There was something about the fellow that always got him, Roland, angry. And now his wrath had got him into a fine mess. He shuddered at the thought he might have to resign – and over something so silly. Of course, there'd been a few times during his twenty years when he'd threatened resignation, but it had been purely for effect. He'd been well aware then that his bluff wouldn't be called. He wasn't so sure now, though. The council had changed over the years. So many of the old, solid, reliable stalwarts had died, retired or been defeated at elections. There was a sizeable gathering in the chamber of the new breed – those ambitious men and women who wanted 'to do things', change the town, squander money, clutter up agendas with resolutions and suchlike. Several of the 'old school' remained, of course, but would they be enough to put a stop to this twinning nonsense? Roland Smith pulled a handkerchief from his trouser pocket and mopped a brow beaded with sweat, despite the coolness of the evening.

'I'm afraid, Mr Mayor, that I have to class Councillor Smith's outburst as the rantings of a dinosaur,' said Ken Wilson in his smooth, superior kind of way. 'I had hoped that such nationalistic, indeed, chauvinistic nonsense, had died long ago, but it would seem I'm wrong. All I can say is that Mr Smith's type of attitude and approach has served this country ill over the years. In fact, I'll go further and suggest that this type of ostrich-like refusal to observe, and learn, from the great strides forward made by so many of our European partners is what has held this country back; for sadly, there are still too many like him in this country. Granted their numbers are getting fewer, but those of opinions and attitudes similar to Mr Smith are still very prevalent in all aspects of life throughout this land. 'Little Englanders,' is what, I believe, some call them. I would call them small minded, bigoted people totally lacking in vision.'

'Just a minute, Mr Mayor!' roared Councillor Edgar Phillips – a generally quiet member of the council but one who was always quick to defend a principal or a fellow councillor whom he thought unfairly attacked – jumping to his feet. 'That's a scurrilous attack by Mr Wilson. Everyone's allowed to express their opinion in this chamber and that's all Mr Smith's been doing. And I would remind Mr Wilson, and all other members of the council that Councillor Smith, with his long years of distinguished war service, has more right than most to express opinions about the direction in which the nation appears to be going. And also the right to expect some sort of protection from Mr Wilson's shameful personal attack.'

Roland Smith gazed at Phillips, an expression of deep gratitude flitting across his face. Good old Graham, he thought; one of the best – and straight as a die. He'd liked the bit about 'distinguished war service', too. He'd never really considered himself to have had a particularly 'distinguished war service', but then, Edgar Phillips was a perceptive man, so could well have been right. It was true he'd never actually left British shores, only having been in the army for 2 years, doing his National Service, called up as an 18 year old in the late 50s, and had only risen to the rank of corporal in the catering corps, but who was to say that he had not performed his duties with distinction and dedication? No, Councillor Phillips could well be right – in fact, almost certainly was right.

'I do tend to agree with you to a certain extent, Mr Phillips,' said the mayor. 'Mr Wilson' – he glared at the erring councillor as he spoke his name – 'I do feel that your attack on Mr Smith was rather strong and, indeed, unnecessary. He was only expressing a view as is his privilege, so I hope that you refrain from such personal attacks in future.'

Ken Wilson got to his feet. 'Mr Mayor, if I've offended you, then I apologise,' he intoned, not the slightest note of contrition in his voice. 'I certainly intended no offence to anyone, but I do feel most strongly upon this matter of twinning – and I feel a certain obligation to the people of this town to try to ensure that outmoded ideas and prejudices do not stand in the way of their taking a full part in the building of bridges between this country and Europe – all of which is going ahead with such speed, and success, in so many other towns throughout our land.'

Dorothy Parsons caught the mayor's eye and got to her feet.

'Mr Mayor,' she said, 'it's all very well us talking about twinning with this French town – Guip – Guip – Guiplonk. . .'

'Guipapont,' corrected Wilson.

'Well, that's what I said, more or less,' snapped the somewhat irascible Miss Parsons. 'What I'm getting at is simply this – we're talking about twinning with this French town, but how do we know they want to twin with us!'

'Oh, but they do, they do!' cried Wilson. 'That's the whole point of me bringing up the subject. They are very keen to establish a twinning link with a town in England. I found this out when I had a chat with the Mayor of Guipapont, Monsieur Darleau. I had a most pleasant talk with him one afternoon, in his office in the town hall at Guipapont. A most charming and courteous man, he made me feel very welcome. Certainly I was glad I went round to his office to introduce myself. I felt I should, Mr Mayor, as a member of this council. I felt it was most certainly the courteous thing to do.'

'He would,' muttered Dick Conway, sarcastically, to Jim Bennett.

'I naturally gave him your best wishes, Mr Mayor,' he continued, 'and he reciprocated; and it was during this conversation that he put forward the idea of our two towns investigating the possibilities of an official twinning. Guipapont is already twinned with a West German town and another in Holland, but the mayor, and his council, as well, apparently are keen to establish links with an English town. So it was most fortuitous I called on Monsieur Darleau that afternoon. When he discovered from me that ours was a town of similar size to theirs and that we weren't twinned with anybody, he became most enthusiastic for us to consider formal links with them. I told him I thought it an excellent idea, and would bring it before this council when next we met. That is what I have done. I do hope we will grasp this hand of friendship extended towards us over the English Channel, and establish official twinning links with Guipapont, and do so as soon as possible.'

'Mr Mayor, the only thing I know about this twinning business is that it's the same as any other situation where entertaining guests is concerned – it's going to cost money,' said Sam Simmonds, 'council tax payers' money. And they won't be very keen to see their hard earned cash frittered away on nonsense such as that.'

'I quite agree with Councillor Simmonds,' said Dick Conway. 'This council already has enough trouble in finding sufficient money to fulfil our commitments; there's no way we could justify squandering any on a tom fool idea like twinning with a French town. Anyway, if the truth be told, I don't hold with twinning; it's a load of mischievous nonsense. My father always said that there were only two races in the world – British and foreigners; and he was right. This country, Mr Mayor, has had nothing but trouble with foreign countries right through its history – especially European ones. During the past century millions of Britons have died fighting them. To establish these twinning links is to spit on the graves of the brave men who fought and died for this country.'

'But we've not fought the French, for heaven's sake!' cried an exasperated Ken Wilson. 'Mr Mayor, they were our allies in the two World Wars – not our enemies.'

'And a fat lot of good they were as well,' snapped Roland Smith. 'More trouble than they were worth. In the First World War they only stayed at the front 'cause our lads were behind them with bayonets, whilst in the Second they caved in almost

169

h

before a shot had been fired in anger and left us to fight the Jerries on our own. No, I've got no time for the Frogs.'

'Mr Mayor, I really must protest at this – this – this narrow minded bigotry.'

'Who's Mr Wilson calling a bigot?' roared Smith, his face almost purple with anger. 'I'll not stand for that. I'm a fair minded man – always have been. But I'm a patriot first and foremost – and like Mr Conway, I do not like foreigners – well, Europeans, anyway. I've nothing against those in the old Empire, or Commonwealth, I suppose, as it is now. They supported us, fought with us in two World Wars, though they didn't have to.'

'So you're what I just said – a bigot,' snapped Wilson.

Smith seemed to be about to burst a blood vessel, but whilst he was in the process of trying to turn his wrath into words, Mrs Vera Hooper got to her feet.

'I still don't believe that twinning is a council matter, Mr Mayor,' she opined, 'but if we're making it so then perhaps I might be permitted to venture an opinion. Basically I feel that twinning is a good idea. After all, it surely has to be to the benefit of us all to broaden our outlook and our knowledge by coming into contact with the culture and the way of life of other nations. I have, though, a major criticism of the twinning pursued by most towns in this country: it nearly always lacks originality, adventure and – and I do feel this is so very important – a sense of social awareness and responsibility. What I'm getting at, Mr Mayor, is that comfortable, reasonably well off towns and villages in this country habitually twin with similar places in France or Germany – sometimes, perhaps, in the likes of Holland or Belgium. That's all very well as far as it goes, but I would like to feel that this council, if we decided to seek twinning links, should look beyond France, and, in fact, all of Europe. We should be bold, Mr Mayor, and make our twinning a highly significant gesture in a world where the gaps between the rich and poor nations gets ever wider. What I'm saying is that we should forget this Guipa place and seek twinning links with a town in Ethiopia, or the Sudan or Bangladesh, or some such Third World Country as that. I'm sure that if we were to pursue such a bold policy, others would soon follow.'

'You've got to be joking,' rasped Dick Conway, not sure whether to laugh or cry. 'Mr Mayor, who in their right mind would want to pay a small fortune to go to Ethiopia? Let's face it, the whole purpose of twinning is to have a mutual booze up. I reckon in Ethiopia and the Sudan and suchlike, about the only drink you'll get is water – and that'll probably kill you.'

'Mr Conway has totally missed the point I'm making, Mr Mayor,' protested Mrs Hooper. 'And probably deliberately as well,' she added darkly. 'What I'm trying to get over to the council is that we should not be lemming-like regarding this twinning business. Just because virtually every other place twins with a European counterpart, it doesn't mean we should do the same. If we were to twin with a town in, say, Ethiopia, we could send them – in fact, possibly, we could take them – things which would help them in their very hard lives. Food, blankets, medical supplies – all of these things and more we could take to these unfortunate people and receive, in return, those things which mark their own unique culture. . .'

'Like a bucket of sand and a few thousand flies,' snorted Dick Conway. 'Mr Mayor, I've never heard such a load of tripe in all my days. All twinnings are a waste of time in my estimation, but to even consider such links with the countries Mrs Hooper is talking about is plain daft.'

'I wouldn't agree with that at all,' said Ken Wilson, somewhat piously. 'Mrs Hooper's idea has much merit. In fact, her vision of twinning is the correct one really – the exchange of cultures, mutual help and so on. However, having said that, I do believe that links with underdeveloped Third World Countries would be a somewhat ambitious prospect for us at present. Far better, Mr Mayor, for us to forge formal links with Guipapont in France and once we've established strong ties with them, then we could well look much farther afield for our second twinning – possibly a Third World country as she suggests.'

'Mr Mayor, the only thing I want to forge any links with is my bed,' said Sam Simmonds, wearily. 'This debate has gone on long enough. All we're doing is to go round in circles. Let's make some decision on this, for heaven's sake.'

171

'I quite agree with Mr Simmonds,' retorted Wilson in his suave way. 'We should make a decision on this matter – here and now. With that in mind, I propose that this council establish formal links with the French town of Guipapont.' He made to sit down, but promptly straightened up again. 'I would deem it a privilege, Mr Mayor, to be the – what shall I call it – well, the link man in this business. I get on very well with the Mayor of Guipapont, so feel that I would possibly be the ideal man to actually negotiate the twinning.'

'Big headed bugger,' muttered Roland Smith.

'Mr Wilson has proposed that we establish formal twinning links with Guipapont,' droned Basil Parfitt. 'Do I have a seconder?'

'Point of order, Mr Mayor,' rasped Dick Conway. 'We can't vote on an important resolution like this without having a full debate on it – and learning more about it, and its implications.'

'Mr Mayor, what Councillor Conway says is nonsense,' stormed Ken Wilson. 'After all, what have we just been doing if not debating this issue? It's possible to debate for ever – and do nothing. I feel that we've given this business a very good airing, so let's now vote on it and then get on with organising this twinning.'

'Assuming the council's in favour, Mr Wilson,' interjected the mayor somewhat reproachfully.

'And I don't know that the council will be in favour,' snapped Dick Conway. 'I shall certainly vote against it at present. The fact is, we know nothing about the implications of twinning. We don't know if it will be supported by the town. We don't know if other organisations will be interested in getting involved – which has to be important. Most of all, though, we do not know just how much all this business will cost this council. I mean, it would be absurd to vote in favour of twinning, then find we don't have enough money to carry it through. A sub-committee, Mr Mayor – that's the way, at present. We should set up a sub-committee and they should go into it all thoroughly, then report back to this council at a later date.'

'I quite agree,' said Sam Simmonds, desperately looking for a

172

way of bringing the proceedings to an end. 'A sub-committee's the answer.'

'Yes, I think perhaps that would be the best course,' agreed the mayor.

'But Mr Mayor,' cried Wilson, 'this will mean that we'll waste weeks – perhaps even months!'

'Possibly, Mr Wilson. But I do feel it's important we don't rush into this business – attractive though the idea might well be,' added the mayor quickly. 'No, I think a sub-committee is the best plan here. Members agree that we should set up a sub-committee to go into all the implications of a formal twinning with the French town of Guipapont?'

There were mumbled 'yesses,' 'noes' and a fair amount of coughing. Basil Parfitt looked cross. The way things were going, he'd be lucky to get home by dawn.

'Perhaps we'd better have a formal vote on it,' he snapped. 'All in favour of setting up the sub-committee? One, two, three, four, five, six. . . Now, those against? One, two, three, four, five, six again. Which means I've got the casting vote. I vote for the setting up of such a sub-committee. Right,' he continued briskly, 'who's going to be on this committee?'

'I propose the usual members, Mr Mayor; yourself, the deputy mayor, chairman of finance and chairman of properties.' Dick Conway had rattled off his proposals so quickly that there was a brief pause after he sat down as members considered it. Ken Wilson was the first to spot its weakness – from his point of view.

'But, that doesn't include me,' he whined. 'Surely I should be on it; after all, the entire thing is my idea. And I've background knowledge which I think will be vital to the sub-committee.'

'Yes, I think it's only right that Mr Wilson be on it, Mr Mayor,' said Mrs Hooper. 'I feel he will have quite a bit to contribute.'

'Load of rubbish, that's what he'll contribute,' muttered Roland Smith.

'Yes, I think perhaps Mr Wilson should be on the committee,' agreed Basil Parfitt. 'He is, after all, our French expert,' he added, with a hint of sarcasm in his voice. 'Members agree with Mr Conway's proposals, plus Mr Wilson, for the sub-committee?'

Members did, indeed, agree. All, that is, except Roland Smith, who neither agreed nor disagreed. He just sat slumped in his seat, a doom-laden expression on his face.

Basil Parfitt glanced at his watch – and winced. These meetings seemed to ramble on forever. It was time to bring it to a close. 'I trust there's no other business,' he said – and when Basil Parfitt put on such a demeanour few argued with him. Not that he gave them the chance anyway. 'There being no other business, ladies and gentlemen, I declare the meeting closed at 10.20.'

Everybody got up from their seats and prepared for home except for Roland Smith. He just sat in his chair gazing straight ahead, blankly. Dick Conway walked around, and sat down beside him. 'What's the matter, Roland?' he asked cheerfully. 'You look like death warmed up.'

Councillor Smith shook his head sadly. 'What took hold of me Dick? I must be mad. I let that big-headed fool Wilson get up my nose, and before I know it, I'm threatening to resign. And I don't want to, Dick, I don't want to. I enjoy being on the council. I know I've threatened it in the past, but there was never any real chance that I would have to. It's different now though. I'm looking down the barrel of a shotgun.'

'You won't have to resign,' assured Conway in a soothing tone.

'But I will. After all, there's no way that this council won't eventually propose a formal twinning with this French town. It might take a while, but it's bound to come. I've been around long enough to know that. Far too many people in favour of it, both on and off the council.'

'Oh yes, I reckon it'll come – sometime. But it's a long time in the future, don't you worry.' Conway's tone was confident rather than soothing now. 'I made sure of that when I proposed that sub-committee.'

'How do you mean?'

'Well, think it through, Roland. Who's on it? Basil Parfitt for a start. Now old Basil's no great bridge builder; a conservative by nature and probably politically as well. And he's not the most energetic of mayors, either: He won't want anything to do with this twinning nonsense whilst he's in office, for certain. And the

174

deputy mayor's very similar. In fact, I reckon Sam Simmonds will be even less keen on it than Basil. No lover of foreigners – Sam. Dorothy Parsons will be there as chairman of properties, of course, and she'll probably be in favour of it, to start with. But you know Dorothy; easiest thing in the world to brow beat her. And then there's the chairman of finance – me. And I shall certainly oppose twinning. We're short enough of money now. Certainly there's nothing like enough to do half what we should be doing as a council. So there's no way I shall ever support twinning, Roland. A complete waste of time and money. So our friend Mr Wilson will find himself isolated on the sub-committee. Might well come one day, of course, with some changes in the council after an election or two, but that's way to the future.'

'But it'll still mean I'll have to resign one day,' muttered Smith, gloomily.

'Rubbish. After a year or two everybody'll forget you ever threatened to resign. People don't remember things for very long – you know that. In fact, they might well forget it by this time next month.'

Roland Smith nodded his head. 'Something in what you say, boy, I must admit. They do forget things.'

'Of course they do. I reckon there's not a chance you'll have to resign from this council over twinning, Roland.'

Smith got jauntily to his feet, grinning broadly. 'I must say you've made me feel a fair bit better, Dick. Tell you what – you've got to pass my place on the way home; how about coming in for a quick drink?'

'Yes – all right Roland. Excellent idea. Thanks very much.'

They walked briskly towards the exit, Smith still looking mightily pleased with life. He glanced at his companion as they walked through the door and into the lobby which led to the street. 'Over that drink we could perhaps talk about who's going to be deputy mayor to Sam Simmonds when he takes over. Only a few months away, you know. Soon be with us. How would you fancy it, Dick? You'd be the ideal man in my opinion.'

'Well – I'd not really thought about it. But I could be interested,' said Dick Conway as they walked out into the street, a hint of a smile playing around his lips. Whilst he'd not given solace to the troubled Roland Smith with any ulterior motive in mind, this sudden suggestion from his elderly colleague was much to his liking – and assuredly would be to his spouse, Helen, who would certainly enjoy being the deputy mayor's wife, and, if custom was followed, mayoress the following year. A gift horse had leapt before him – it's mouth would not be inspected.

IX

The Foxhounds

Frank Jackson announced the result of the vote – 'eight against, four for, two abstentions.' There was weariness in his tone. Not the best, fairest or most logical decision in his view; the town council refusing the local Lions Club permission to hold an open air concert in the park this coming June – to raise money for local charities. It could 'disturb the peace', said one councillor. This view could possibly have been sustained had the concert not been scheduled to finish at 9pm, and had not they granted permission a few weeks earlier for a pop concert to take place in the same place on Easter Monday. 'We always seem to be catering for the older generation in this town. It really is time we thought about the youngsters,' such were Councillor Mrs Julia Beckett's earnest words when proposing that this application be granted – one passed, amazingly in the view of Mayor Jackson, with little debate and even less dissent. How raucous guitars connected up to cutting edge, ear shattering amplification, going on to midnight, was less disturbing of the peace than the rich, but gentle tones of Mozart, or evocative compositions of Elgar, was beyond him. Still, this was democracy – logic did not come into it. Time to move the meeting forward, he mused to himself.

'Item five on the agenda, ladies the gentlemen – the works supervisor's report. This has been circulated; anything you wish to bring to members attention, Mr Benson?'

The perpetually melancholy looking Billy Benson got to his

feet, said briefly, and quite softly – as was ever his way – 'No, nothing, Mr Mayor, thank you,' and promptly sat down.

Jackson gazed out at the ranks before him – 'Anything on the report which anyone wishes to raise?' No sooner had he posed the question than he re-opened his mouth to move business on, anticipating nothing would be brought forth. He was to be proved wrong. Councillor Mrs Sally Gilbert's right arm shot into the air:

'Yes, Mr Mayor, if I may.' A largish lady, she pulled herself slowly to her feet. 'On page two of the report, Mr Benson has a brief paragraph regarding complaints he has received following the annual meet of the local hunt outside the Glanville Hotel on Boxing Day. I've also had a complaint only today from a resident of the town concerning this, and I am wondering if that which has come my way is the same as received by him? His report on the matter is so brief, so terse and lacking in information, it is impossible to know.' She fixed the works supervisor with an unsympathetic glare when saying the words – not a council officer upon her 'Christmas card list', was Benson. She had little faith in him in his role as the custodian of council property and practical administration (a little unfair as he, generally, was more efficient than immediately apparent). Indeed, she was ever critical of his casual and vague approach to reporting matters to the council and dealing with the residents of the town (this possibly somewhat justified and a view held by several other councillors).

The officer got to his feet once more, an expression of mild puzzlement joining solemnity upon his lean, rather lined features. 'Well, Mr Mayor, clearly I don't know the nature or the grumbles that have come the way of Mrs Gilbert, but I have had two or three people approach me complaining that the pack of hounds had left – well, droppings – all over the pavements and road outside the hotel and in the square beside it. Also, they felt that – well, well, I'm a little taken aback by this – but in accordance with recent local rules, all the hounds should have been on dog leads. I've not put any of this in my report, Mr Mayor, because frankly I think it's all a load of non . . . of . . . of petty complaints that are of little relevance, and which . . . well, Mr Mayor, which

I feel possibly should not, with respect, be taken particularly seriously by this council. Anyway, the issues raised do not really come within the remit of this authority at all. Essentially they are district and county council matters. I only put it in my report because it is customary to inform members of all issues brought to me, no matter how trivial, inconsequential or, in fact, irrelevant they might be to us as an authority.' The works supervisor spoke the words in tones which combined surprise, mild exasperation and a touch of laconic indifference. When attending meetings, he had ever given the impression he wished he were somewhere else (indeed, he would admit, if pressed, that it was more than just an impression), 'And, also, Mr Mayor, I'm not sure those complaining lived in the town – one certainly didn't. And the nature of the complaints suggest to me – with respect,' that hackneyed brace of words were added, hastily – 'that these were just folk with nothing better to do than to cause trouble for others, especially those who hunt. There are many people even in a rural area like ours who are always gunning for the hunt, folk who I feel – well, who tend to look for any ammunition to use against fox hunting. Even the most minor issue is magnified by them to cause trouble. Obviously they've a right to do so if they wish, Mr Mayor,' added Benson, with uncharacteristic haste, aware that he was in danger of voicing opinions when it was merely his job as a paid officer to report facts. He was, though, from a farming family (his grandfather had pursued such) and his brother was a current member of the hunt. 'Anyway, as I've said, I don't really feel that this is a matter for this council, as we've no direct say in the matter unless the hunt goes across any land or property owned by us.'

The mayor nodded. 'I tend to agree with you, Mr Benson. These are matters which come within the wide areas of responsibility of authorities other than ourselves. Also, it could be you are right in that there are those making somewhat trivial complaints in pursuance of their own agendas – their own personal prejudices and dislikes. Also. . .'

'I'm sorry, Mr Mayor,' interjected Mrs Gilbert, rising, again slowly, from her seat, 'but I really do not think we as a council can just ignore these complaints. The issues raised may not be directly under our control as a local council, but all this happened in our town so we have to take some responsibility for matters, and the fact the works supervisor feels it is nothing to do with us – and certainly nothing to do with him – carries no weight at all in my opinion. We make the decisions here as elected representatives of the people, and his job is to ensure these decisions are put into practice.' She glared once again at Benson as she said the words – again she made no real effort to disguise her lowish opinion of his ability, competence and dedication in terms of his role, even though he had occupied the position for some fifteen years. 'The complaints I've had are exactly the same as those that Mr Benson refers to in the absurdly brief entry he has inserted into his monthly report – the street and the square fouled by dogs, and the animals not on leads contrary to the by-laws introduced by the district council only a year or so ago. So the question I ask, Mr Mayor, is what do we do about it?'

'Do about it, Mr Mayor – do about it? Nothing, that's what we do about it,' exploded Councillor Jim Sparks. 'I have never remotely heard such nonsense in my life – and mischief making. There are some people out there who cannot let hunts alone – cannot leave them in peace. There is nothing illegal in hunts going about their business as long as they keep within the law and ensure hounds do not actually savage foxes. Nothing wrong with them meeting every Boxing Day outside The Glanville Hotel as they've been doing for generations. Yet these wretched, bigoted people cannot leave them in peace. I do believe they'll not rest until they've seen every foxhound put down, every ridden horse, also. My God, I feel there are times they could teach the Taliban a trick or two.'

'I'm not sure I necessarily agree with Mr Sparks, Mr Mayor,' opined Councillor Nigel Hollins. 'Dog fouling does concentrate my mind, that's if the roads and square are left as these complainants say. I've never attended the meeting of the hunt so I do not know if there is truth in this or not.'

'No truth,' stated the town clerk, Cecil Conway. 'To my knowledge – and I fancy the works supervisor will confirm –

there are members of the hunt who clear up the mess immediately after they move off, and do a thorough job.'

'Quite so, Mr Mayor,' agreed Billy Benson – with unusual alacrity, and a rare touch of asperity in his tone. The dislike Councillor Mrs Gilbert had for him – the lack of respect – was something he had long been aware of, and it was offensive to him. Attacks on him by councillors such as her made him relieved he had only three years to go before he retired.

'Yes, definitely correct,' interjected the deputy mayor, Douglas Denny. 'I usually go down to see the hunt on Boxing Day and they always clear up after the dogs have moved off – and they certainly did this time because a work colleague of mine was involved in doing it. I remember because I had a brief conversation with him. I must say they leave the streets in that area as clean as they are all year round.'

'Yes – fair point,' agreed Councillor Sidney Bartlett, wheezing even more than usual, his rather portly build and chain smoking habit (for a lifetime) more a cause than his 80 plus years. 'Shocking the state of the streets most of the time, Mr Mayor. District council's fault that is – they keep cutting back on staff and at the same time put up the council tax. I get hell from people about it, which is understandable even though it's not my fault as there's nothing I can do about it.'

'I must agree with Mr Bartlett, Mr Mayor,' said Councillor Mrs Liz Crosby in her soft but precise way. 'Far too often the streets of the town are in a state which none of us would tolerate on our own paths or gardens. And I have to say that the Gentleman I see out and about every day in his yellow jacket picking up the litter is certainly not selected for his speed – and he seems to have a chat with virtually every passer-by, often at some length.'

'Yes, I know the chap,' agreed Councillor Arthur Phillips. 'Mrs Crosby is right – slower than a three-legged donkey. I don't know how he. . .'

'Thank you, Councillor,' the mayor's interjection was sudden and authoritative. 'We're not here to talk about the state of the town streets (or indeed the speed of council employees), even though it is something which needs addressing, and soon. It is the

181

complaints regarding the hunt we are discussing at present, and it would appear that there is no truth in the allegation that dog mess was not picked up.'

'Mr Mayor, could I have some clarification here?' Councillor Tom Gaskell sounded somewhat puzzled – a rare event, he being a fellow with a mind like a razor. 'Indeed, perhaps I'm seeking to raise a point of order, more than anything else; I mean, what are we doing wasting our time even discussing this. The fact is that the areas where this took place are not under the control or the responsibility of this council, as has already been stated. I know Mrs Gilbert feels we should do something about it, but I have to disagree. There are many problems we face – often expensive ones – looking after those affairs which are the direct responsibility of this town council without concerning ourselves with those which clearly are not. Let us just pass these complaints on to district and county and let them sort it all out.'

'Yes, I agree,' rasped Jim Sparks. 'Pass it up to them. In fact, I'm prepared to move we do so. With that in mind, I. . .'

Councillor Sparks was not destined to make his proposal, being interrupted by what was little less than a bellow from Arthur Phillips, a councillor who, even though he'd been on the council for fifteen years or so, often ignored – indeed, forgot totally – the courtesies and protocol of formal proceedings when gripped by a train of thought. 'The hounds should be on leads? Was one of the complaints that the hounds should be on leads? Did I hear that right, Mr Mayor? Surely not – nobody could be so daft as to suggest that.'

'Well – yes, it would appear such was one of the complaints, Councillor,' conceded Frank Jackson. 'And I have to say that if it wasn't so absurd and petty, it would almost be funny.'

'I don't know there is anything absurd or petty about the matter, Mr Mayor,' opined Nigel Hollins in the somewhat superior tones which he adopted on occasions – and which tended to irritate many councillors, exceedingly so at times. 'The law is the law – it is what we all have to live by, what keeps this a civilised country, or, at least, a reasonably civilised one. If these new rules state all dogs have to be on leads in an urban environment, then so be it; I doubt it makes any allowance for foxhounds. Thus the hunt have to keep to the rules just like all others – just like the people of the town, members of this council, in fact, who keep dogs and take them for a walk. We would not expect to be exempted, so nor should they. After all, we have our own local by-laws concerning what people can and cannot do in, say, our parks and so forth. We would not be too tolerant of anybody who felt they had no obligation to obey them, of that I'm very sure. Still, perhaps the town clerk will enlighten us as to this recent ruling. From what I've heard it would seem the hounds should be on leads – but we really do need to have the law spelt out to us, to the letter.' As he sat down, he looked in the direction of the town clerk as did most of the members of the council, including the mayor.

'Well, Mr Conway, I feel Councillor Hollins makes a fair point,' stated Jackson in his usual measured tones. 'It would be helpful to know what these new rulings state – essential, in fact. Can you enlighten us?'

One glance at Cecil Conway's face, with its expression of bemusement and mild panic, was more than sufficient to tell members, loud and clear, that the town clerk could not enlighten them, even in the remotest fashion.

'Well, Mr Mayor – well – well, I cannot honestly say I know a very great deal about these new rulings regarding dogs. Certainly as I understand it, fouling in public places, and them being on leads, figure large in the matter, but the technicalities, the minutiae of the laws are something else. They have not come my way, and they would not, of course, as they are the responsibility of the legal departments at the district and county councils. Should it become our direct concern, Mr Mayor, should we be called upon to actually administer these new requirements, then, of course, I will ensure I know what they are and, indeed, ensure they are adhered to in all our properties.' The town clerk ended his reply with infinitely more confidence than had been his when he began it, more than a little pleased by the way he had handled a difficult and most unexpected situation.

Nigel Hollins, however, always a precise, pedantic and

persistent man, started to rise to say that despite all the town clerk had said, it was his job – his responsibility – to know the 'ins and outs' of the law even though it might not have been the town council's duty to enforce it. Before he could say anything, however, he was forestalled by an observation from the highly regarded Jack Dawson, a councillor who would sometimes sit through an entire meeting without saying a word, but whom, when he did speak, was listened to in respectful silence, he rarely saying anything which was not well thought through, logical, even wise.

'Mr Mayor, I cannot pretend to know these new regulations well, but my brother is a farmer who keeps sheep – and, thus, has a couple of sheepdogs; and I fancy he said recently when for some reason he mentioned the new 'dog laws' which had come in, that when they were in public places, it did not apply to sheepdogs as they were classed as working dogs. Thus he could use them to shepherd sheep along the public highway without them having to be on leads. Nor would he have to clean up after them – nor the sheep either,' he added with a gentle smile. 'With that in mind, Mr Mayor, surely it can be argued that foxhounds are working dogs, therefore exempt from the law. I certainly feel that such is a logical conclusion.'

The mayor nodded – 'A sound point, Councillor,' he agreed, 'very sound indeed – compelling, in fact. If that's correct then it would seem the hunt are not required to put their hounds on leads.' There was much relief in his tone – the absurdity of foxhounds on leads was, to him, almost beyond comprehension.

The works supervisor got to his feet with some alacrity – truly an event in itself. He nodded enthusiastically (well, almost), seeing an avenue of escape; he would almost rather hand in his resignation than have to go around making huntsmen put their hounds on leads – or, to be more exact, trying to achieve such. 'Yes, I fancy Councillor Dawson is correct, Mr Mayor,' agreed he. 'I don't know for certain, but I'm sure one of the officers up at the district council has said something of the sort. Which makes sense, of course. Certainly, if that is the law, then the hunt are doing nothing wrong.'

The mayor nodded once more. 'Common sense would suggest you are correct, Mr Benson. It would also suggest we take no further action on this. I so move from the chair – do I have a seconder?'

Jack Dawson did just that, and the mayor, after thanking him, said simply, 'All in favour of the council taking no action, please show.'

However, before arms could be raised, Nigel Hollins was again on his feet. 'Mr Mayor, before a vote is taken, I feel we must consider whether or not foxhounds are working dogs. The point that an exemption in the law regarding having canines on leads might well be the case if they are for the purpose of work – such as a sheepdog – is quite logical and, indeed, right, but an argument could well be put forward that foxhounds are not working dogs in the eyes of the law.'

'Of course they are,' rasped Jim Sparks, his voice pregnant with exasperation and bemusement at what he saw as being the lunacy of both the complaint and the debate. 'For Heaven's sake, a hound's not out for an afternoon stroll with its owner, it's there to flush out foxes – vermin, Mr Mayor, and a menace to so many other creatures, and, these days, they're found in towns as well as in the countryside.'

'But that's the point, Mr Mayor,' persisted Hollins, 'they're there to flush out foxes. They're there to provide sport and excitement for those following them on horseback also, for that matter, those following in cars or on foot. I will not pretend to be a fan of fox hunting with hounds, and I was pleased to see the law come in some years ago which banned hunts from allowing these dogs to kill foxes. However, in terms of law I would say – in my view, of course, which is merely a layman's opinion – that back in the days when they could, and did, actually kill foxes, then they could clearly be classed as working dogs; they were doing a job of work, objectionable though it was to many of us. These days, however, they are merely a sideshow in what, to some, is an enjoyable afternoon's entertainment.'

'But what they do is work, Mr Mayor – it has to be. If it's not work, then what is it? A lot of the foxes they turn out are shot, and

185

farm animals are a lot safer.' A farmer's son, Councillor Sparks was no lover of foxes. 'Of course it's work – I don't know where Councillor Hollins is coming from. He's talking nonsense.'

'That'll do, Councillor,' snapped the mayor. 'Mr Hollins is putting forward reasoned arguments as is his right. We may or may not agree with what he says, but I have served on this council many years with him and know him to be a man who never puts forward opinions which are not well thought through, even though I might not always agree with him.' Frank Jackson was sincere in this – he had never liked the rather haughty, slightly condescending Hollins, but the man was intelligent, articulate, clear thinking, honest, a good councillor and his views could never be dismissed lightly.

Nigel Hollins was about to make his own reply, but Sally Gilbert forestalled him; 'Mr Mayor,' she cried in her rather shrill voice, 'I've just had a thought.'

From Tom Gaskell there was an audible groan at such news. Experience suggested that any thought from Councillor Gilbert, whether wise or plain daft, would be articulated at great length – with every point made in pedantic fashion. She launched forth:

'We are talking here regarding the streets of the town – the public highways – where we do not have jurisdiction. Yet we are ignoring an area which is very much under our control – a larger open space; and I don't mean the park – it's highly unlikely the hunt will ever go through there. The Downs though, up by Dartmoor on the edge of town, is a very different matter, for the hunt often go across there, and we are the authority in charge of it.'

'No we're not,' snapped Councillor Sparks. 'It's common land – moorland, in effect. Nothing whatsoever to do with us.'

'It is to do with us, Mr Mayor,' retorted Mrs Gilbert. 'Oh yes it certainly is land where the commoners have grazing rights, and true, nobody actually owns it, but we are the landlords of that area, which includes the golf course; so we have responsibility for it. So as the hunt crosses it regularly, then we have a duty to ensure they do so within the law. I accept it would be difficult to pick up the droppings, but we could – indeed, we must – ensure the hounds are kept on leads if that's what the law demands.'

'What? Did Mrs Gilbert say the dogs had to be on leads? Is she serious, Mr Mayor?' Douglas Denny was every bit as incredulous as he sounded. 'Is she saying that every time the hunt passes over that part of the moor which comes under our jurisdiction, we have to ensure that all the hounds are on leads?'

'I fancy that is exactly what she's saying,' responded the mayor in weary tones.

'Yes, it is,' retorted Sally Gilbert. 'If the law says dogs must be kept on leads when in public places, then in those areas for which we are responsible, we must ensure they are. Clearly, the enforcement of such rules on other parts of the moor is down to the National Park Authorities, but it is up to us to uphold the rules on that which we control. Granted we have to be certain what this law states, and that is something I feel the town clerk should clarify as a matter of urgency – first thing tomorrow, in fact. But if it is now incumbent upon us to impose these new rules, then we really should do so. Councillor Hollins is right in what he says – the law has to apply to everybody; without fear or favour, as they say.'

'So folk out hunting will have to chase after hounds, holding God knows how many leads in their hands, as they hurtle over rough, boggy terrain chasing a fox. Those doing that will have to possess the strength of Samson and the pace of Usain Bolt.' Douglas Denny shook his head wearily as he spoke the words. 'Mr Mayor,' continued he, 'I've been a member of this council now for some twelve years, and I've heard, and been involved in some pretty daft debates, but nothing can equal this. I cannot believe that any law can be as ludicrous as this; even the EU couldn't come up with anything as crass. That there are such statutes regarding dogs on leads and the like, I do not doubt. Certainly I read of it a while back and was struck then by the feeling it was taking a sledgehammer to a walnut – yes there are problems with dogs running around, fouling and the like, but it never really needed legislation. If the laws now are demanding such lunacy as hounds having to be on leads when chasing a fox – thus huntsmen and women have to be staggering after them, then the world has gone crazy. Let us stop this nonsense now, Mr

Mayor. To proceed any further will do nothing other than waste our time, officers' time – for which there is a cost – and make us look like a bunch of idiots. There are plenty of folk out there who lack faith in our levels of wisdom at the best of times; if they hear we want to have foxhounds put on leads when hurtling over the moors, they'll want all of us sectioned.'

'Nonsense, Mr Mayor,' snorted Councillor Gilbert. 'The opposite is the case. We live in a decent town inhabited by good, law abiding people – on the whole, anyway. They will applaud us for standing up for law and order – or a majority will, of that I'm certain. It is vital we find out exactly what the law says, and if it states that all dogs in public places have to be on leads, then we put such a policy into action immediately – which will include foxhounds.' She was fixed with a glare from Douglas Denny (not quite malevolent, but assuredly unfriendly).

The deputy mayor's anger, though under control, was palpable. In this mood, he was formidable in all aspects of his life – which most certainly included his council work. Thus, from him, came an explosion of articulate, disciplined fury. 'Mr Mayor,' he rasped, 'I do not believe we should even contemplate instructing the town clerk to waste his valuable time in any clarification of the law. I cannot believe that these new regulations require foxhounds to be kept on leads – if they do, then in the words of Dickens' Mr Bumble, the Beadle, the law is an ass. To me the most sensible words spoken this evening were by Councillor Dawson when he stated that all logic pointed towards these hounds being classed as working dogs. With that in mind, I move that we have nothing more to do with pursuing this – this nonsense regarding leads; I formally propose no action, Mr Mayor.'

'Seconded,' cried Councillor Sparks, instantly.

'I must protest, Mr Mayor,' cried Councillor Gilbert. 'I really must protest. This is iniquitous.'

'I'm not sure what you are protesting about, Councillor,' responded Frank Jackson in a fashion far more urbane than he actually felt – he was not impressed by the, to him, trivial, pedantic and, as far as some councillors were concerned,

188

prejudiced nature of the debate. 'The motion has been proposed and seconded in accordance with standing orders. I cannot see you can have any argument regarding that.'

Sally Gilbert, on occasions – especially when riled – could have the tenacity of a limpet. 'Surely, then, Mr Mayor, if a motion is put before this authority, then we should debate it; we must be permitted to have our say.'

'Debate it – have our say? We've spent hours debating it, or so it seems to me,' wheezed Sydney Bartlett. 'If we talk about it for much longer then half the hounds we're on about will have died of old age.'

'I agree with Mr Bartlett,' opined Liz Crosby. 'It really is time to put this to bed – so that we can all do likewise. I move that the motion be put.'

The mayor did not hesitate: 'It's been moved the motion be put. Do I have a seconder?' Councillor Tom Gaskell raised his hand, and nodded. 'It's been proposed and seconded the motion be put. All those in favour – that we take no action?' He counted the arms thrust into the air. 'Nine,' said he – adding his own vote. 'Those against?'

The clerk gave the score: 'Five, Mr Mayor – and two abstentions.'

'So, by a clear majority, the motion is carried – we take no action,' stated Frank Jackson with authority and a large measure of satisfaction.

The rest of the meeting took less than ten minutes – folk just wished to get home to their beds, or their televisions. Indeed, within a couple of minutes of the mayor declaring it closed, the chamber was virtually empty. The mayor and his deputy moved towards the exit, leaving the town clerk to put out the lights. Just as they were about to reach the door, a female figure passed them. 'Good night, gentlemen,' said she.

Jackson was first to respond, 'Oh – oh – good night, Ruth,' spluttered he as Mrs Ruth Blythe, Deputy Editor of the *Clarion* passed by on her way out to the street and home.

'Ruth Blythe,' groaned Douglas Denny. 'Do you know, I'd not thought about her. 'Course, she was there at the back right

j

through the debate. It wasn't in committee, so she could report everything that was said. How I never thought about that, I don't know. Good Heavens, Frank, she'll have a field day, some of the nonsense that was talked tonight. She'll make us look the biggest bunch of fools that ever walked the earth just by reporting the truth – stating that which was actually said; and Ruth always writes accurately all that is said – that's her great quality, total honesty. It's Elections this spring – half of us will not be voted back when folk read of some of the idiocies that came out tonight.'

'I quite agree, boy,' replied the mayor in very calm fashion. 'But for you and I – and several other members – there will be more plusses than minuses. Just think about it, Doug. As you said, Ruth will report that meeting with complete accuracy. Every quote she uses will be exactly as it was made – that's her great quality. I doubt the length and breadth of the land, there's a reporter, local or national, more wedded to the truth than Ruth Blythe. I don't know about you, but there've been times in the past when I've forgotten exactly what I said in debate and have had to read her report in the *Clarion* to remember; and it will be word for word what you said, you can depend on that. Now, she will be reporting the debate on the hounds on leads idiocy exactly how it happened. Who do you think is going to be made to look fools, and who will come out of it with some semblance of common sense?'

The deputy mayor looked a trifle confused: 'Well, I don't really know, to be honest. You can never be sure how people will react.'

'I think you can in this instance, boy. We live in a rural, Devon market town. Farmers and country people are very much in the *Clarion*'s circulation area – traditional folk with like values and beliefs. Also, on the whole, it is a community a touch older than the average. Certainly the readership of the *Clarion* will be highest amongst those over 50 – those most sympathetic to hounds and country life. When they read about the nonsense of putting foxhounds on leads, those in favour will lose votes – those opposed will be viewed most favourably; of this, Douglas, my dear chap, I have not the slightest doubt, and Ruth will have noted down the names of those voting for and against the motion – and it will be in her report, you can be sure of that.'

They reached the street, wished each other 'good night' and proceeded home. Perhaps, mused the mayor, it had been a worthwhile debate after all, tedious though it had been – for long term he could see no way most of the positives, electorally, could fail to accrue to the common-sensical pragmatists who eschewed pedantic, dogmatic, oppression even though that, technically, might be the legal edict. If it was, then in his view, the law was totally daft.

X

The Bridge

'We come now to 'any urgent business' brought forward at the discretion of the mayor,' said Frank Jackson, in somewhat melancholy tones. 'And I'm sorry to say, it really is urgent. Mr Conway, please.'

'Thank you, Mr Mayor,' replied the town clerk. 'As I informed you right at the beginning of the meeting, Mr Mayor, we have run into considerable problems with the footbridge over the river linking the playing fields with the park. As members might be aware, a safety inspector checks it every four or five years to make sure it's up to standard. Well, he came after lunch today, inspected the bridge – and promptly condemned it.'

'What does that mean?' asked Councillor Sandra Miles.

'It means that the bridge will have to be closed to the public,' replied the town clerk. 'Actually, I'm using the wrong tense, Mr Mayor; it is closed to the public. I took it upon myself to instruct the works supervisor to get his staff down there this afternoon and block off the entrances to the bridge – and put up signs saying that the bridge is closed from now on. I believe that work's been done, Mr Benson.'

Billy Benson, the works supervisor, nodded wearily from his seat on the other side of the mayor, then got slowly to his feet.

'Yes, it's all closed off now,' he said in his laconic fashion, 'but we had a right caper doing it.'

'In what way?' asked Conway.

'Well, we put these big sheets of hardboard each end of the bridge – which blocked off the entrances beautifully. Then we put up the warning signs, and went back to the depot. Well, I don't suppose we'd been back there more than ten minutes when one of our men who'd been down the park trimming a hedge came in to say that vandals had knocked down all the woodwork we'd just put up and heaved it into the river.'

'Unbelievable,' muttered the mayor.

'Shocking!' snapped Councillor Sally Gilbert.

'God knows what the answer is,' said Councillor Jack Dawson sadly.

'I blame their parents,' grunted Councillor Douglas Denny.

'I'd birch the buggers,' rasped Councillor Tom Gaskell.

'I thought Mr Benson said the bridge was closed off, Mr Mayor,' said Councillor Liz Crosby, getting to the point – as was her custom.

'It is, Mr Mayor,' replied Benson, still without any urgency in his tone. 'When I heard that the boards had been thrown in the river, I went around immediately to Maxwell's the farm suppliers and bought a roll of this new kind of barbed wire – the stuff that's made of steel and so hard that only special wire cutters can slice through it. There's a razor element to it as well.'

'They'll find some way of cutting it, don't you worry,' interjected the cynical Jim Sparks.

'I certainly hope not, Mr Mayor,' retorted Billy Benson. 'If the wire was cut away and somebody got onto the bridge, and it collapsed – well, I shudder to think what would happen.'

'This council would be sued, that's what would happen,' said Liz Crosby. 'In fact, it could be that we as members of the council could be sued. . .'

'I fancy that somewhat unlikely,' interjected the town clerk, urbanely. 'There's no way this council – or its members – can be liable as long as we take all reasonable precautions to close the bridge off. And this we have done, of course. Anyway, I don't think the bridge is in any real immediate danger of collapsing even if somebody did walk on it.'

' 'Course it's not going to collapse, Mr Mayor,' snorted the veteran Sidney Bartlett. 'You could march the household cavalry across that bridge – and their 'osses as well – in perfect safety. Built, that bridge is – built when they knew how to put things together. Over a hundred years old, that bridge. My grandfather helped build it. Craftsman he was. But then, they all were in those days. That bridge, Mr Mayor, will last as long as the Pyramids. How anybody can say it's unsafe is beyond me.'

'The inspector gave it a close examination, and was in no doubt that the bridge is unsafe,' explained the town clerk. 'Apparently one of the support struts has rusted through and is literally swinging in the breeze.'

'Get on, it's been like that for years,' rasped Douglas Denny. 'But does it matter? I agree with Mr Bartlett – that bridge is sound as a bell. It'll stand for generations. I propose we ignore what the inspector says and keep the bridge open.'

'Keep it open, Mr Mayor?' The town clerk sounded aghast. 'But we can't keep it open. The inspector has condemned it. The bridge is unsafe – it's as simple as that. If we keep it open we'll be breaking the law, as well as endangering people's lives.'

'Endangering people's lives, be damned,' snapped Tom Gaskell. 'There's nothing wrong with the blasted bridge, Mr Mayor. I often walk over that bridge when walking the dog, and there's nothing wrong with it at all. I shall continue to take my dog over it.'

'I'm afraid Mr Gaskell won't be able to do that,' retorted the town clerk, 'unless he's willing to crawl through barbed wire.'

'Don't reckon I'll have to do that,' rasped Gaskell. 'Knowing the hooligans around here that wire's probably been cut through already.'

'I hope not,' said the mayor. 'This entire business is costing us enough money as it is without any more vandalism on top. Where the money will come from to take down this bridge and build another, I really don't know.'

'Take it down?' spluttered an incredulous Douglas Denny. 'Build another? Mr Mayor, with respect, I've never heard such nonsense in my life. It'll cost a fortune to knock it down and an even bigger one to put up another.'

'Quite so, Councillor,' retorted the mayor. 'Unfortunately, though, we've no option. We must have a sound footbridge over the river.'

'We have got an option, Mr Mayor,' persisted Denny. 'We can repair the old one – simple as that.'

'That we cannot do, I'm afraid,' said the mayor.

'Quite so,' agreed the town clerk getting to his feet. 'The bridge is beyond repair – according to the inspector. Rust, metal fatigue – you name it, the bridge is suffering from it. We've not had his full written report yet, naturally, but the inspector was most insistent that the bridge be closed down immediately, then demolished. Whether we build another is up to us, of course, but it will cause a few problems to many people in the town if we don't.'

'Of course, it will, Mr Mayor,' opined Sandra Miles. 'For a start the changing rooms for those using the football, rugby and hockey pitches, and the tennis courts, are on the other side of the bridge in the park. If we've got no bridge it means that they'll have to change then walk to the end of the park, pass over the road bridge, then walk up the main road to the west gate of the playing fields.'

'That's not very far,' grunted Sidney Bartlett.

'Not very far?' retorted Mrs Miles. 'Why, it's – it's a huge distance. Mr Mayor, the bridge has to be replaced and as quickly as possible.'

'I quite agree,' snapped Councillor Nigel Hollins. 'The park and the playing fields have been one unit thanks to that bridge for – for over a hundred years. Think of the thousands of people every year who use that area – and use the bridge out of necessity. Of course it has to be replaced – no matter what the cost.'

'It's all very well saying that, Mr Mayor,' said Jack Dawson in his slow, thoughtful way, 'but where's the money to come from? It'll cost thousands to demolish the bridge and scores of thousands to rebuild it.'

'I think we'll probably be able to get a grant towards it,' opined the town clerk – blithely.

'Towards what?' asked Councillor Gaskell sharply. 'The knocking down or the rebuilding?'

'Well – well – well, I'm not totally certain,' replied Cecil Conway slowly, pulling a handkerchief from his pocket to mop his brow – a habit of his when things were getting a little difficult. 'But I'm sure we can get some financial help towards an emergency project such as this.'

'Who from?' asked the persistent Gaskell.

'That's a fair question,' agreed the mayor. 'Mr Conway?'

'Well, Mr Mayor, well . . . I feel . . . well I'm sure,' stuttered the town clerk, 'I'm sure there are grants to be had. There are always grants to be had for such work as this – or usually, anyway. Obviously, though, I've not had time to go into it all, Mr Mayor. It was only this afternoon, after all, that the inspector condemned the bridge.'

'Yes, that's quite true,' agreed Councillor Mrs Julia Bartlett. 'It's most unfair to expect answers of this nature at this stage from the town clerk. He must be given some time to find out just what money there is available. With that in mind, I would propose that we defer any decisions on the bridge until our next meeting, by which time Mr Conway will no doubt have obtained details of assistance we can get towards replacing this bridge.'

'I don't object to deferring it for a month, Mr Mayor,' said Douglas Denny, 'but I'll tell you now, there'll be no money forthcoming from anybody to sort the bridge out. I still reckon we should keep the bridge open; but if the council decides it's got to be closed off, then so be it. But for sure, we'll never be able to afford to replace it, so it's best, in my estimation, just to leave it as it is. We've got the barbed wire across the entrance at each end to stop folk walking across it – and that's all we need do. Far better to spend what little money we do have on something else.'

'But that's plain silly!' cried Councillor Miles. 'We can't just leave the bridge. Quite apart from anything else, look what an eyesore it would be – a rusting, decaying heap of metal straddling the river.'

'Why should it be?' queried Tom Gaskell. 'It's not an eyesore at present, so why should it be later on. Just the opposite I would think; a structure like that built by craftsmen in the age when such people produced only workmanship of the highest quality, should be kept for future generations to see – just like they keep the *Cutty Sark* and Nelson's flagship. Folk enjoy seeing them, so why shouldn't they want to see our bridge? Why, it could even become a minor tourist attraction.'

'With respect to Mr Gaskell, Mr Mayor – that's plain daft,' snorted an exasperated Councillor Beckett. 'There's absolutely no point in preserving a bridge which cannot be used.'

'Then why do they preserve the *Cutty Sark*?' snapped Gaskell. 'I've not heard of it carrying any cargoes of tea for some time.'

'That's different – obviously different,' she retorted. 'Mr Gaskell's being deliberately stupid.'

'Nothing's deliberate about it in Tom's case,' muttered a smirking Arthur Phillips to his 'neighbour', Jim Sparks.

'Who are you calling stupid?' roared Gaskell. 'Mr Mayor, I protest. I've been on this council for over twenty years and nobody's ever insulted me like this before. I demand an apology.'

'I'm sure Mrs Beckett meant no offence, Mr Gaskell,' droned the mayor in as soothing a tone of voice as he could muster. 'However, I do feel that you should be a little more careful in how you speak of, or to, other members of this council, Mrs Beckett.' He gave her a look of gentle reproach as he said the words.

'I didn't mean to offend Mr Gaskell, or anybody else for that matter, Mr Mayor,' retorted Julia Beckett in an uncharacteristically aggressive way. 'I was just speaking my mind. What he said was stupid, as I'm sure most members would agree. However. . .'

'The Victorian Society, Mr Mayor, that's the answer,' interjected Sandra Miles excitedly. 'We must apply to them for a grant. They'll pay something towards renovating the bridge, I'm sure.'

'Who's the Victorian Society?' asked Councillor Liz Crosby.

'Well, I don't know that they're called that exactly,' retorted Mrs Miles, 'but there is a nationwide society who concentrate their efforts on preserving our heritage – especially things Victorian. I went to a lecture and slide-show about it a couple of years ago, held in the church hall. It was given by – let's see, yes, it was Mr Jenkins the butcher in Fore Street. Very knowledgeable he was about so many things, and I'm sure he said the society gave out grants to preserve ancient monuments, buildings and suchlike – with Victorian being very much to the fore. Perhaps Mr Conway could have a word with him, before the next meeting, about the possibility of getting some money from his society for the bridge.'

'You'll have to take a shovel with you,' snapped Douglas Denny, directing his words at the town clerk. 'He died about twelve months ago.'

'Yes – of course he did,' agreed Nigel Hollins. 'We used to get our meat there until he died. His shop's an estate agents now.'

'Yes, I remember now,' chipped in Tom Gaskell. 'Criminal it was, that the planning committee let that go through. Dammit, we seem to have as many estate agents in this town as we've got houses.'

'Well, you know what happened there,' said Jim Sparks. 'It's obvious there's one or two on the committee. . .'

'I fancy we're straying from the subject, gentlemen,' interjected the mayor. 'Mrs Miles was telling us about this society who give out grants – and that the late Mr Jenkins was connected with it. What we obviously have to do now is to find out if there's anybody else in this town involved with this society or, failing that, the address of the society at county or national level. Perhaps we could leave that with you, Mr Conway.'

'Yes – yes, of course,' agreed the town clerk with a grimace. How, he asked himself, was he supposed to go about finding an organisation which nobody knew the name of and whose only local member, of which anyone was aware, was a dead butcher?

'Waste of time I fear,' opined Councillor Dawson.

'Why do you say that, Mr Dawson?' asked the mayor. 'It would seem to me to be a reasonable idea. After all, even if we were to get a grant of just a few hundred pounds out of this society then it would be worthwhile.'

'I agree – but the fact is that we won't get a grant from them, will we?'

'Why not?'

'Simply because such a society will most certainly only be interested in paying out good money if it's going to be used to preserve something Victorian – not to knock it down, Mr Mayor.'

'That's a fair point,' agreed the mayor. 'I suppose it's impossible to actually renovate the bridge, Mr Conway?'

'Well, yes, according to the inspector, Mr Mayor. Of course, he only gave me a verbal report. It'll be some weeks, no doubt, before we get a full written report on the matter. He did say, though, that there was no way in which the bridge could be repaired. Its deficiencies are so numerous and widespread that the only realistic course is to take it down – and rebuild it.'

'And it's impossible to build a Victorian bridge in this day and age,' said Dawson.

'Why,' asked Mrs Shearer.

'Because if a bridge is built now, it's not Victorian, but a twenty-first century one, or, if you like, an Elizabeth the Second bridge. It'll be all concrete and girders – like the things they put over motorways. There's not an historical society in the world that'll give a grant towards that.'

'I see Mr Dawson's point, Mr Mayor, but there's no reason why we shouldn't build the bridge in a Victorian style, surely,' argued Sandra Miles. 'If we were to do that, then it's possible we might be able to get a grant. Besides, it would look nice – in keeping with the character of the town.'

'There's no way that any new bridge could be built in an old style,' opined Tom Gaskell, 'simply because there's no real craftsmen about these days. I doubt there's hardly a man in this country, let alone this town, who would have the skills needed to work on such a bridge. Skilled men like that passed on years ago. We'll not see their like again.'

'Mr Mayor, if I might make a suggestion,' said Jack Dawson in his ever courteous way.

'Certainly, Councillor.' He would be pleased to hear anything sensible which would direct them to some course of action and bring the debate to a close; and if anybody could bring sense to the discussion, then that person was Jack Dawson.

'Well, Mr Mayor, it seems to me that the obvious place to look for a grant to help fund the replacement of the bridge is to the district council. I am, of course, as you know, a member of that council as well as being on this town council, and generally there are funds put by to help in situations such as we face now. How much there's available, mind you, I don't really know. What with the government cut-backs and the added expense faced by the district owing to the problems with the roof over the Council Chamber and the subsidence of the swimming pool, I reckon there's not exactly a fortune available. But having said this, there's no reason why we shouldn't have a share of what there is. I'll bring it up at the next meeting of the policy committee – which is on – well – sometime next month. Unfortunately, Mr Duncan and Mrs Bevan, who're also on that committee from the town, aren't here tonight, but I'm sure they'll give full support. So I formally propose that we seek a grant from the district council towards the replacement of the footbridge, and we defer any other action on the bridge until we know whether or not any money is forthcoming.'

'Thank you, Mr Dawson,' said the mayor briskly, relieved that they were getting somewhere at last. 'Is there a seconder?'

'Seconded!' cried Nigel Hollins.

'Those in favour?' A sea of extended arms swayed as they were held aloft.

'Against?' There was not the slightest movement.

'Carried,' droned the mayor. 'Now, there being no further business – or none that I've been informed of at any rate,' he added in a tone which brooked no argument, 'I declare the meeting closed.'

Never a man to linger behind after meetings, Frank Jackson was out of the chamber almost as soon as his gavel had come to rest on his desk, and was followed, a little more slowly, by the members of the council in ones and twos. Last to leave were Jack Dawson and Tom Gaskell.

'Do you reckon there's any real chance of getting any money from the district for this blasted bridge?' the latter asked as they passed through the doorway leading from the council chamber.

'Sadly, not a hope in hell,' retorted Dawson. 'To start with the district's got hardly any money left and secondly, as you well know Tom, they wouldn't give the town council a brass farthing even if they had. It'll be a long time before they forgive us for refusing to allow them to park their environmental pollution advisory caravan in Broad Square car park last summer. So there'll be nothing coming from them.'

'Why did you propose we approach them then?'

'So we could get home tonight. That debate could have meandered on for hours. Frank is a good mayor in many ways, but there are times when he allows a bit too much debate – too much democracy if you like;' a grin played around his lips as he said the last few words.

'But what'll happen when the town's told there's nothing coming from the district?'

'Nothing – that's the whole point, Bill, isn't it?' said Dawson with a shrug of his shoulders. 'Let's face it, nothing's going to be done to replace the footbridge – not in the foreseeable future anyway. You will get your wish; the bridge will be left there probably until it falls down – and I reckon we'll all be retired from the council, and the world itself, by the time that happens.

'You think that?' Gaskell sounded somewhat amazed.

'Certainly,' replied his companion, urbanely. 'After all, where's the money to come from to even take the bridge down, let alone replace it? As I've said, there'll be nothing coming from the district – though it'll take about five meetings and a like number of months for them to make that a final decision. There'll be nothing coming from any other outside body, will there? After all there's nobody to apply to as far as I'm aware – certainly such daft suggestions as applying to Victorian Societies, and suchlike, is a real non-starter. And last, and most importantly of all, the town council haven't got enough spare money to take out one rivet. So that's that.'

'We could put up the council tax.'

'You're joking, Tom. We put it up last May to help pay for the new ceiling in the town hall – and there was all hell let loose as you well remember. If we put it up again, I reckon we'll all be tarred, feathered and thrown off the blasted bridge.'

Gaskell laughed. 'We could well be tarred and feathered, Jack, but there's no way they'll be able to throw us off the bridge. That's out of bounds – barbed wire both ends, razor wire too.'

Jack Dawson smiled in his laconic way, nodded his agreement, and walked slowly towards his car parked further down the street. He stopped abruptly, and gazed at his companion, a serious expression upon his face. 'Barbed wire both ends – I'd not thought about that, Tom. We could have problems there. Boarding up is one thing, but barbed wire – no, worse, razor wire, health and safety could have a field day. What if some young devil out for mischief – vandalism, in fact – cuts himself on it, or some such thing; there'll be all hell let loose. The council could well be in trouble. Daft, of course, but that's the age we live in. Health and safety is the new religion – sanity has melted away like snow before the sun. So perhaps something else should be put there, and the wire taken down.'

'And cost the council even more money? No, not the way forward in my view, Jack. You've got a point, though. What, I fancy, is that there needs to be signs both ends, not just saying the bridge is closed, but warning of the possible danger of the wire. That might deter some little heller bent on causing mayhem. More important, though, it should clear the council of responsibility if anybody did injure themselves. I'll phone Cecil Conway in the morning suggesting a sign is put there immediately – that's if it's not been done already.'

Jack Dawson smiled, then nodded agreement: 'Yes, good idea boy. That should cover us as councillors. This is a litigious age – we've got to cover our backs. If we don't, there'll be those who will thrust a knife into them.'

'Too true, I'm afraid,' agreed his companion. 'One thing for sure is they will have to keep repainting the sign – it'll be there for decades! Good night Jack.'